PRAISE FOR THE ROXY REINHARDT MYSTERIES

"Wow! This series gets better and better."
"Roxy is one of my all time favorite characters."
"The story was brilliantly plotted out and wonderfully written, you could barely wait to turn the pages to see where the tale would take you next."
"Excellent story, very clever."
"I read your book until the wee hours last night.... couldn't put it down!!"
"All the food made me very hungry and really wanting to visit New Orleans!"
"Absolutely loved it!!!"
"You've done a great job. Truly. This one shines."
"I just want you to know how much I like Roxy. She makes me smile."
"Loved the book, looking forward to the next installment. I think you've got a winner!"
"I like Roxy and her new friends and look forward to more books including them."
"Love Roxy's posse."
"What a great book!"

CAJUN CATASTROPHE

BOOKS IN THE ROXY REINHARDT MYSTERIES

Mardi Gras Madness

New Orleans Nightmare

Louisiana Lies

Cajun Catastrophe

COLLECTIONS

Books 1-3

Mardi Gras Madness

New Orleans Nightmare

Louisiana Lies

Published by Mesa Verde Publishing
P.O. Box 1002
San Carlos, CA 94070

ISBN: 979-8392823499

"Keep reading. It is one of the most marvelous adventures that anyone can have."

- Lloyd Alexander -

CAJUN CATASTROPHE

ALISON GOLDEN
HONEY BROUSSARD

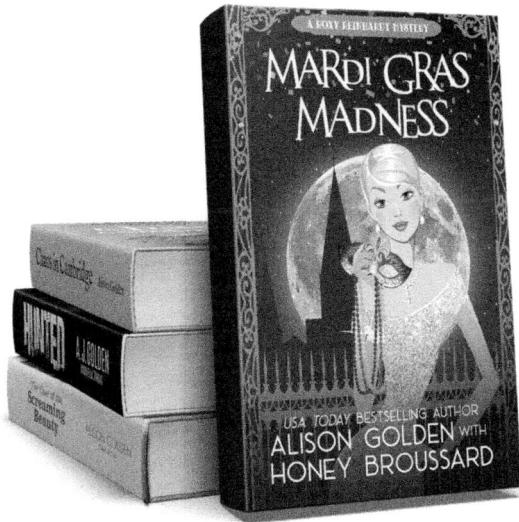

"Your emails seem to come on days when I need to read them because they are so upbeat."
- Linda W -

For a limited time, you can get the first books in each of my series - *Chaos in Cambridge, Hunted* (exclusively for subscribers - not available anywhere else), *The Case of the Screaming Beauty, and Mardi Gras Madness* - plus updates about new releases, promotions, and other Insider exclusives, by signing up for my mailing list at:

https://www.alisongolden.com/roxy

CHAPTER ONE

"SOMETHING'S HAPPENING ACROSS the way," Sage announced, standing at the hotel entrance, staring out. "Something *big*."

The tall, African American woman looked spectacular, as usual. She was wrapped in a purple-and-pink sari, the thin fabric swirling around her strong frame. Her green and blue hair was braided and wound into a bun on the top of her head. Her cheekbones glittered in the morning light.

Breakfast was over, the guests getting up and out early. Behind Sage, Roxy, manager and part-owner of the Funky Cat Inn, flitted about clearing tables and straightening cushions.

"Here we go again," Nat said. The hotel's girl Friday rolled her eyes and wiped her hands on a towel. She looked a little forbidding in her tight black jeans, black metal-band T-shirt, and Doc Martens. On her wrists were studded bracelets. She tossed the towel across her shoulder and looked skeptically at Sage. "What is it this time? Did the hotel's aura shift into Capricorn? Have the spirits misaligned the crystals?"

"No." Sage smiled at Nat, knowing this was just a game they played. "There's a film crew outside Elijah's bakery."

Suddenly alert, Roxy and Nat darted quickly to the large windows. Sure enough, the alleyway outside was filled with people and activity. Men hauled equipment from large vans parked on the main street. People were shouting instructions at each other. A crowd of ten or so stood watching. Roxy recognized some of Elijah's regulars.

"They're setting something up," Roxy mused. "Look, there's lights." The early morning sun reflected off Roxy's short, blonde hair. She was wearing a T-shirt with ripped jeans and sneakers for this part of the day. Her blue eyes matched the denim of her jeans and the bright, clear sky outside.

"And cameras," Sage added.

Nat gasped. "There's a TV truck. Has something happened to Elijah?" she said, fear in her voice.

"I don't believe so," Sage said calmly. "Look, the crew doesn't seem to be in a hurry, and I sense a very happy, positive energy about them." Nat turned from the window to look at Roxy for confirmation, as if Sage's words weren't quite enough to calm her.

"She's right." Roxy shrugged. "They don't seem like a news crew, and most of them appear in good spirits. Look, they're laughing." One crew member slapped another on the shoulder.

The three of them continued to peer through the windows for a little longer until, like a comet hell-bent on destruction, Evangeline's voice burst from the kitchen, her small, chunky frame following it.

"Where's that Elijah with the beignets?" she cried. "Ain't no good bakin' the best beignets in the city if they don't get here in time!"

The elderly woman—former owner of the hotel prior to Roxy and an excellent chef—stopped when she saw the three women peeking outside. Nat turned and said, "Something's happening at his bakery. Looks like a film crew setting up."

Evangeline toddled to her side. "Scoot over. Let me take a look . . . Oh Lord, what's that flamin' fool got himself involved with this time?" Evangeline was officially retired now that Roxy had taken over but couldn't quite seem to stay away.

Roxy withdrew from the window and moved to the door. "I'll go find out."

"No, you won't," Evangeline said.

"Yes, I will!" Roxy argued back.

"No, you won't, cher," Evangeline repeated. "Look, our new guests are about to knock on the door. I know a new guest when I sees one."

"Oh!" Roxy exclaimed, looking quickly about the lobby to check nothing was out of place. She looked down at herself. She was hardly dressed to meet new guests, but there was nothing she could do about that. "Well, get away from the windows then! Sage, why don't you go find out what's happening while I welcome them." Roxy looked at her watch. It was eight thirty a.m. "What are they doing checking in so early?"

Sage glided to the door. Roxy opened it for her, and after Sage had passed through into the courtyard outside the hotel, she kept the door open to greet the new guests and wave them inside.

"Welcome to the Funky Cat." She smiled.

A tall, photogenic brunette turned to Roxy. She looked formidable in her white silk blouse, business pants, and heels. "I'm Paige Crawford," she said in a strong, commanding voice. "I'm an executive producer with UB Productions."

"I'm Roxy Reinhardt, the manager. It's a pleasure to welcome you here."

Paige gestured to an equally tall and confident-looking man beside her. He wore an expensive, tailored suit and had silvery, thick hair that looked as well cut as his clothes. "This is Alan Conway," she said, "head of NOLA-09."

"Oh!" Roxy had not known her guests were from a TV network.

"How do you do?" the man said, shaking Roxy's hand and smiling. There was an old-world charm about his manner.

"And this is Frank Ancelotti," Paige said, turning to a short, stout man in a pinstripe suit and trilby hat. He had a big, bushy handlebar mustache. "My fellow executive producer."

"Executive producer, investor, restaurateur—and my béchamel sauce cannot be beat!" Frank laughed. He took off his trilby and wiped his bald head as he looked around the hotel lobby before turning to smile at Roxy. He looked full of mischief, but as if his mood might turn quickly.

"One hell of a place you got here," he said as he handed Roxy his business card. "Last time I saw a joint like this there were enough bullet holes in it to grate parmesan! Haha! Ah, but it was a different time back then. I've heard plenty about this place. I thought I'd stay the night so I could check it out. A vacation in my own city!" Roxy noticed Paige Crawford share a raised eyebrow with Alan Conway before turning back to point to two men carrying bags into the lobby.

"This is Zach and Mickey," Paige said. Sleeves rolled up and collars undone, the two men looked as though they anticipated a hot day's labor. "Zach's our lead cameraman," Paige said, pointing to a dark, tough man with a heavy, square jaw set in a grim line, grizzly stubble, and messy black hair. "And Mickey is our sound engineer," Paige added, smiling at a lanky dude with stringy muscles and loose, blond, surfer-style locks. The two men nodded before dropping the bags and returning to the courtyard.

"Great," Roxy said, still beaming her cheerful, welcoming smile. Her face was beginning to ache. She noticed that the bags the two men had brought in had tags on them. "I'll have somebody take the luggage upstairs to your rooms. You're staying for two nights, correct?"

"Just one," Paige said, already busy typing something on her phone. "But I booked two just to be sure. We'll pay for both even if we leave tomorrow morning."

"Okay, very good," Roxy said. She wondered what they were doing here, especially since she now suspected they were involved with the goings-on at Elijah's bakery. She wanted to ask, but Paige was engrossed in her phone. "Would you like some breakfast?"

"No, thanks," Paige said quickly. "I've got to supervise the setup. Alan?"

"Ditto for me, I'm afraid," the TV network man responded.

"I'm game. What you servin'?" Frank said, not bothering to wait to be asked. He rubbed his hands together.

"This morning, we have eggs hussarde—that's eggs in a red wine sauce, rusks, and bacon. You could have bananas Foster French toast—French toast slathered with sauce made from butter, brown sugar, cinnamon, dark rum, banana liqueur, and topped with vanilla ice cream. There's also a Creole breakfast skillet—shrimp, French sausage, mushroom, grilled with a lot of rich cheese and plenty of spices that our cook—"

"Stop, stop! I'm sold!" Frank shouted happily. "I'll take the skillet and the French toast. Sounds like much more important work than hanging around the crew." Roxy noticed Paige and Alan share another look. Paige Crawford was obviously not Frank Ancelotti's biggest fan. Her eyeroll communicated her feelings perfectly.

"We'll see you later, Ms. Reinhardt," she said.

"Please call me Roxy. Yes, of course. I'll make sure your bags are in your rooms on your return." Crawford and Conway walked outside, while Roxy led Frank to the dining room to take his order. Paige and Alan might not want to spend time with Frank, but Roxy was keen. She wanted to know what was happening across the way.

CHAPTER TWO

ONCE SHE HAD settled Frank at the dining table, Roxy rushed into the kitchen to fix him a café au lait. Nat stopped her washing at the sink to look at her, but Roxy was too focused on making the coffee to pay her any attention.

"Roxy," Nat said, making her jump.

"Oh!" Roxy put a hand to her throat. "Sorry, I was deep in thought."

"No probs. I was just wondering if I could duck out early tonight, immediately after dinner?"

Roxy busied herself tapping, tamping, and turning knobs. "Yes, of course, if you clean up before breakfast."

"I'll deal with everything when I get back before going to bed. I won't be too late."

"Going anywhere nice?"

"Oh, er, nowhere special," Nat said, suddenly scrubbing the bottom of a pan as hard as she could. "So?"

"So what?"

"What's going on at Elijah's?"

"I don't know. Sage hasn't come back. I've got a guy

from a TV show here though. I think he might have something to do with the fuss. I'm going to see what I can find out."

Evangeline grabbed a couple of plates and laid them noisily down on the counter. "What's the order, cher?" she asked.

"One breakfast skillet, the French toast for dessert," Roxy said.

Evangeline froze and glared at Roxy. "Just one? What happened to the rest?"

Roxy shrugged. "They left. I think they're involved somehow with the crew at Elijah's."

"Who is it?" Evangeline asked. "For breakfast. The blonde ice queen?"

"No. The short, bigger man in the pinstripe suit. His name's Frank."

"Not the Mafia guy!"

"He's *not* a Mafia guy, Evangeline!" Roxy exclaimed as she placed some biscotti on the coffee cup saucer. "He's quite cheerful. A bit strange maybe. But he seems fine."

Evangeline laughed dismissively as she filled a plate with cheesy grilled shrimp and sausages. "You young'uns think the Mafia are just a myth they made up for the movies, but these old eyes have seen things, cher. Mafia used to run this city. I can spot 'em a mile off."

Nat swapped a smile with Roxy and wriggled her eyebrows. *Here we go.*

"The clubs, the bars—they ran them all," Evangeline continued as she filled the plate with mushrooms and more sausage. "*Cheerful?* That's the Mafia alright. They'd crack jokes right up until they broke your legs. And *after* too."

"I'm going to eat with him," said Roxy. "Plate me up too, Evangeline."

"Me three," Nat said.

Evangeline cast a quick glance at them, then pulled out more plates. "I suppose I'm eatin' as well then. Not going to leave you naïve young'uns alone with a killer."

A minute later, the three of them were exiting the kitchen laden with plates of food and drink. Roxy and Nat served Frank first.

"*Now* we're talkin'!" Frank beamed, his eyes gleaming at the sight of the food in front of him. He tucked a napkin into his collar. "You were *torturin'* me havin' me sit here smellin' how good it is!"

He laughed. It was a big, open-mouthed, room-filling sound. Evangeline shot Roxy a look. Roxy had to admit— Frank *did* sound like a Mafia guy. At least what she thought they sounded like based on what she'd seen in movies.

"I hope you enjoy it, Mr. Ancelotti." Roxy smiled as she took a seat opposite him.

"Where did you learn to cook like this?" he asked her as he stacked his fork. "You're not from around here—I can tell from your accent—and this sure as hell looks like the kind of food only a local could cook."

"That's Evangeline," Roxy said, nodding at the older woman, happy to give her the credit. "And Nat. They run the kitchen here at the Funky Cat."

Frank nodded appreciatively at the two women. His mouth full, he still managed to smile as he chewed. Evangeline turned her head sideways and squinted. She raised her chin, assessing him.

"It's a nice little setup you have here," Frank said through his chewing. He was already piling food on his fork in anticipation of his next mouthful. "I like it."

"Morning, Sam," Nat said. Roxy turned to see the tall, blond laundryman-cum-handyman-cum-hotel owner walk in. He carried his toolbox. He wore a pair of loose slacks and a white shirt. His skin was flushed a little from the rising heat outside, but his sandy hair was perfectly swept.

"Morning, everyone," he said. His eyes focused on Roxy. Sam was her business partner. Together they owned the hotel. For the longest time, that was enough to ignore the connection they had. But his eyes would sometimes linger a half second too long, and Roxy would find herself smiling at him for no reason. Strangers would often mistake them for a couple. But nothing had happened between them except for an impulsive kiss some time back. Since then, shyness seemed to have overwhelmed them, and they had reassumed their business partner roles without any acknowledgement of there being anything between them other than laundry, repairs, and the accounts.

For Roxy, there were still too many unanswered questions swimming around the enigma that was Sam. The subject of money was always so hush-hush with him. It made him mysterious, and not in a way that made her feel good. She didn't like secrets. They made her nervous and mistrustful. Sam had been seen handing out brown packets to people on street corners, and Roxy was sure that laundromats, Sam's main business, didn't throw off the kind of money he seemed to possess.

"Ya hungry, cher?" Evangeline asked, already getting up from the table to ready him something.

"No, I'm good. Just a coffee and a beignet for me," Sam said. "I'll get it myself when I'm done fixing that towel holder that's broken."

Roxy stood. "I fixed it myself last night," she said. "But you can help me carry these bags up to the rooms since you're here."

Sam smiled. "Whatever you say, partner," he replied as she led him to the bags in the lobby. Roxy smiled back.

"Since when did you become so handy?" Sam asked as they began up the stairs.

"Oh, I was just preparing the rooms last night and came across it. I messed around a little and . . . it just needed a couple of screws tightened. Simple, really."

Sam laughed. "Good for you. I'm impressed. I like a woman who can get involved and figure things out." Roxy felt heat rise in her cheeks but hid her blush by fiddling with the keys to open the door to one of the guest's suites.

They went from room to room depositing bags. Sam would take them inside while Roxy made a quick inspection to make sure the room's presentation was up to her exacting standards.

"What's going on at Elijah's?" Sam asked as they moved around.

"We don't know," Roxy replied. "Sage went to find out, but she hasn't come back yet. I was going to ask our breakfast guest but haven't had a chance."

"I hope everything's alright."

"Me too," Roxy said.

"Maybe it's something to do with the renovations Elijah's planning for the bakery."

"You mean like a news report?"

"Could be, although I was thinking it might be something more. His building is historic. Perhaps they are planning a documentary on the building and its history."

"Or maybe it'll be a show on the renovations. You know, the before, after, and a disaster."

Sam put down the last bag. "I guess that's it."

"Thanks a lot, Sam."

He turned around to face her but didn't move. They

stood looking at each other. Roxy felt her cheeks warm and pressed her lips together. "Come on. Let's get you that coffee—but no beignet, I'm afraid. Elijah hasn't brought us any. We need to find out what he's up to."

Sam left the room and Roxy locked the door. "Say, that guy at the table. Who is he?" Sam asked.

"Frank Ancelotti. He's part of the group that's staying. The TV people. I think he's something to do with the film crew that's doing . . . *whatever* they're doing . . . at Elijah's."

"Huh . . ."

As they reached the landing, Sam looked deep in thought. "Do you know him?" Roxy asked.

Sam thought a little longer, then shrugged. "I don't know. He looked a bit familiar, that's all."

"Evangeline thinks he's a Mafia guy."

Sam laughed. "How come?"

"I guess all it took was the Italian name and the pinstripe suit."

In the dining room, Frank was still wolfing down the breakfast skillet. Roxy guessed it was his second serving. He was alone at the table. Nat was clearing away some plates. Evangeline had disappeared.

"Nat, would you fix Sam a coffee?" Roxy asked. It took a moment for the tattooed girl to understand the insinuation in Roxy's voice.

"Huh? Oh, sure," Nat said. She quickly disappeared.

Roxy swapped a frown with Sam as they sat at the table. A blast of sounds—clattering and banging—came from the kitchen. Evangeline, probably, taking out her mood on the pots and pans.

Frank hoovered up the last of his skillet and, without pause, eagerly replaced the empty plate with the bananas Foster French toast. He was too busy eating to even stop to speak. Instead, he raised his eyebrows and gave a thumbs-up sign to express his pleasure.

"So, Mr. Ancelotti . . ." Roxy said.

"Frank," the man blurted out quickly, just before shoveling another enormous bite into his mouth.

"Frank . . . You're an executive producer?" Frank nodded as he ate.

"At a TV company?" Another nod.

"If you don't mind me asking, do you have anything to do with the film crew at the bakery across the road?" Frank nodded happily, smiling as he chewed, a twinkle in his eye.

"What exactly are you filming?" Sam asked.

Frank held up a finger, asking them to wait while he finished his food, when his face lit up at a sight behind them. Roxy turned to see what he was looking at.

"*Sor-ry!*" announced Elijah loudly. He struck a dramatic pose as he stepped into the room. Leaning on one hip sideways to them, his foot pointed, he held one arm high in the air as he pushed his chin out, flicking his hair as he did so. Sam and Frank stared at him in silence, perhaps with a little horror. Roxy was in awe. She wished she had the confidence to make such a showstopping entrance.

Slowly, in the silence, Roxy's gaze drifted to Elijah's skyward hand. In it, he balanced a big, white cardboard box. So finally, they were here. Better late than never. The beignets had arrived.

CHAPTER THREE

AS ELIJAH RELAXED his pose, two women appeared alongside him. One was Sage. The other was a cheerful, plump woman around thirty years old. She had rosy cheeks. Her hair was scraped into a tight ponytail, and she wore a pink cardigan over cream leggings, the outfit matching her complexion perfectly.

"Elijah!" Roxy called out. "We were worried about you!"

"I know, I know," Elijah sang, twirling into the room in a show of energy. "I wanted it to be a surprise."

"A surprise?" called Evangeline. She'd come to the swing door at the entrance to the kitchen, having overheard the commotion, and was now leaning against the doorframe. "I'll give you a surprise, cher! Let's get those beignets on the table already! They're hours late."

"Elijah, my boy!" Frank said happily, finding a moment between bites. "Good to see you. Come and try this banana thing. It's incredible!"

"Frank, you old dog," Elijah said. "I should have known

I'd find you where the food was at." Frank laughed heartily, and it was clear they were good friends. Roxy felt even more confused.

"Are you wearing . . . *makeup?*" Sam asked Elijah.

"Of course!" the baker said as he took a seat beside Roxy. "Do you know what a camera can do to you without it? Even someone like *me* needs an artistic genius to smooth out a few flaws. And luckily, I have one of the best. Everybody, this is Jocelyn—my MUA." Elijah gestured to the pink and cream woman next to him as though he were announcing a star. Jocelyn giggled happily, blushed some more, and gave them a little wave.

"Oh, Elijah," she said, her cheeks going from rosy to crimson. "*Stop!*"

Nat arrived with a fresh coffee pot and several cups. Evangeline brought over a plate of the bananas Foster French toast for everyone to help themselves and another piled with fresh beignets.

"Your *what?*" Nat said.

"My MUA," Elijah said proudly. He quickly grabbed a slice of toast and began eating while Roxy, Sage, Sam, Nat, and Evangeline stared at him, waiting for an explanation.

Jocelyn piped up. "He means makeup artist." Five pairs of eyes swiveled to look at her. Frank kept on eating, the food keeping him from saying anything. "I'm his makeup artist."

The friends were silent as they took in this information. Five pairs of eyes swiveled back to Elijah. "Well?" Roxy asked eventually. Elijah looked up, his cheeks full of food. "Are you going to tell us what's going on?"

"Oh, Roxy, I'm sorry," Elijah said, quickly swallowing. "Everything's happened so fast. I've been up since three baking and getting everything ready. I don't even have much time now. I have to get back in fifteen minutes. I only came by to drop off the beignets and see how you were doing. I wanted it to be a surprise, you see."

"Wanted what to be a surprise?" Sam asked. "We're all still clueless."

"Here's the thing," Elijah said. He paused. "Try not to all scream at once." He jiggled a little. "Are you ready? I'm in the running to be the third judge on *New Orleans Ultimate Baker*!"

There was a clatter at the other end of the table. Everyone turned to see Evangeline had dropped an empty cup.

"*New Orleans Ultimate Baker?*" Evangeline repeated, her eyes as big as tractor tires. "Ain't that somethin'?"

"It sure is." Elijah grinned.

"What is that?" Roxy asked. "*New Orleans Ultimate Baker.*"

"It's a TV show," Nat explained. "You haven't heard of it?"

"It's not just a show," Elijah said. "It's a *phenomenon*. People go crazy for it. Ask Frank, he's worked on it from the start." At Elijah's elbow, Frank nodded as he shoveled in more slices of banana.

"Anyway," Elijah continued, "one of the judges has gone on to other things, so they need a replacement. Frank has known me for years, so he put my name forward. Now it's down to just me and somebody else. I'm *this* close." He held up his two forefingers, half an inch apart.

"How did you keep *that* a secret?" Nat asked.

"Yes," Sage added. "You're not known for keeping secrets."

Elijah laughed, then said, "Well, honestly, I never really expected to get this far. Frank put me forward six months ago. There were about a hundred candidates back then. I figured 'what the hell,' but I never thought I'd be in the final two. I didn't want to tell you all and for my application to go nowhere . . . Yet here I am. Seriously, even if I don't nail the gig, I'm amazed I've gotten this close."

"I'm not amazed." Sam slapped Elijah on the back. "I've always said you were made for TV. But what's with the film crew over the road? You say you haven't got the job yet."

"Not *yet*. That's why they're filming me. My day. My kitchen. They want to see how well I work on camera. And, of course, if I *do* get the job, they need some footage for my bio, my introduction in the show. Isn't it *exciting?*" He growled like a lion about to feast on a carcass.

"*New Orleans Ultimate Baker* . . . my friend Elijah . . ." Evangeline repeated dreamily, staring blankly into midair.

"Who's your competition?" Roxy asked.

Elijah looked at Jocelyn and pulled a face. Jocelyn giggled, then covered her mouth quickly.

"Patrice Marveau," Elijah hissed. "Have you heard of him? He owns Patisserie Paradis in the French Quarter. Great baker, terrible person. If you think *I'm* a handful, then Patrice is a whole wagonload."

Jocelyn giggled again nervously. She leaned in a little and spoke in a thin, high-pitched voice. "His specialty is making people cry. The judges have to be critical, but in auditions, I've seen Patrice take it way too far. He's just *mean*. And he's not the easiest person to work with, either. To be honest, I think the whole production team is rooting for Elijah. Patrice really can be difficult. I've never known anyone complain like he does about his makeup. I have to spend twice as long on him as I ever do on anyone else."

"Me, for example." Elijah smiled. "But then, you do

have more to work with." Jocelyn laughed, and so did the others around the table.

"You're our guy," Frank said, poking his fork at Elijah. He leaned back, stuffed and satisfied. "I'm pushing for you, Elijah. You know that."

"Who's deciding between the two of you?" Sam asked.

"Paige, Alan, and myself," Frank said. "Though we'll run our decision through a few other people at the network."

A pang of concern made Roxy shiver. She looked down at her food, trying to hide her frown. She remembered how Paige had rolled her eyes when Frank spoke. Perhaps having Frank on his side wasn't the best for Elijah.

"*Ultimate Baker* . . ." Evangeline said again, sighing.

Sage had been gazing at Elijah with her calm, serene expression for a while. Suddenly she spoke, and as always, her words sounded deep and important. "I feel good things," she said. "You have a lively spirit, Elijah. A spirit that's destined to shine far and bright. TV is perfect for you. The universe aligning."

Nat looked up from her phone and raised her eyebrows. Roxy noticed and nudged her. Nat shrugged and said, "I agree, actually. Elijah is clearly meant for bigger, better, brighter things."

"Thanks," Elijah said, checking his reflection in the back of a spoon. "But let's change the subject. I don't want to jinx it." He widened his eyes. "Nothing's certain yet."

"Indeed," called a voice from the doorway. "Nothing's certain yet *at all*."

Everyone turned. Like Elijah, the man was tall and skinny. He had fair hair that reached his shoulders. He roughly ran his hands through it and shook it out. His blue eyes burned like headlights, but his skin seemed shiny and waxy, much like his red leather pants. He wore a tight T-shirt and alligator shoes with huge buckles. Like Elijah, he posed: one hand high and limp, his head at an angle, his smile well-practiced. Gleaming, overly large teeth split his face in two.

Roxy stood up quickly. "Hello. Welcome to the Funky Cat," she said. "Are you looking for a room?"

"Ha!" the man cackled. He looked around with distaste. "I wouldn't *dream* of staying here."

"Ignore him, Roxy," said Elijah with a sigh. "He's nobody. That's just Patrice Marveau."

CHAPTER FOUR

"THE ONE AND only," Patrice said as he sashayed around the table. He looked at the food as if it was off-putting. "These are your beignets no doubt, Elijah? I could smell the grease the second I walked in."

Sam half rose. "Now hold on a second, buddy. You can't. . ."

Elijah stopped him with a raised hand. He shook his head. "Don't worry about it, Sam. This is normal behavior for Patrice. It's who he is."

Roxy noticed how Jocelyn's smile had vanished. She had shrunk a little and was staring at her plate, as though she wanted to jump into it and hide among the food there.

"What brings you here?" Frank asked. "We're not filming your bit until Thursday."

"Just thought I'd pop by," Patrice said, sitting down. "Offer my . . ." He paused to pick up a beignet delicately. He grimaced and quickly dropped it back on to the plate. "Support."

Roxy could see exactly what the others meant about

Patrice. He was mean and catty. Everything he said contained an insulting subtext.

Turning to Jocelyn, Patrice said, "What's your name again?"

"Jocelyn," the woman said meekly.

"Did you find a better range of powders like I asked?"

"Not yet, Mr. Marveau. I'm going to buy some as soon as we're done with Elijah today and . . ."

"Make sure you do before Thursday. Get a few different ones for me to choose from."

"Of course, Mr. Marveau."

"What roast are you using in your coffee?" Patrice asked Roxy as he reached for the coffee pot.

"French."

Patrice winced again. "I mean . . . I don't *mind* French," he said as he poured himself a cup. "But it's very last year. *Everyone's* drinking blonde these days."

Roxy shot a glance at Sage across the table. She looked deeply uncomfortable. A frown rumpled her usually ultra-smooth skin. Sage was a spiritual woman who perceived all kinds of energies in her surroundings. She was intuitive and empathetic enough to feel the emotions of others as her own. Patrice had single-handedly and in just a couple of minutes set the whole table on edge.

Meanwhile, Nat glared at Patrice. Roxy could tell she was close to making a scathing comment about him. Out loud. The Goth girl had learned quite well how to hold her tongue since Roxy had known her, but it wouldn't take much more for her to explode. Across the table, Sam spoke quietly with Elijah, while Evangeline continued to daydream about *Ultimate Baker*, completely ignoring everyone at the table.

Frank slurped the last of his coffee and took the napkin

from his collar. "Well, that's me full and fat," he said, patting his stomach as he stood. "Thank you for the *primo* breakfast. Best I've had in a long time."

"I'm glad you liked it." Roxy smiled back, then gestured at Nat and Evangeline. "I'm proud of my kitchen, so that means a lot."

"Oh my, is that the time?" Elijah said, glancing at the clock. He quickly stood. "I should be getting back. Jocelyn?"

"I'm right behind you, Elijah."

"And I'm right behind *you*," Frank said.

"Anything we can do to help you with the filming over there?" Sam said.

Elijah paused for a moment to think. "Actually, we're probably going to run short on kitchen towels. I threw out my dirty, old ones and now I'm paying the price."

"Oh, I'll bring some over," Roxy said, getting up.

"No rush," Elijah said. "We're good for now, but if you could drop them by in an hour."

"Sure thing."

"See you later, sweethearts," Elijah said. Frank gave a smiling nod to the crowd around the table and gestured for Jocelyn to step ahead of him.

Roxy showed the trio to the door. Across the way, she saw three people standing in front of the two men who'd brought in the TV company's bags earlier. The dark, square-jawed man had a camera hoisted on his shoulder. The fairer, skinny one held a microphone out of shot. Paige Crawford stood to one side talking. "Who are they, Elijah?" Roxy said.

"Wh—oh, that's Annie Broolan, Xavier Jean-Pierre, and Lacey Gregory. They're interviewing them about the café reno. Gosh, Rox, if I get this gig, I'll be able to go ahead with it. Tear it down and build it back up. Wouldn't that be fabulous? Annie's my construction manager for the reno. We were at school together. Xavier Jean-Pierre's the historical restoration consultant. The other person is Lacey Gregory, city planning box checker and all around pain in the ass. She is a stickler for the tiniest of details." Elijah clenched his fists and squished up his face. "It's all so exciting! Gotta go!"

Patrice remained at the table quietly watching this interaction from the dining room. He seemed without a care. Eventually he stood, and without saying a single word of goodbye or thank you, swept through the front door.

"Wow," Nat said.

"Can you believe that guy?" Sam added.

"There's something very dark in that man," Sage said. "I could almost smell it, the bitterness, the envy. The sourness of hatred. It would take a lot of work to heal such a soul."

"Well, I think he deserves a smack in the mouth," Nat said in her British accent. She began to gather up the plates to take them into the kitchen.

"Is something wrong?" Sam asked Roxy as she came back in the room. Her lips were pressed together in a thin line, and she was flapping a napkin against her thigh.

"Hmm," she said. "I was just thinking . . . Patrice Marveau . . . What did he come here for? He doesn't want to 'support' Elijah during his filming at all. Is he up to something?"

"I suspect he's intent on mixing up his dark energies with Elijah's good ones. Perhaps to bring him down. I'll come with you when you take those towels over. We'll each do what we can to support our friend," Sage said. "I'll prepare a short protection blessing for him."

"That's a good idea," Roxy said.

"I'd come too," Sam said, "but I've . . . There's something I've got to do."

Roxy looked at him, and he forced a smile. She could tell that whatever he *had to do* wasn't about to become public knowledge. Just when she was trying to make her mind up about him, his secretive ways got in the way again.

CHAPTER FIVE

THE CAMERA CREW had done their thing at Elijah's bakery and left. The producers had stayed the night. A quiet, young couple arrived at the Funky Cat for two nights. Two tourists from Italy were visiting for a week. Underneath all this activity, everyone was on tenterhooks waiting to hear if Elijah had won the job as third judge on *Ultimate Baker*.

"It would make such a difference to me," Elijah had said to Roxy at one of their coffees. Once a week the pair got together to talk about their businesses, a sort of mastermind. "It would put this place on the map." He nodded at the bakery building. "And it would raise my profile stratospherically. Who knows what it might lead to?"

"Presumably, more income," Roxy said.

"It certainly would. I'd be able to do that refurb, no problem. Not only could I update the bakery inside, but I could also expand upward to the second floor *and* have the historical external features preserved and restored too." Elijah pressed his hands between his thighs and shut his eyes tightly. "Oooh, Roxy, I so want this. I can't sleep!"

Roxy patted his hand and squelched her misgivings. She still remembered the glances exchanged between Paige Crawford and Alan Conway behind Frank Ancelotti's back, Elijah's champion at the TV company. "I hope it all works out for you. When are they going to give you their decision?"

"Any time. They've done Patrice's screen test. Now it's up to them to choose and let us know. I'm just trying to distract myself while I wait."

Roxy felt almost as nervous as Elijah. It was as though he had transferred some of his agitation onto her. Now she needed to know the outcome of the decision as much as he did. Like Sage, her empathy was strong, although at times, Roxy felt her sensitivity was a curse.

For everyone else though, life continued as normal. Nat had quietly continued to disappear immediately after dinner to places she hadn't cared to share with Roxy. Sage was completely engrossed in a new project: taking beautiful photos of the hotel and updating all mentions of the Funky Cat online. Evangeline was besotted with her puppy Pinkie but still showed up to make the odd breakfast and dinner despite her "retirement." Elijah flitted in and out, a ball of nervous energy. Roxy hadn't seen much of Sam; he'd sent someone else to pick up the laundry, and she wondered why.

A week after the camera crew had shown up at the bakery, Roxy arrived at the dining table for her morning café au lait and beignets. All the guests had breakfasted and left the hotel early. Sage was there, working on her laptop. Nat sat across the table from Sage, sipping coffee and tapping away on her phone. Roxy moved to glance over her shoulder to see what she was doing.

"Oh, that looks amazing!" Roxy said when she saw a picture Sage had taken of one of the rooms.

"Thank you," Sage said, putting the finishing touches to the filter she was using. Sage flicked through some more of the shots.

"They all look so great," Roxy said. "Wow. They really show off the hotel."

"I think it would be good to put some pictures of us up as well," Sage said. "People like to see faces. Especially yours, Roxy. This hotel is an extension of your character now. Your spirit fills this place."

Roxy laughed. "I don't know about that," she said, then thought about it a little more. A year ago, she would have immediately run away from the idea of putting a pretty picture of herself in promotional material for the hotel. But now . . .

"Actually, why not? I'm up for it. What do you say, Nat?"

Nat didn't look up from her phone. "Huh? No chance. I hate having my picture taken."

Of course, Nat would hate it. Her visa had expired. She'd found cash-in-hand employment with Evangeline and had been living on the down-low ever since, unable to face leaving New Orleans for the rainy weather of England. She had made a happy life for herself in the city, but she constantly lived in fear of the authorities finding her. Parading herself on the hotel's social media pages would not be a good idea.

"How about just me and you then, Sage?"

"Let's do it," Sage said.

A loud clatter from the kitchen reverberated around the dining room. "Is Evangeline alright?" Roxy asked.

Nat rolled her eyes and said, "Elijah's late with the

beignets *again*. You know Evangeline, she gets cranky about that kind of thing. She hadn't any fresh ones to offer the guests. One of them insisted she reheat yesterday's leftovers, saying that was better than nothing, and you know how Evangeline hates that."

Roxy looked at the door as if she hoped Elijah might come through it. She frowned. The last time Elijah was late with the beignets, he had a big surprise for them.

Five minutes later, the door banged loudly as it was flung open. Roxy was on her second cup of coffee, flicking through the hotel's mail. Elijah stood in the doorway, dramatically balancing a platter of beignets in his hand. "Good morning, ladies!"

"You look in an exceptionally good mood, Elijah," Roxy said.

"Unlike Evangeline," Nat added. "She's furious with you for being late with the beignets again."

"She'll forgive me when I tell her my news," Elijah said. He struck one of his trademark poses, his leg out, his toe pointed, his chin high. "It's my time to shine!" he announced proudly.

"Isn't that the case every morning?" Nat said.

Elijah laughed as he strode toward them. "True, but now," he said, "it will also be every Thursday evening prime time between eight and nine thirty. I just got the call. I'm officially a judge on *Ultimate Baker*. I start today!"

CHAPTER SIX

LATER THAT MORNING, Sam, hastily recruited for the job, drove Elijah, Roxy, and Nat to the studio in his Rolls Royce. Sage and Evangeline stayed behind to hold down the Funky Cat fort.

"I'm to arrive in style!" Elijah cried when he saw the car.

"You're a celebrity now, man," Sam replied.

"Well, I'll be your friend forever if this is how I'm treated on the regular," Nat said as she settled into her padded, luxurious leather seat. "I could get used to this."

"So glad you guys are coming with me. I feel quite overwhelmed." Elijah fanned his hand in front of his face. Roxy patted his thigh and smiled reassuringly at him.

"Have you heard from Patrice? Perhaps to graciously extend his congratulations?"

"Goodness, no. In fact, I don't think anyone has heard from him for a few days."

"This street?" Sam asked Elijah over his shoulder.

"Yeah," Elijah answered, looking through the windshield. "That big blue building at the end."

"Got it."

"Ladies, look," Elijah said, pointing out of the window. "That's Patrice's bakery right there."

Roxy and Nat leaned over to look at the large shop front that sat under a pink canopy, the words *Patisserie Paradis* in gold letters spread across it. Most of the tables outside were filled with people, and as they passed by, Roxy noticed that the queue at the counter extended to the sidewalk.

"It actually looks quite nice," Sam said, glancing over from the driver's seat.

"Oh, sure," Elijah said. "Patrice is a lot of things—and the owner of a good bakery is one of them."

"But new judge on *Ultimate Baker* he is not!" Nat said quickly. Sam and Elijah laughed. Sam pulled the car over as Nat continued. "He's going to have to watch you go to the studio every day. That'll teach him."

Roxy smiled. She found it endearing how defensive Nat was of her friends, including Elijah, even if she was a little prickly at times. Nat would probably never forgive Patrice for acting the way he had toward her friends when he had visited them at the Funky Cat. Sometimes having someone as fierce and protective as Nat on your side was a very good thing.

Sam stopped the car, and before anyone could move, he'd opened the door for Elijah. He even nodded as if he were Elijah's chauffeur, making Elijah laugh as the friends entered the studio. "You are going up in the world, Elijah. You have an entourage," Nat cried.

"Mr. Walder!" called a woman as soon as she saw Elijah enter the huge glass lobby with his "entourage."

"That's me," Elijah answered happily, throwing out some jazz hands. Being recognized clearly delighted him.

"I'm Jenny," the woman said, holding out her hand. "I'm

here to look after you. I'm your wrangler. It's my job to get you what you need and make sure you are where you need to be at the time you need to be there. I've got your ID. The *Ultimate Baker* team is up on the third floor. I'll bring you to them soon, but I'd like to give you a quick tour beforehand."

"Great," Elijah said, taking the ID and putting the lanyard over his head, careful not to mess up his hair.

"You're all with Mr. Walder?" Jenny said, looking at the others.

"Call me Elijah, please." Jenny smiled. "And yes. They're with me. They came along to offer some support. That's alright?"

"Of course," Jenny said, smiling even more broadly. "Follow me."

For the next thirty minutes, the group was led around the New Orleans television studio. Jenny carefully explained to Elijah the protocols for the building, where his dressing room was, from whom to order his choice of food, and how he could get hold of her for anything else he might need. They took the elevator to the studios. On the way, Jenny allowed the group to peek into other studio projects. "But only if you're very, very quiet."

They saw the newsroom and watched the weather-person give the daily report in front of a green screen. They quietly snuck into a morning chat show. Three women sat on a couch interviewing a local musician who had just returned from a tour in Europe.

Jenny calmly explained everything to Elijah, answering his questions and showing him where things were. Behind them, Sam, Nat, and Roxy quietly whispered to each other.

"Wasn't that Donna Perry, the chat show host?"

"And wasn't that Megan Rothkopf, the soap opera star?"

Eventually, Jenny led them all to the *Ultimate Baker*

studio. It was a vast space. A kitchen was being assembled at the back. There were dozens of crew members carrying, lifting, fixing, and setting everything up. It was noisy with the sounds of drilling and hammering.

Suddenly a familiar voice called out to Elijah from the corner of the studio. They all turned. It was Paige Crawford, the executive producer. She approached them with confident strides.

"We were just wondering where you were," she said as she got close. She smiled cheerfully at Roxy. "Oh, hey! Nice to see you again."

"Likewise," Roxy said.

Paige turned to Elijah. "Come along," she said. "I'll introduce you to the team."

"Should we stay here?" Nat asked.

"No, you're welcome to come too," Paige said. "We're not filming yet, so it's all very informal. But when we do start, watch out!" She smiled again. "There are a lot of protocols to observe."

Elijah looked back at his friends and wiggled his shoulders. Roxy could tell his nerves had been replaced with a giddy excitement. They followed Paige across the studio, weaving between the busy crew members and their equipment. It was then that they heard it.

A sound far more sudden and shocking than any work tool pierced the air. They froze. A scream stopped them in their tracks.

The activity in the studio came to a halt, and every single person turned toward the bloodcurdling sound. The scream had come from a young woman. With her clipboard and headset, she looked like a showrunner. She held a phone to her ear, as pale as snow.

"Andrea?" Paige said, taking charge. She quickly walked over to the frightened young woman. "What is it?"

"It's . . . it's . . ." The girl stuttered, staring into space. "It's Patrice."

Paige frowned and carefully put a hand on the girl's shoulder. "What about him?"

Andrea shivered a little but managed to meet Paige's eyes. "He's . . . they found him . . ." She pressed the phone harder to her ear to listen again, maintaining eye contact with Paige. "At his bakery. He's been found . . . dead."

CHAPTER SEVEN

T THE NEWS, silence followed gasps. Shock rippled through the air. It was as if an icy wind had flung open the doors and brushed against their cheeks, the backs of their necks, anywhere their flesh was exposed.

Nobody moved. Nobody said anything. Time seemed to slow down. It felt to Roxy like a whole hour passed. Then, something inside her forced her to move quickly forward toward the door.

"Roxy!" Sam called quietly after her. "Where are you going?"

Roxy stopped just long enough to turn and answer him. "I'm going to find out what happened. His bakery is only a block from here."

"What about . . ." But Roxy was already trotting away.

"Good idea," Nat said, hurrying after her.

"I'm coming too," Elijah said adamantly.

Sam looked around him at the shocked faces, then quickly followed his friends out of the studio. He loved

Roxy's new confidence, but it made her much harder to keep up with.

When they arrived, there was already a police cordon around Patisserie Paradis. A small crowd focused on a narrow alleyway beside the bakery. A couple of police cars were parked diagonally on the street in front stopping traffic.

Roxy, Sam, Nat, and Elijah joined the crowd and peered down the alleyway like everyone else. The sight was uninspiring. It was rundown and littered with trash. Graffiti marred the end wall of the bakery and that of the business on the other side. It was dark and uninviting, even in daylight. In the gloom, all the friends could see was a fire escape snaking up the side of the building and the outlines of a few dumpsters. In the distance, a young man in kitchen work clothes leaned against an outer wall, smoking anxiously.

Two police officers walked slowly around the three dumpsters that lined the walls of the alleyway, inspecting the grimy ground. A third officer held one of the dumpster lids open so that the detective next to him could peer inside as he held a flashlight overhead.

"Is that . . ." Nat began the question but didn't finish it. The detective glanced up and over the crowd.

"Humph. Yes," Roxy said. "It's Detective Johnson."

As she said it, Johnson's eyes met hers. Recognition passed over his bulldog face. Roxy groaned quietly to herself. She and the detective had history. The glowering fire in his eyes made Roxy realize he hadn't forgotten any of it. He started walking over to her.

"Harman," he growled at one of the officers. Johnson always sounded as if he'd had a terrible night's sleep and was dying of thirst. "Get rid of this crowd. It's a crime scene —not a street performance."

Roxy prepared to walk away, but Johnson's voice stopped her. "Not *you*," he said, coming up to her on the other side of the police tape. Roxy turned around to face him. His eyes scanned her, then Nat, Sam, and Elijah, slowly recognizing them. Nat hung back a little. "What are you doing here?" Johnson said to the group.

"We heard someone was found dead," Sam said.

"Did you now?" Johnson replied, squinting and frowning. "And you thought you'd all pass some time by coming to have a good look, did you?"

"Of course not!" Nat said defiantly, her indignation causing her to forget momentarily her aversion to authority.

"We *know* him!" Elijah added. Johnson raised his eyebrow, apparently interested in this juicy piece of intel. Elijah meekly backpedaled. "I mean . . . if it's who we think it is. And we barely know him really at all."

"Well, why don't you come and see what you came to see then?" Johnson said. He lifted the police tape and nodded for them to join him on the other side of it. Leading them to the dumpster, he pulled on a glove he had in his pocket and lifted the lid.

Elijah gasped so hard it came out as a yelp. Sam groaned and turned his head away, his hand over his mouth.

"Oh. My. God." Nat said, her enunciation even more precise than usual.

Roxy felt her body go cold and stiff. Lying on top of black garbage bags, and looking just as crumpled, was Patrice. His bright yellow shirt was patched with dried blood, his limbs strewn around awkwardly. Blackened, sticky goo marred his waxy face. Flies buzzed around him.

When everyone averted their eyes, Johnson brought the dumpster's lid down.

"So," he said loudly, as if proving a point, "is that the guy you know? But not really. But kind of do. But barely at all?"

Elijah looked like he was about to weep. He nodded slowly. Detective Johnson scanned all of them, ending with Roxy. He swatted a fly before speaking.

"Why am I not surprised?" he said. "What's that now? The third or fourth death I've investigated that you're associated with?"

"That's not fair!" Roxy exclaimed. Somehow, everything Johnson said to her sounded like an accusation, or as if he were building up to one. Even with her new level of confidence, Roxy felt exasperated and ill at ease under his hard gaze.

"Perhaps not," Johnson said without missing a beat. "Yet here I am investigating a bloody murder on the other side of town from your hotel and, suddenly, up you pop."

"Now hold up," Sam said, stepping forward. "You can't go around saying stuff like that." Roxy put her hand on Sam's arm to let him know she was okay.

"Maybe," Johnson said. "But then again, I don't much like civilians meddling with my investigations, and whenever she's around, I know she's going to be getting in my way."

"What are you even talking about?!" Elijah cried angrily. "There's a man dead and all you can do is pick on Roxy!"

Detective Johnson glared at them again before yanking a notebook from his pocket and flipping it open. "Let's get to it then," he said, licking his pencil. "Which one of you knew Patrice Marveau best?"

CHAPTER EIGHT

NOBODY SAID ANYTHING, but Nat unconsciously turned her body toward Elijah. Johnson noticed. He shifted his gaze. Elijah, who still looked like he might burst into tears, sighed heavily and then shook his head as he searched for the words and the strength to say them. "He was a baker—just like me. I knew *of* him for years, but I never really met or spoke to him until . . ." Elijah trailed off, and even Roxy thought he sounded evasive.

"Until what?" Johnson prompted.

"Until we . . . you see . . . we were both going for this role on a TV show . . ."

Johnson's eyes narrowed until they were like chips of coal. He pointed at Elijah, then at the dumpster. "You and him were in competition with each other?" Johnson said. "For what? A job?"

"It wasn't really like that," Elijah said quickly.

"When was this?"

"Recently."

"How recently?"

"Um, I got the call this morning."

"You got the call about what?"

"That I'd won the job."

"What kind of job?"

"A TV job. Third judge on *Ultimate Baker*."

"Never heard of it."

"Oh, it's quite popular." Elijah brightened for a moment before sobering.

"This man has been dead for days. And now you're telling me that he was your rival for some TV thing . . . and you just learned that you beat him out?"

"Yeah."

Roxy winced. She knew how it sounded.

Johnson swatted another fly buzzing around his head. "That's a mighty fine coincidence, isn't it?"

Roxy had had enough. In a flash she remembered all her meetings with Johnson, including the very first one where he had interviewed her in a cramped closet and another when his officer had interrogated her in a toilet. Johnson had been just the same with her then as he was now with Elijah—treating him as if he was guilty from the start. Back then her head had spun. She was newly arrived in New Orleans. She had been an insecure, frustrated, and aimless young woman whose boyfriend had dumped her on the same day as she had lost her job.

But now, things were different. She was no longer timid. She would no longer be intimidated. More than that, she wouldn't stand by while Johnson pulled this routine on Elijah. Especially when he was clearly shell-shocked, almost speechless.

"Now you listen . . ." Roxy began. She pointed a finger at the detective.

But before she could continue, the detective's expression changed. His pupils shrunk to tiny pricks. All the power and authority seemed to disappear from them. Roxy saw something else there. Fear? Johnson wasn't even looking at her now; he had noticed something behind her. She turned slowly.

"Billy boy!" Frank Ancelotti cried as he walked up to the group. Seeing him in daylight, Roxy realized how short and chubby Frank was. He wore a light gray suit this time, and a navy-blue shirt with a dark grey tie. He also wore a toupee. "Long time, no see!" Roxy, Sam, Elijah, and Nat stood aside as Frank paid no mind to the police tape and ducked underneath it.

"What are you doing here, Frank?" Johnson said. His irritability had instantly evaporated, leaving his voice cold and emotionless. "Last I heard you were buying a stake in a media company."

"That's right. And the production arm of my burgeoning empire is just up the road." Frank smiled at Johnson as if he were a friendly dog. Johnson glared back like Frank was an enemy of old.

"The same TV production company that this guy"— Johnson pointed at Elijah—"and the dead guy inside the dumpster were competing to work for?"

"So, Patrice *is* dead?" Frank said, his smile disappearing. He sounded surprised and shocked, but Roxy wondered if it was genuine. "That's terrible."

There was a strange tension in the air now. Roxy assessed Johnson. She hadn't seen him like this before. He seemed humbled, and a little . . . frightened. A van screeched to a halt beside them, followed by the sound of slamming doors.

"Forensics is here," Johnson said. He slapped his notebook shut and stepped aside to let the team through. "None

of you leave the city. I'm going to want to talk to you later."
He leaned toward Frank. "You too, Frank."

"Of course!" Frank said. "You know where you can find
me."

Johnson let out a low noise that might have been a growl
before storming off to his vehicle. Other police officers
quickly approached the group.

"Out of the way please. Return to the other side of the
tape," they commanded.

"You look shaken, Elijah," Frank said when they were
out on the sidewalk. "Why don't you skip the meeting
today. Don't worry, I'll explain to the others. We'll probably
cut it short anyway . . . under the circumstances."

"What was that all about?" Roxy asked, sounding
confused as Frank began walking back in the direction of
the studio. Her mind spun. Patrice's death, Johnson's berat-
ing, and his strange reaction to Frank had bamboozled her.

"What do you mean?" Nat snapped. "Johnson's always
like that. It's amazing he makes any progress as a detective
considering how he treats people."

"Not that," Roxy said. "The weirdness between him
and Frank. Didn't you pick up on it?" She turned to Sam.
Sam glanced at Elijah and shrugged.

Roxy frowned at him. It wasn't the reaction she
expected of Sam. He was usually quite astute. *Did he know
more than he was letting on?*

"Isn't it obvious?" Nat said. "Evangeline even told us—
Frank is a mafioso. A gangster. He and Johnson probably
know each other well."

"Is that true, Sam?" Roxy asked, reflexively turning to
him.

Sam shrugged again and took his time answering. Sam
was New Orleans born and bred. "I don't know . . . There

are rumors he was involved in some shady stuff at one time. Just like there are rumors about almost every club and restaurant owner in the city—except you, of course. Everyone knows you are completely aboveboard and whiter than white. But Frank . . . rumors abound. I've never seen evidence of him doing anything illegal, though. It's probably nothing; just people jumping to conclusions because he's Italian and successful."

"What about you Elijah?" Nat asked. "Do you know anything about it? Frank and the Mafia?"

Elijah sighed heavily. He put a hand to his forehead as if he was about to faint. "All I know," he said, "is that I want to get out of here."

"Come on," Sam said. "Let's get to the car. I'll take us all home."

Roxy stared out of the window on the car ride back to the hotel. She had plenty to think about. Patrice was dead. Elijah had got the *Ultimate Baker* job. And Frank was looking more like the Mafia guy Evangeline had said he was.

For once, she almost didn't blame Johnson for jumping to conclusions. She could guess his thinking: Frank wanted Elijah to win the *Ultimate Baker* gig, so he killed Patrice, or more likely had him killed, just before the decision had to be made. Elijah would get the job by default. Ordinarily Roxy would consider that kind of thinking crazy, but now that she knew Frank's reputation as Mafia wasn't restricted to Evangeline, it made more sense. Wasn't that exactly the sort of thing Mafia did? Put hits out on people they didn't like? But why would Frank care so much about Elijah getting the job that he'd kill his rival?

Roxy leaned her head on the window of the Rolls Royce and let the coolness of the glass calm her. Elijah was Roxy's friend, and she trusted him completely. She knew Elijah would never kill anyone. But did he *know* something about it? Or perhaps he knew someone who was *capable* of it and *suspected* something. Was that why he was so shaken?

When they got back to the Funky Cat, Roxy poured herself some coffee. She picked up one of the morning's long-forgotten beignets and went to sit by the window in the lobby to think. Of course Elijah would be shaken, she thought. You don't need to be friends with someone to feel terrible about their death. Especially one like Patrice's. Doesn't mean they know anything about it.

Roxy gazed out beyond the hibiscus plants in the court-yard to Elijah's bakery. It was quiet now, just a few midday stragglers. It would get busy again as the afternoon wore on. Questions whirled about her mind like cotton candy in a windstorm as she sipped. How had Elijah met Frank? Why did Frank want to help him so much? Was Frank really a gangster? So many questions.

She was starting to feel as stressed and lost as she had back in Ohio. She needed to gather herself. She had a hotel to run.

CHAPTER NINE

J OHNSON ARRIVED LATE that evening. It was a quiet night in the hotel. Roxy's two Italian guests had gone out to eat while a handsome, tired-looking businessman had checked in and gone straight to bed. A honeymooning couple only had eyes for one another in the dining room, while a table of three had dropped in on spec and been treated to a feast of catfish jambalaya and dessert with a New Orleans twist—a sticky toffee pudding drizzled with Creole cream cheese made from cream, buttermilk, and rennet.

Roxy was the lone staff member on duty when Johnson arrived. With dinner over, Nat had gone out, and when the bell rang at the front desk, Roxy was taking inventory in the supplies closet. She hurried out but immediately slowed down when she saw who it was.

"Hello, Detective," she said. "You've caught me on my own."

"Where's the tattoo girl?"

"Good evening to you too," Roxy said calmly and firmly. She wanted to point out that Nat had a name but thought better of it given the precariousness of Nat's legal position. "She's gone out."

"Where has she gone?"

"I don't know," Roxy said, coolly walking up to the detective with a placid smile. "Would you like some coffee? Tea?"

Johnson narrowed his eyes. "What's with the act?" he growled.

"Whose act? Yours or mine?" Roxy smiled.

"Don't you get clever with me."

"Shall we sit down?" Roxy said, leading him to the dining room. Johnson followed her.

They sat at the table, the detective never taking his eyes off Roxy. He produced his notebook and opened it in front of him, then pulled out a pen from the inside pocket of his coat.

"I've already interviewed your baker friend. Things seem a little sus there. He certainly has plenty of motive, but I want to hear from you. Let's start with how you know Patrice Marveau," he said. "What do you know about him? Everything. Now."

Carefully, Roxy explained what had happened since Elijah had first burst into the hotel a few days earlier and announced that he was a contender for a judge's position on *Ultimate Baker*.

"So, the last time you saw Patrice Marveau, he left looking angry, having insulted you and your hotel," Johnson said when she was finished.

"*First* and last time, Detective. I'd never met him before that. And I understand he was always angry about something. And critical and unpleasant. He was just like that. I don't think we were exempt or special in any way. I hear he treated everyone the same—nastily."

"Sounds like you didn't like him very much."

Months ago, the question would have panicked Roxy. She would have squirmed and sweated and tried to find some way to backpedal to avoid the insinuations Johnson was making. But the old Roxy didn't exist anymore.

"That's right," she answered. "I only met him once, but I didn't get a good impression of him. I don't think a lot of people did. He was mean and catty and vain. I suspect he had a lot of enemies."

"And now he's dead," Johnson said.

A little shudder rippled through Roxy at the word. Under the table, she gripped her hands together so Johnson wouldn't spot the tension she felt whenever she was in his company.

"You seem to be suggesting that I had something to do with that. Just because I didn't like him it doesn't mean I *killed* him," she replied. "The idea is ridiculous. I only met him the one time."

"Doesn't look good though, does it?" Johnson said, still pushing. "You could have been in league with your friend across the alley. Marveau was rude to you and standing in the way of your friend. You could have done it together."

"Don't be silly. It's not a big deal that I didn't like Patrice," she said calmly. "I mean, you don't like Frank Ancelotti."

"*What?*" Johnson spluttered. "I . . . What . . . Who . . . What has that got to do with . . . Why are you . . . Who told you that?"

"No one. But I saw how you acted around him earlier. It was obvious."

"What's that got to do with anything?"

"I'm just saying," Roxy replied calmly, "that not liking

someone is normal when they aren't a very pleasant person."

Johnson pointed a finger at her. He was breathing heavily out of his nose. His complexion was blotchy, red patches appearing on his neck as he shook his finger. "You're trying to act clever, and I don't like interviewees getting clever with me!"

"I'm *not* trying to be clever, Detective," Roxy retorted, matching Johnson's irritation. "I'm trying to *help*. But every time you question me it feels like you think I'm guilty. And I'm *not*! I had nothing to do with Patrice Marveau's death. And I don't know why you'd even begin to believe that I had!"

This last word came out high-pitched and exasperated. Roxy had kept her emotions bottled up for so long around the detective that they were spilling out. She hated that she sounded childish and as if she was protesting too much. Immediately she felt uncomfortable and anxious.

But it seemed to work. For a moment—only a moment—Detective Johnson looked genuinely ashamed and embarrassed. He couldn't look Roxy in the eye and hung his head, looking down at his notebook. His angry, hot breathing slowed now to a long sigh, and his shoulders slumped.

After a few seconds, he looked back at Roxy, his expression more open than she had ever seen it. "You're right. I am tough on people who sometimes don't deserve it. That's just the way I do things. It works. That's all I know."

"So would treating me nicely," Roxy said, allowing herself a small smile.

Johnson narrowed his eyes. "You're not the pushover you used to be."

"Not anymore," Roxy replied, feeling her back straighten and her chin rise. She smiled.

Johnson didn't return her smile, even though the beginnings of one seemed to flicker at the corners of his mouth. Roxy tried to remember if she had ever seen the gruff detective smile, or even show any sign of pleasure at all. He closed his notebook and put it away in his pocket. Then he stood up from the table.

"That's all for now, anyway," he said. "I'll come find you if I need anything else."

"Okay. Goodbye then, Detective."

Johnson turned and took three steps to the front door before stopping. Roxy stood waiting for him to do something. Slowly, he turned and, looking back over his shoulder, said, "Two things. One: I don't want you getting involved in this. Don't go playing amateur Sherlock Holmes and getting in my way—or worse, getting yourself killed. I don't need two murder cases on my desk. And two . . ." Johnson took a long time before speaking again, as if unsure whether he should say anything at all. "Two . . . be careful around Frank Ancelotti."

CHAPTER TEN

A T ONE A.M., Roxy finally went to bed. As usual, there had been something of a party in the dining room until, at around midnight, the mood of the guests had morphed from energetic and upbeat to tired and mellow. The alcohol and food had settled in their stomachs and made them sleepy.

Sage, Sam, and Elijah said their goodbyes and left the hotel for their homes. Nat had left midevening, and without her there, Roxy had taken care of the guests. She reminded the tipsy Italians where their room was and brought fresh towels for the honeymoon couple.

With the guests in their rooms crashed out, Roxy cleared the table. Sam had offered to help her clean up, but she had insisted she could do it alone, partly because he'd helped enough tonight, and partly because she was worried what might happen if they were alone together again. There was too much to think about to worry about the state of their "romance."

Finally, with the dining table looking decent and a gigantic pile of washing up left for the morning, Roxy made her way to her room. Evangeline had promised to come in the next morning, as would Nat. They would clean up.

Nefertiti was already curled up at the foot of Roxy's bed. When Roxy entered, the cat raised her head slightly, and when she saw who it was, she lay her head back down and quickly returned to what she did best—sleep. Roxy slipped out of her dress, took a quick shower, then put on her pajamas and turned out the light. Finally, she could sleep.

Five minutes . . . perhaps ten . . . maybe even a quarter of an hour passed. Roxy was almost gone. Her body was exhausted and had sunk into the soft, downy layers of the bed with relief. Her eyes closed, her thoughts meandered, illogical. And then she heard something outside.

The soft clicking of a bicycle mechanism. The gentle squeak of its brakes. Footsteps.

It was one of those warm early-summer nights where every tiny sound seems to travel for miles as clear as a high piano key right after it has been tuned. The Funky Cat's small cul-de-sac was usually silent during the night. Roxy had left her window open so her room wouldn't get stuffy.

Roxy perked up when she heard the sounds. Whoever made them was right outside her hotel. When silence descended again, she opened her eyes and waited. Her first thought was that Nat had returned from wherever she had gone. But the bicycle noises didn't make sense. She'd never seen Nat on a bike. Nat would have walked—or taken a cab if she'd gone far. So who else could it be?

Perhaps it was a guest. She'd had a few people turn up randomly looking for a room in the middle of the night before. Once, a musician from Chicago had shown up at midnight looking to stay for a night. He said he'd heard "good things" about the Funky Cat at the gig he'd just played. Maybe this was someone like that.

All these thoughts passed through Roxy's mind quickly, until her curiosity forced her out of bed. She pushed the covers aside, careful not to disturb Nefertiti, and silently moved over to the window to take a look.

She pulled the curtain aside a little and peeked out. A young man was standing in the courtyard, looking up at the windows. Only a little of the streetlight caught part of his face, yet there was something familiar about him. Roxy leaned against her wall, holding the curtain aside only an inch, just enough to squint at him, wondering why he seemed to trigger her memories in some way but not enough for her to be clear who he was.

The young man didn't seem interested in entering the hotel. He started to pace up and down, moving in and out of the light. Roxy noticed him wring his hands. Just as she was getting discomfited enough to want to confront him, he turned around and walked back to his bike. Roxy watched him quickly mount and ride away.

Her thoughts spinning, she clambered into bed, not bothering so much about Nefertiti this time, and lay there thinking about what she had just seen. Sleep seemed elusive now, and it took her a long time to drift off. She was *sure* she had seen him before from somewhere . . .

CHAPTER ELEVEN

V ERY EARLY THE next morning, Roxy was in the kitchen whipping up chocolate dip for the beignets while Evangeline scouted the kitchen fridges and pantry thinking about what to prepare for a big evening dinner. Three more guests were arriving today. It was also the last night for the two Italians. They would likely have dinner at the hotel and an early night.

The weather was turning hot and sunny, so Roxy wanted to dress for it. She wore a blue sundress with blue Chucks, a small silver clip in her pixie-cut hair. Her pale skin was developing a slight tan, though she was wary of the sun. She burned easily.

However, as light and cheerful as she looked whisking the cream into the chocolate, her mind swirled with heavy thoughts. Detective Johnson's warning about Frank Ancelotti echoed in her mind. She worried not just for herself, but for Elijah, whose friendship with Frank was troubling. If he was a thug, Elijah needed to be careful. What if Elijah did something to upset Frank? Crossed him in some way? And what if Elijah got blamed for the

murder? Even Roxy had to admit it was obvious who bene-
fited most from Patrice dying.

"Roxy?"

Roxy was so lost in her thoughts she hadn't even noticed
Nat standing beside her, yawning and trying to catch her
attention.

"Good morning, Nat," she said.

"I think you've stirred that sauce enough." Nat sprinkled some chili powder into the bowl and chased it with a
few drops of vanilla. Roxy looked down at the sauce she had
been stirring absentmindedly for a long time now.

"Oh yeah. Here," Roxy said, stepping aside. "You take
over. I've got to check the rooms before the new guests
arrive. Things to do, people to see . . ."

Nat took the wooden spoon from her, and Roxy ran off.
She stopped quickly in her office to check that all the paperwork for the guests' check-in was ready, then took a small
watering can, filled it, and went outside to water the new
plants in the courtyard that Sage had planted there. They
were very fragile and needed daily watering, especially as
the weather got warmer.

Nefertiti was out there too, lounging in a spot of sun
while a ginger tom prowled around her, showing off. Roxy
ignored what that might mean and concentrated on
watering the plants. She had plenty enough to think about
as it was.

It wasn't long after sunrise. There was a quiet, peaceful
calm in the courtyard. Elijah's bakery wasn't yet open.
Soon, the steady drip of his early morning customers would
build into a morning rush, then fade away as the workers
went to work and school-run moms moved on. The temperature was warm but comfortable. Something about the
morning sunshine always seemed clean and magical to

Roxy. The beautiful French architecture of the old buildings shimmered and sparkled against the clear morning sky,
making them seem even more alluring. Roxy found it easy
to get up early when her mornings were like this. She
smiled as she realized how different it was to the dread she
used to feel getting up for her call center job in Ohio. What
a difference it made having work you loved and friends who
loved you.

Behind her, footsteps on cobbles caught her attention.
She turned from the plants to see who it was. "Morning,
Elijah," she said as he sauntered across the courtyard
carrying the beignets. "You're early."

"Glad you noticed." He smiled. "I hope Evangeline
does as well. I'm trying to make up for my late deliveries."
Roxy laughed and Elijah smiled, but then his face turned
serious.

"I hear Johnson visited you last night," Roxy said. "He
came here too."

"Yeah, he just asked me a few questions, you know,
about my relationship with Patrice and the *Ultimate Baker*
job. I couldn't tell him anything important. I hadn't seen
Patrice since he showed up at your place that morning, and
I've been in the bakery ever since surrounded by people. He
seemed satisfied." Roxy considered how *un*satisfied Johnson
always seemed to be with her and wondered what the
difference was.

"Actually, I want to ask you something," Elijah said.

"Sure. What is it?"

"You see, I'm heading into the studio again today. First
time since, well, yesterday obvs. I don't know. It all feels a
little bit weird. I wondered if you would mind, if you can, if
you have time"—Elijah took a deep breath—"would you
come with me?"

"Oh," Roxy replied. "Of course. I just need to arrange what we'll do about the new guests arriving . . ."

"If you're busy, never mind," Elijah said, waving the idea away. "I'll manage."

"No, no, of course I'll come," Roxy insisted. "I mean, it *is* weird, everything that has happened. I completely get why you feel uncomfortable. I'd like to come and support you."

"Thanks so much, Roxy. I'd be so grateful," Elijah said, smiling widely. He let out a deep breath and the worry lines across his forehead disappeared. Roxy could see how genuinely, deeply relieved he was.

"I'll ask Sage to welcome the guests," Roxy said. "She always makes such a strong first impression. I'd ask Nat, but . . . well . . . have you noticed she seems preoccupied these days?"

Roxy put down the watering can and moved to hold the door open for Elijah. He glided into the hotel.

"I haven't," Elijah said in a low voice. "What's going on with her?"

Roxy shrugged. "I don't know. She keeps leaving dinner early to go out in the evening. Often as soon as dinner is done. I figure if she wanted us to know where she's going, she'd tell us."

"Have you asked her?"

"She always evades the question," Roxy said.

Elijah didn't say anything else. He walked into the dining room and put the box of beignets down on the table.

"Would you look at that!" Evangeline called from the kitchen. "He's early for once!"

Nat had prepared the coffee and finished the chocolate dip Roxy had been working on earlier. She and Evangeline brought cups to the dining table, along with the dip. None of the guests were up yet.

"I've been bringing beignets here for five years," Elijah said in a playful tone. "I'm late two times and she won't let me forget it!"

"It's not breakfast without beignets!" Evangeline grumbled, then gave him a gap-toothed smile to let him know she was only joking.

The smell of the beignets, coffee, and spiced chocolate dip was too appealing for further conversation. The four friends were soon reaching for pastries and dipping them generously in the chocolate sauce as they sipped coffee. The only sound was a few murmurs of satisfaction.

As they dipped and munched, Sage arrived. "Sage, would you mind helping our guests this morning?" Roxy asked her. "I'd like to accompany Elijah to the studio today."

"Sure, honey. I'll spend some time uploading the photos while I wait for them."

Elijah got up from the table and shot Roxy a look. "Are you ready?" he asked. "It would be great if we could go now. I'd like to get it over with."

"Absolutely. I'll get my things."

CHAPTER TWELVE

GOING TO THE studio was, for Elijah, even more challenging this time. Not only was he meeting a bunch of new people whom he would work with, be filmed with for the first time, and receive lots of attention from, the person he beat out for the job was dead, and by default, he was involved in a gruesome murder case. All those new introductions he would have to make would be twice as awkward and complicated. And the specter of suspicion lay heavy across the atmosphere.

Roxy did her best to help Elijah relax. She cracked a few jokes and kept him talking. It seemed to work only a little though. She wished Sam was with them. He was good at that sort of thing.

When they reached the studio, she noticed Elijah slow down. "Don't worry," Roxy said, holding his arm gently. "I'm here. It'll be fine."

Elijah looked at her and smiled, then put his hand on hers. "Thanks, Roxy. I don't know what I'd do without you."

Roxy laughed gently. They entered the studio together.

Straight away they noticed Jenny, his wrangler, waiting for them.

"Mr. Walder, Elijah. It's good to see you. How are you feeling?"

"I'm okay," Elijah said. "A bit shaken, you know?"

"Yes," Jenny said. "We all are. Can I get you anything?"

"No. I'm good. Let's get things over with."

"Okay, they're waiting for you. I'll take you up. Follow me." As Elijah and Roxy made their way up to the studio, Jenny chatted with them. "People here have been shocked about what happened to Patrice, but they're professionals and have a job to do. They're getting on with things."

When they arrived in the vast, cavernous studio, there was less activity than there had been the day before. The kitchen was set up, and now just half a dozen people busied themselves arranging cameras and lighting. Elijah and Roxy looked around for a familiar face and soon saw Paige Crawford chatting with a show runner. After a few seconds they caught her eye, and she immediately broke off from her conversation to greet them.

"Elijah, I'm glad you came," she said, looking relieved.

"Of course I came," Elijah said. "I said I would."

Paige smiled warmly. "Well, we should have a meeting with the team. We've lost some time so we're going to have to reschedule a few things. Are you ready?"

"Sure," Elijah said, then looked at Roxy.

"I guess I'll see you at dinner tonight perhaps?" Roxy said. She turned to Paige. "Would it be okay if I take a little look around before I go? I've never been in a studio before. Well, not since yesterday."

"Of course!" Paige said. "Take your time." She smiled kindly. "Knock yourself out."

Roxy gently patted Elijah's arm as he traipsed off to a

side office with Paige. It was more of a corner screened off with fabric nailed to a wooden frame, to be honest. Roxy was surprised at the rough improvisation evident in the studio. The set was pristine—an elaborate working kitchen, well lit and expensive—but the rest of the space away from the cameras was dark and beat-up. Not at all what she expected.

When Elijah and Paige had gone, Roxy stood in the middle of the studio looking around at the equipment and crew. She wasn't sure what she was doing there, but she felt she had some kind of opportunity to do something, learn something. She scanned the crew, looking for a familiar face, and then she saw one.

Big, tough cameraman Zach who had brought in luggage on the day Elijah had been filmed in the bakery was kneeling by a camera unit. He was fiddling with some wires. Roxy moved slowly toward him until she was in his peripheral vision. He looked up.

"Hi, Zach," she said cheerily. He glanced at her, his hands still wrestling with the wires even though he wasn't looking at them.

"Hey," he said. He frowned before a look of recognition flickered across his stubbly face. "You're the girl from the hotel, right?"

"I'm the woman who *runs* the hotel," Roxy said, then laughed to show she wasn't offended, even if she was. A bit.

Zach nodded and returned to his cables. He yelped and brought his hand up quickly. Blood ran down it.

"Oh dear!" Roxy said. "Let me find a bandage for you."

"Nah, you're alright. It's nothing. They'll just want to write it up. It's not worth it. Leave me be."

"But that looks nasty." Roxy saw that Zach's hand was swollen.

"Part of the job. Did you want something?" Zach put his hand behind his back to indicate he was truly done with Roxy's attempt to care for him.

Roxy pursed her lips. "I'm sorry about everything," she said.

"Huh?" Zach replied, keeping his eyes fixed on his wires.

"Patrice," Roxy explained. "It's terrible what happened to him."

"Yeah," Zach said, getting up from messing with his cables and now checking the camera beside him. "Shame."

"Did you know him well?"

Zach shook his head. "No more or less than any of the other talent," he said. "Barely knew him, really."

Roxy watched him check the camera viewfinder, adjust the lens, press some buttons, and otherwise continue with his work. He didn't seem willing to say anything else, and she couldn't think of anything more to ask. Eventually, she drifted away.

After checking out the large kitchen and watching showrunners test the facilities, Roxy grew bored and decided to head back to the Funky Cat. This filming malarkey wasn't as interesting as she'd expected. As she left, in a small corridor that led off the studio, she heard a noise behind her. Turning, she saw a woman come out of the bathroom and quickly walk away from her. The door swung again, and Jenny, Elijah's wrangler, emerged. She was messing with her hair but smiled brightly when she saw Roxy.

"Can I help you?" she asked. She fingered the ID card on the end of her lanyard.

"Oh, no. Just having a wander around. I'm leaving now."

'Well, if there's anything I can help you with, please let me know." Jenny smiled her toothpaste ad smile again. "I'll leave you to it." She walked away.

Roxy's phone pinged, and as she investigated, the bathroom door opened again. A familiar face peered out.

"Jocelyn!"

"Huh? Oh . . . Roxy." Jocelyn's eyes sprung wide with surprise. There was a little redness about them. Her cheeks flushed. The makeup artist had glowed with happiness and energy before. Now, she looked stressed, perhaps had even been crying. She was dressed in black, a big contrast to the pink and cream ensemble she had worn when Roxy met her last.

"How are you?" Roxy asked.

"I'm . . . yeah. I'm good. Great," Jocelyn said, stumbling over her words. She laughed, but it sounded forced. Roxy remembered how, at the Funky Cat, the bubbly makeup girl had laughed often and easily. Now though, Roxy could tell something was worrying her. And meeting Roxy seemed to have had made her anxiety even worse.

"Is everything alright?" Roxy asked.

"Yes. Mm-hm. Sure," Jocelyn said quickly, forcing another laugh. "Are you here to watch the filming?"

"No. I came to support Elijah after everything that happened."

"Oh, yeah. I see," Jocelyn answered. "Well, it was nice seeing you again. Have a great day."

Before Roxy could say or ask anything else, the woman scurried past her and headed into the studio. Roxy watched her go, replaying the strange conversation in her head while wondering what was going on.

CHAPTER THIRTEEN

I T WAS SHAPING up to be another exciting evening at the Funky Cat. The new guests were infecting the hotel with their excitement about being in New Orleans, with the quiet, young couple livening up, encouraged by the Italians and determined to enjoy their last night. Evangeline had come in to supervise the cooking of dinner. Elijah had gotten over his nerves and was full of stories after his first day at the television studio. Even Sage had good news about her photographs of the hotel attracting plenty of positive attention on social media.

Roxy, however, felt a little detached from it all. She couldn't stop thinking about Patrice. Even though she hadn't really known him and disapproved of virtually everything she had seen or heard about him, she felt a deep sense of injustice that his killer was roaming free.

"Penny for them?" Nat walked up and offered Roxy a glass of wine.

"Oh, I'm just thinking about Patrice. It's madness that his killer hasn't been found. It's been over twenty-four hours since his body was discovered, longer since he was missing.

Given that he had so many enemies, you'd have thought whoever it was would have been caught right away."

"That's probably the problem," Nat said gravely. "There are so many possible suspects. They've gotta go through them all."

"Yes, I suppose you're right. I'm even feeling a little sympathy for Detective Johnson."

"Steady on . . . Don't get carried away now. How did you get on at the film studio? Elijah seems full of beans again."

Roxy shook her head. "I found Jocelyn coming out of the studio bathroom. She looked like she had been crying."

"About Patrice?"

"Could have been about anything, of course, but what if it *was* something to do with Patrice? Does she know something, d'you think?"

"Maybe she was just upset about his death?" Roxy flicked Nat a skeptical glance. "No, no, you're probably right. Too unlikely. He *was* very unpleasant to her over breakfast that time."

What Roxy didn't reveal to Nat was that she thought Frank Ancelotti was the *really* worrying prospect. Johnson's warning to her was pretty clear. Perhaps Evangeline was right in believing he was a Mafia guy. Murder was nothing to them—Roxy had seen enough gangster films to know that much. It was their bread and butter. But surely they wouldn't kill Patrice because they wanted Elijah to get the judge job. Why would they? And if that wasn't the motive, what was?

"What's the matter, cher?" Evangeline exclaimed, standing behind Roxy as she sat at the dining table. "You haven't touched your *pompano en papillote!*"

Roxy snapped to attention. She had been daydreaming

while everyone else was chatting and eating around her. She looked down at her food: the fillet of fish in wine and parsley was cooked in a paper package and looked impressive when opened on the plate. It also tasted delicious, so it was understandable for Evangeline to be surprised, possibly offended, that Roxy wasn't tucking in.

"Oh, sorry." Roxy laughed, taking a bite. "I guess I'm so tired I can barely bring my fork to my mouth."

"Never mind, cher. I know you've been working yourself to the bone. Give me that plate. I'll bring out the main and it'll perk you up for sure."

"What is it?" Elijah asked, handing his empty plate to Evangeline.

"Fried chicken with red beans and rice. Willy Mae style. The chicken's been brined in Coca-Cola and thyme before bein' rolled in three different kinds of paprika and a choice of spices that'll put fire into your soul, cher."

"Sounds great," Roxy said, smiling to show she was focused and present now. It was a wonder nobody else had noticed how quiet she was. The dinner was already lively.

Sage was once again entrancing their guests with stories of New Orleans's spiritual history. Elijah slipped onto the piano stool, tinkling the keys in the background while he waited for his main course. He sang an old tune in a silly voice that one of the guests knew and was soon joining in with. Sam poured more wine for one of the Italian women, playing the charming Southern gentleman.

Nat helped Evangeline clear the table of the empty starter plates and then brought out the chicken and rice. Instead of taking her seat beside Roxy, however, Nat casually tapped her shoulder.

"I'm just heading out now. I'll see you in the morning."

"Oh, okay. See you," Roxy said, surprised. Where was

Nat going now? Roxy watched her collect a sports bag she had left in the kitchen and saunter out of the room. When she turned back to her plate, the full, spicy aroma of the chicken wafting up to her, she saw Sam smiling. His eyes were full of concern, however.

"Everything alright?" he said in a low voice, leaning into her so she could hear him.

"Sure. Why wouldn't it be?" she replied, taking a bite of her chicken.

Sam laughed gently, still leaning in close. "I don't know," he said. "I just worry about you."

Roxy almost choked on her chicken. She swallowed and smiled at him. "You don't need to."

"I know I don't. But I do anyway," he said. Roxy tried not to blush, but the spicy chicken and the warmth of the room made it impossible. "I can tell you've got a lot on your mind these days. I just want you to know that if you need any help, you know where I am."

"To be honest, I *do* have a lot on my mind."

"Then tell me about it."

Roxy paused to think. Elijah began singing another song. One of the guests waved her arms to join in with him and knocked over some wine. There was chaos for a while as Elijah, Sam, and Roxy all rushed to clean it up, then everyone laughed, and the raucous dinner continued as if nothing had happened.

"Is it about Nat?" Sam asked. He had moved close again. He seemed more interested in Roxy than his food. "I noticed she just left. You seemed surprised."

"Well, that's one of the things on my mind, sure," Roxy said, returning to her chicken. "She keeps disappearing. I hope she's not in any trouble."

"You really have no idea where she's going?"

Roxy shook her head. She wished she had more to tell him. "You know I don't like invading Nat's private business. I don't want to ask her what she's doing. I prefer to wait until she feels comfortable telling me herself."

Sam smiled back at her. "Who said anything about asking her?" he said. "This all sounds to me like a perfect opportunity for you and me to have a night out. If Nat's hitting the town, then we are gonna find her by hitting the town ourselves."

CHAPTER FOURTEEN

"**N**AT, I NEED you and Sage to handle dinner and cleanup on your own tonight. I'm going out, and I'll leave after I've checked in with the guests. I need a night off."

"It's what your soul has needed for a while," Sage agreed.

"You deserve to go out and have a good time," Nat said. "I'll be going out after dinner is done too."

"Oh, anywhere nice?"

"Nah, not really."

That evening, after she visited each dining table to inquire how satisfied the guests were with their stay, Roxy went to her room to get ready for the evening. As she figured out what to wear, Roxy considered what she was doing. She felt a little silly. The whole idea of barhopping around New Orleans to find Nat made little sense to her now. New Orleans was a big city, and even if they found her, what were they going to do?

Hitting the town with Sam, however, sounded fun.

Even if investigating Nat's disappearances was a ploy to go on a date without it being *a date-date.*

From her position loafing on the bed, Nefertiti watched Roxy move rapidly about the room. Roxy settled on a red, knee-length, figure-hugging dress and black heels. Classic and versatile. Who knew what the night might bring?

She still wasn't sure what sort of bars or clubs Sam had in mind for them. After adding a pair of thin, gold earrings and a gold necklace, she inspected herself in the mirror. "What do you think, Nef-nef?"

Before the cat could answer, Roxy's phone rang. It was Sam. "You ready?" he asked.

"I'm ready," Roxy said as she went to the window to look outside. She peered down the alleyway to the street. He was there. Or rather, his Rolls Royce was there. "I'm coming down now."

Roxy hurried downstairs, said a quick goodbye to Sage and Nat, then walked to Sam's car. Sam got out to open the door for her. She was a little taken aback when she saw him. He was wearing a grey suit, and it made him look even taller and more broad-shouldered than usual.

"Wow," he said with a big smile as she approached him. "We're supposed to be looking for Nat, but how can I look at anything but you?"

Roxy laughed and smacked him gently on the chest to stop him being silly. "And you look mighty fine yourself, sir. I can't believe you got me to do this," she said. "Following a friend."

"We're not *following* anyone. We're just a man and a woman going out for an evening of fun. And if we happen to bump into our friend, so be it," Sam said, opening the car door for her. "Besides, you've been here for months now. You've tried the food, seen Mardi Gras, met the locals—but you haven't really experienced New Orleans until you've been to the clubs, heard the live music, and danced."

"I'm not much of a dancer," Roxy said shyly as she folded herself into the car. Sam closed the door after her, then got in the driver's side.

"That's okay," Sam smiled, firing up the engine. "I'm a good teacher. Is Nat still at the Funky Cat? If she is, perhaps we should wait for her. We could see in which direction she goes."

"And in this conspicuous car, she'd spot us immediately. I mean, you couldn't advertise yourself more if you tried."

Sam grinned. "No, I suppose you're right. Oh well, if we don't spot her, I'll bring my van next time."

"Next time, huh?" They both laughed, excited about the evening ahead.

Soon, they were driving steadily through the streets with music playing. Roxy wasn't quite sure where they were heading. The streets were lively and full of people. Neon signs glowed, and people's clothes, many dressed to the nines, told her that they were out for a good time. They passed women in sequins, bright colors, and skyscraper heels, the men in tuxes, all of their faces wreathed in smiles.

Sam found a place to park the car, and when they got out, he approached Roxy and offered his arm. She took it as he led her out onto a busy street.

"So, what's the plan?" she asked.

"First of all," Sam said as he led her down some steps into an old-fashioned, oak-paneled bar, "we get a drink." Inside, the room hummed with chatter and laughter. A pianist in the corner, tinkling the keys with jazz riffs, added atmosphere to the dimmed lights and antique interior design. Without missing a beat, Sam grabbed Roxy's hand and led her to the bar. "Devon!"

"Sammy boy!" the bartender called back with a smile. He left his customer to come over to them. "Ain't seen you in a while."

"I've been busy."

"I'll bet," Devon said, glancing at Roxy. He touched his forehead. "Pleased to meet you, ma'am. I'm Devon."

"Roxy," she said.

"What'll you have, miss?"

"Um . . ."

"Sazerac, whiskey with sugar, bitters, and absinthe," Sam said. He turned to Roxy. "It's delicious. You must try."

"Sure," Roxy laughed.

"And a beer for me," Sam said. "I need to play it cool if I'm driving."

"Coming right up." With a few deft moves, Devon prepared their drinks. He set them in front of Roxy and Sam before turning his attention to his other customers.

"Okay," Roxy said, after taking a sip. Sam was right; the drink *was* delicious. Sweet *and* bitter. "So, we've got our drinks . . . What's the plan now?"

"I'm thinking we hang out here for a bit," Sam said, playfully clinking his beer bottle against hers, "then go to another bar. Then another. And then when we've had enough of bars, we drive to the club playing the best music in town to check it out."

Roxy took another sip. "And you think we'll find Nat that way?"

"Sure," Sam said. "Maybe."

Roxy laughed. "This is a big city," she said. "With a lot of people. The chances of just randomly bumping into her are slim, it seems to me."

"What you're forgetting, Roxy, is that there are a few things in our favor."

"Such as?"

"For a start," Sam said, "I know this city well. And I know a lot of people in this city *very* well. It might seem like a big place to you, but to me, it's little more than a village. I hear about everything that goes on in New Orleans—whether I want to or not."

"I suppose," Roxy admitted.

"Hey, Devon," Sam called to the bartender again.

"What's up, my man?" Devon replied, coming over while counting some bills in his hand.

"We're looking for a girl who's been around town these past few weeks. About this high. Straight black hair to here. Tattoos all down one arm like this." Sam brought his hand to his shoulder, his chin, and his wrist.

Devon sighed and shook his head. "Lot of girls have tattoos these days, man."

"But this girl's British. She's got the cute accent and everything," Sam added.

Devon looked down and frowned as he thought more seriously now. "I can think of a couple of girls who might fit the bill, but they don't have the accent. I tell you what, I'll keep an eye out and let you know."

"Excellent. Thanks, man," Sam said, cuffing him on the arm. Devon winked, then returned to his customers. Roxy still felt a little uncertain that their plan would succeed, or if it was even desirable that it did. The pair of them finished their drinks.

"Right, let's go on somewhere else," Sam said. Soon they were out walking through the crowds on the street.

Time and again, Sam was stopped by people who recognized him. All sorts of people—smart people, casual people, even homeless people. They all seemed pleased to see him and to regard him positively. Roxy knew that Sam was popular—he was generous, kind, and charming—but seeing people in the street greet him repeatedly was a little mesmerizing. And curious. How did he know so many people?

Each time Sam met someone he knew, he would ask them if they'd seen Nat. None of them had.

Back in Ohio, Roxy had only had a couple of friends. And she didn't see them too often. She had been on decent terms with some of her workmates (and on bad terms with others), but she never saw anyone outside the office. Seeing how well-known and popular Sam was and how embedded he appeared in the local community, she envied him until she realized that there was nothing stopping her from doing just the same. She just needed to get out more, get involved.

"Let's go in here," Sam said, again leading her by the hand into another busy bar. "They have a balcony with a view of the whole street. Perfect for our 'operation.'"

CHAPTER FIFTEEN

ROXY LAUGHED AS, clasping her hand again, Sam hurried inside and led her up to the balcony. After a few words with a security guy he seemed to know, they were let into the VIP area and shown to a table. A jazz band played, and the wood-paneled walls vibrated to the rhythm of the music. Roxy felt intoxicated, even though she'd only had one drink. The atmosphere, the music, Sam breezing about so easily, the sense of the streets being alive with energy and life—it all made her feel dizzy with excitement. She almost forgot they were there with a specific goal—to find Nat.

Before she knew it, drinks were placed on the table between her and Sam—she hadn't even noticed him ordering them. He raised a glass to toast her. She laughed, lifted her drink to touch his, and sipped.

"I haven't been out in ages," Roxy said. "I'm having a good time." She tapped her foot and bobbed in her seat as she shook her shoulders, swaying to the rhythm of the music. Around her, people at tables leaned in to talk or, like her, danced in their seats as they enjoyed the jazz.

"I'm glad to hear it." Sam smiled. He leaned forward to look out over the balcony at the people down below on the street. "You did such a good job with the hotel that you deserve to take some time off."

"Well, I do have a great team around me." Roxy looked over the balcony too. "You're so popular here. How come you know so many people? It's like you're friends with half the city."

Sam laughed. "Well, I *did* grow up here—and it's a very friendly city if you're friendly too. I'm sure you were popular back in Ohio."

"Not really," Roxy said. "I just sort of went through life meeting people and then losing touch. I never really had lots of friends—or even a strong friend group. Before I left to come here, my crowd pretty much consisted of just my boyfriend and the people I knew from work."

"I'm surprised," Sam said. "You're such a warm and kind, generous person. You work so hard. Everyone appreciates you."

"Well, I don't know. I felt like a different person in Ohio. Nothing ever seemed to happen there. Not to me, anyway."

"A lot of things happen in New Orleans."

"A lot!" Roxy agreed. They both laughed.

"I guess playing music helped me get connected," Sam said. "New Orleans is a music town, and if you're a player, you get to know a lot of people. I've also always done charity work, which is another great way to develop friendships. And then there's the laundry. I meet crowds of people through that too."

"You didn't always own a laundry though," Roxy said. She sensed she was treading on treacherous ground, soft enough to stumble, but she couldn't help herself.

"No," Sam replied. His eyelids dropped a tad, and his mouth set in a slightly firmer, thinner line.

Ignoring the signs, Roxy probed gently. "What else have you done?" She hoped he might feel ready to tell her some more about himself, his history, and perhaps even how he made all his money.

"Is that Nat?" Sam said suddenly, pointing down at the street.

"Where?" Roxy said, leaning over the railing to see.

"There, walking past that sushi sign."

Roxy searched the crowd but couldn't see anyone who looked even remotely like Nat.

"Never mind," Sam said, settling down. "Whoever it was just turned a corner. It probably wasn't her. Anyway, I'll get us another round of drinks."

Roxy eased back in her chair, feeling confused and not knowing why. As she watched Sam's back as he headed to the bar, it dawned on her that he had pretended to see Nat to distract her from her question. Whatever his secret was, he *really* didn't want to share it. She decided not to press him any further—the evening was too pleasant to spoil—but she was disturbed by his secretive behavior.

When they finished their drinks, they left the club and walked the streets for a while, Roxy's arm threaded through Sam's. Jazz, blues, and soul music streamed from the bars and clubs that lined the streets. People shouted and laughed, making Roxy turn her head. Sam continued to greet people he recognized as they passed by—though none of them could tell him anything about Nat.

They stopped off in a bar with a band playing raucous blues-rock so that Sam could ask a few more questions. After discovering nothing, they left and walked on a little more. It was deep into the night now, and their hopes of finding Nat had pretty much left them. Still, Roxy was having such a good time that she didn't mind.

"Hey, let's go in here," Sam said, once again leading Roxy into a jazz club. It was small and intimate. The walls were covered with colorful African art and huge photos of jazz musicians exuberantly playing their instruments. Soft orange and red lighting danced across the brass features of the elegant tables and chairs. Red velvet curtains fringed with gold framed a small stage. "This is a pretty hip place with a lot of interesting people."

"Okay," Roxy said, hesitating a little, "but let's make this the last one. I'm tired."

"Sure," Sam said. "One last drink, a few more questions, and then we'll get a cab back. I'll send someone to pick up the car. Despite my best intentions, I've enjoyed myself a little too much in the drink department."

"Okay, good," Roxy said, wondering how he managed to get someone to run such an errand at this time of night.

The atmosphere in this club was more relaxed and subdued than the earlier ones they had visited. A jazz band played on the stage to an audience of well-dressed people who appeared knowledgeable about the genre judging by the way they nodded their heads and tapped their palms on the table, preferring to listen to the music rather than talk over it. A couple was getting up, so Sam led Roxy to their table, stopping to greet a few people and shake their hands on the way.

Eventually, a young, slim server came by. He and Sam obviously knew each other well enough that the server anticipated Sam's drink. Roxy ordered a small martini.

"Coming right up," the waiter said.

"Say, Gerard," Sam added, stopping the waiter from

leaving. "We're looking for a girl—black hair to her chin, tattoos on her arm, about this tall, British accent. You seen anyone like that around?"

Gerard stopped and looked from Sam to Roxy and then back at Sam. He seemed to hesitate. "I mean, I see a lot of girls come through here. Lot of tattoos, British accents, black hair. I can't help you, Sam. Sorry."

Sam nodded his thanks and let the waiter go. "Sam," Roxy said when the waiter was gone.

"Yeah?"

"Is it me or did that server seem uncomfortable?"

"Gerard?" Sam said. "I've known him over ten years. If he knew something, he'd tell me."

"Are you sure?"

Sam thought a bit, then shrugged. "Why wouldn't he?"

Roxy sighed and let it go. When Gerard came back with the drinks, Roxy eyed him carefully, but there was no repeat of the earlier awkwardness. Sam clinked his glass against hers and they both sipped, turning their eyes to the stage where the band was bringing their set to a brilliant, energetic climax.

"I'm disappointed that we haven't found out what Nat is doing around town," Roxy said.

"We did our best, and we'll try again another night," Sam replied.

Just then, the band played one final explosive note. The crowd erupted into applause. Sam and Roxy joined in, standing up with everyone else to show their appreciation. The jazz band bowed and smiled their gratitude before packing away their instruments and moving off stage.

Sam leaned forward. "Do you want to go? Oh . . ." The lights of the club dimmed, pitching it into almost complete darkness. A strange piano melody quite unlike the previous lively jazz set began. A hush came over the whole club, and slowly a spotlight, first just a pinprick, grew large on the stage. Into the light, the shadow cast by a pair of hands formed a rabbit on a screen. It began moving, looking around curiously. The crowd laughed. Seconds later, the rabbit silhouette morphed into that of a whole person—a tall, full-bodied woman.

"Ladies and gentlemen," an announcer offstage said just as the piano melody reached a crescendo. "The femme fatale . . . the mystery maiden . . . the brilliant belle . . ." With each description, the silhouette struck a different pose until finally the announcer called out, "The one and only . . . Ms. Laverne de la Croix!"

The piano erupted into a loud, dramatic rock riff as the woman stepped up onto the stage. She wore a sparkling, sky-blue dress and had enormous bouffant hair colored black and yellow. She walked like a cartoon figure—hips and shoulders swaying dramatically, her chin high. The crowd stood, hooting and hollering, clapping loudly. Clearly, they knew this woman and loved to see her. It was only as she sauntered up the stage steps and stood there proudly, displaying a heavily made-up face and a silly pout, that Roxy and Sam realized that Laverne de la Croix was a drag queen.

"Good evening, my lovelies," Laverne cried as the crowd's yelling and clapping died down. "I hope you're all having a wonderful evening." She walked from one side of the stage to the other. "Because I'm about to sing and bring you all back to reality again."

The crowd laughed. Someone even shouted, "We love you, Laverne!"

Laverne countered with a joke. "A lover of mine once called me a siren. I said 'Why? Because I'm so beautiful and tempting and dangerous?' They said 'No, because when you sing in the car everyone moves to one side.'"

For the next twenty minutes, Laverne de la Croix entertained the crowd with a mixture of bawdy jokes and songs. She even interacted with various members of the audience, although thankfully not Roxy. She would have died of embarrassment. Instead, Roxy laughed for almost the entirety of Laverne's act, her sides aching. It had been a long time since she'd laughed that hard and that much. She was exhausted by the end of it.

"Well, you've been a wonderful audience," Laverne said eventually. Roxy looked at Sam and they nodded at one another, agreeing that they should leave before the crowd. They eased themselves from their seats. "And I hope you like surprises, because one of you will probably be taking me home," Laverne finished. "But now I'd like to introduce someone who—and I don't say this lightly or without bitterness—is more beautiful and can sing better than even me. A dear friend of mine who many of you know and love. I know, I know, most of you have just tolerated my act to hear hers. Well, here she is: the fabulous, the delectable, the songstress whose voice almost puts Aretha's in the shade, the shooting star soon to go stratospheric, the one and only, the Mardi Gras madame herself . . . Madison Keeler!"

Roxy and Sam were already moving from their table when the singer came onstage, the intro to her first song already in full swing. They both glanced casually in her direction as the first note of the woman's beautiful voice soared over the heads of those in the club. Sam and Roxy both froze.

For, on the stage in a beautiful, silver, strapless, full-skirted ballgown, her black hair plastered to her head in a gelled twenties style, her hand clutching the mic, was a woman wearing a crystal-encrusted silver mask. Her voice was unmistakable. It was Nat!

CHAPTER SIXTEEN

T HE NEXT MORNING, Roxy woke up late. By the time she had showered, pulled on a pair of denim shorts with a red T-shirt, and gone downstairs, the hotel was already hopping. Elijah had delivered the beignets, Sage sat at the table working on her laptop, and the guests had finished breakfast and were milling around the lobby. Nat and Evangeline were in the kitchen doing the dishes.

"Morning, Sage," Roxy said as she passed her.

"Good morning," Sage replied.

"Morning, Nat, Evangeline," Roxy said as she walked into the kitchen.

"Good mornin', cher," Evangeline said cheerfully. "The others told me you went out last night. I'd ask how your evening went, but considering how late it is, I suppose I don't need to."

"I had a great time, yeah," Roxy said with a smile.

"I'll bet," Nat said, turning away from the dishes to wink at Roxy. "If I were Sage, I'd come up with some mumbo-jumbo about you glowing with energy right now."

Roxy moved around the kitchen checking supplies, unable to stop smiling. After last night, it was strange seeing Nat being her typical sarcastic, spiky self in her dark, metal-band T-shirt and faded, black, ripped jeans. Not to mention she seemed as bright as a daisy. Roxy knew that Nat had a wonderful voice and had heard her sing many times before, but Nat—or Madison Keeler—had been something else at that club. So glamorous and sultry, so confident and alluring.

Nat had only sung five songs, but it had felt like an entire concert. For every second of them the audience was silent, not a single word spoken, all eyes wide and staring, utterly engrossed. Only in between songs did the audience move, and even then, only so they could stand, shout, and applaud loudly before the next one.

"How was your evening?" Roxy asked.

Evangeline decided the question was for her and began to answer it. She was mixing up some of her special spice mixture at the counter and didn't turn around.

"I slept in my armchair! Pinkie fell asleep in my lap, and I just couldn't bring myself to disturb him. I've got a neck ache because of it, but it was worth it for my Pinkie-pal."

Roxy laughed gently, then said, "How about you, Nat?"

"Oh, fine," Nat said without turning around from the sink. "Just hung out. You know."

Roxy didn't say anything else. She still couldn't stop smiling and didn't want Nat to notice. Presumably, Nat had been singing at the club—or perhaps many clubs—for a while now. The audience's reaction to her made it apparent that she was quite familiar to them. Nat—or Madison Keeler—had built quite a reputation.

Sam and Roxy had agreed they would keep Nat's nightly singing a secret between themselves for now. Nat was taking a risk, but Roxy was happy to know that she wasn't in danger or coming to any harm. Her thoughts racing and her smile still plastered on, Roxy grabbed a coffee from the kitchen and went to sit in the dining room with Sage.

"Thank you so much for handling the guests' breakfast today, Sage."

"It was no problem," Sage said smoothly. "They're all going to be out seeing the sights today, so we won't have to worry about them until this evening. Sam will be here soon with clean sheets for the rooms."

"Excellent."

"Oh, and one more thing," Sage said, sipping her coffee delicately. "Elijah said he might drop by for lunch. He's filming today. He said he would bring Jocelyn too. Apparently, she loved the food you laid on last time she ate here."

Immediately, Roxy's mind shifted. Her smile disappeared as she stared at her coffee. She remembered the last time she had seen Jocelyn, rushing out of the studio bathroom looking emotional.

"Roxy?" Sage said, making her realize that she had gone silent. Roxy snapped to and smiled at Sage to show she was alright.

"Okay, let's see what we can rustle up for lunch," Roxy said breezily. She was constructing a plan. Suddenly, she stood up from the table and marched into the kitchen.

"Alcohol," Roxy said to Evangeline.

"Alcohol?" Evangeline replied, looking up. A confused frown furrowed her brow.

"Yes," Roxy confirmed.

Evangeline stared at Roxy like she was crazy. "Cher, I asked you what you wanted me to *cook* for lunch, not what you wanted to drink."

"I know, I know," Roxy said, calming down a little so that she could explain more clearly. "I'm just saying I'd like you to make some dishes that have alcohol in them. Rich, boozy flavors. Rum, bourbon, wine . . ."

Evangeline scratched her salt-and-pepper hair that was tied back in a bun as she considered Roxy's request. "Okay, cher." The old woman squinted at Roxy as she tried to work out the intention behind her words.

"Something with a lot of *kick*," Roxy said, punching the air in front of her as she said it.

"Why though? You want to get us all wasted in the middle of the day?"

"Let's just say I'd like people to relax and open up a little."

Evangeline looked at her again like she was crazy, then shrugged. "One lunch with a hell of a kick coming up then, cher," she said before banging a pan down on the counter.

Roxy returned to the dining room. Sage looked up at her. She had been listening to the conversation from her position at the table. "What are you trying to find out?" Sage asked. "And from whom?"

"Jocelyn," Roxy answered. "The other day when I went to the studio with Elijah, I saw Jocelyn rushing out of the bathroom. She looked distraught about something. It made me wonder."

"It could have been anything," Sage said. "Perhaps her boyfriend broke up with her, or she had some bad family news."

"Yes, perhaps . . ." Roxy said, trailing off, less sure of herself suddenly. "I don't know. I just have a strange feeling about her."

Sage smiled. "You're learning to trust your instincts," she said. "You're beginning to read between the lines, to hear not just what people say, but what they mean. You're becoming more perceptive, Roxy."

Roxy laughed gently and said, "I'm not sure about that. Maybe you're rubbing off on me a little though!"

"No," Sage said calmly. "It's not because of me. It's because you're growing as a person. Discovering yourself. Your frequency is getting higher. Everyone has the power to see the truth once they start living their own."

"That *sounds good*. But I don't think I'm quite there yet," Roxy replied.

Sage tilted her head and turned back to her computer. "I suppose we'll see at lunchtime," she said.

CHAPTER SEVENTEEN

ROXY LEFT SAGE and went to help Nat clean the rooms. That took most of the morning, but once it was over, Roxy went to her office to do some paperwork while the hotel filled with the smell of Evangeline's cooking.

Around midday, Elijah arrived. Roxy heard him all the way from her office. He seemed in high spirits. She also heard Jocelyn laughing as he cracked jokes. She finished filling in one last form and went to join the others at the table.

"Then it was *my* turn to try the contestant's dish." Elijah was regaling Evangeline and Sage with tales from the studio floor. "And I'm supposed to be the big, bad judge, you know? But I was more nervous than the contestant!" His words sparked another round of loud laughter from Jocelyn. "I was holding my fork like this," Elijah said, picking up a fork and shaking his hand violently. Jocelyn was loud enough to make the others wince now. "In the end I was so relieved I'd put the fork in my mouth rather than up my nose I just said 'outstanding' without even really thinking about it!"

Jocelyn continued to laugh, and as she slowly relaxed, she added, "He's lying. Elijah was great! Really, really fantastic."

"I'll take the compliment, if you don't mind!" Elijah said, turning to her and wrinkling his nose.

There was plenty more laughter as they sat down; Elijah was in good spirits. Roxy made sure to sit next to Jocelyn. Nat remained in the kitchen while Evangeline came to sit with them. She didn't want to miss any of Elijah's *Ultimate Baker* stories.

Soon Nat brought out the food and attention turned from Elijah to the intensifying savory, boozy smell that by now had their stomachs rumbling with hunger.

"Wow," Jocelyn said, her eyes as wide as her plate. "What *is* that? It smells incredible."

"Oh, you'll like this, cher," Evangeline told Jocelyn as Nat put a wide plate of shrimp in mushrooms and a heavy sauce in the middle of the table. "Shrimp cooked in Ponchartrain sauce, made with plenty of Madeira wine. Some of the finest you can get in the city. And those," she continued, pointing at the big plate of oysters which Nat set beside it, "are oysters Rockefeller." Evangeline glanced at Roxy and winked.

Jocelyn giggled loudly. "Rockefeller? Like the businessman?"

"That's right, cher. They call them that because they're as rich as he is. Broiled oysters with a puréed sauce made from greens and a good dash of anise liqueur. I like it topped with bacon myself, so I fried some up."

"Wow," Elijah said. "I don't know how you keep coming up with this stuff, Evangeline. I only came here for a quick po'boy before heading back to the studio for the afternoon."

"Well, this is enough to fill you up and stop your hands shaking," Evangeline said as she started spooning food onto the plates. "Take your pick. And if you're still hungry, I've got a Bourbon Street steak in the kitchen too. A lovely piece of beef marinated in sugar, soy sauce, and a great smokey whiskey."

"I'll try a plate of both," Jocelyn said, then laughed at her own eagerness. "No way can I leave without tasting it all!"

As soon as she started eating, Roxy realized Evangeline had taken her instructions to heart. After a few bites she felt woozy and light-headed. She decided to slow down and eat some bread while the rest of the table continued to eat the mains. Increasingly enthusiastic laughter and joking filled the room.

Beside her, perpetually noisy Jocelyn was getting louder. She had eaten a lot and was now giggling at the smallest thing. Her cheeks flushed red, and she bobbed and swayed on her chair.

"What are you doing to us, Evangeline?" Elijah yelled with a smile, gesturing at the last oyster on the big plate. "Did you really think that would be enough? I could eat another plateful all by myself!"

Jocelyn laughed heartily at this, and Evangeline stood up. "Shall I bring out the steak?"

"If you don't mind!" Elijah shouted happily.

"Bring it out! Bring it out!" Jocelyn chanted, then exploded into another round of giggles.

Since lunch had begun, Roxy had tried to figure out a way of broaching the subject of what had bothered Jocelyn so much when she had seen her coming out of the bathroom at the studio. But she couldn't think of a diplomatic, tactful way of bringing it up. Now, on seeing the bubbly makeup girl so joyous and happy, Roxy began to feel like it didn't matter how she approached her. Jocelyn was so high on atmosphere and alcohol that she wouldn't mind a direct, serious question.

"Jocelyn," Roxy asked, touching her arm to get her attention. The makeup artist turned to her slowly as if only now realizing she was there, then laughed at her own silly reaction. "I just wanted to check if you were okay," Roxy said to her. "Last time I saw you, you seemed upset about something." Jocelyn frowned. "You were coming out of the bathroom at the studio."

"Oh *that?*" Jocelyn said without any inhibitions now. "I spent that whole day crying in the bathroom!" She rolled her eyes and laughed before being immediately distracted by the bourbon steak brought out by Evangeline. With her eyes, she tracked the plate the elderly woman was carrying.

"Why?" Roxy asked.

"It's so silly, really," Jocelyn said, handing a clean plate to Evangeline. "It was about Patrice."

"Oh?"

"Yeah," Jocelyn said, eyeing her plate hungrily. She spoke as she cut into the juicy, alcohol-soaked meat. "He was *so* terrible to work with that every time I had to deal with him, I'd pray for something bad to happen. I'd been feeling so guilty. I almost wondered if I was to blame for what happened to him! Silly, huh?" Jocelyn giggled, quickly putting a piece of meat into her mouth, closing her eyes, and swooning at the flavor.

"I see," Roxy said. "Yes, I can understand why you'd feel bad about it."

"The idea of having him be the judge on the show and

having to handle him every day for the length of his contract, possibly years and years . . . it would have been torture," Jocelyn said. "But everyone felt the same, you know. We were all praying they wouldn't choose him. Me, the production assistants, the camera crew, everyone. It was such a relief when Elijah got the job, I can't tell you. But we didn't wish him dead! At least I didn't."

Roxy turned back to her own steak. Suddenly, she pushed her chair back and stood up. She needed to get water. The alcohol content of the food made it delicious, but she needed a clear head.

"Excuse me, everyone," she said.

"Roxy! Where you goin'?" Evangeline said. "You've hardly eaten anythin', cher!"

"Get back here, blondie!" Elijah laughed. "I'm not done telling my story!"

"Is it okay if I finish this?" Jocelyn called after her, pointing at Roxy's plate with her fork. But Roxy wasn't listening. Her phone had pinged. She stared at her screen.

Seeing her shocked face, Elijah spoke up. "What is it honey? You've gone pale."

"It's Johnson. They've arrested a homeless man for Patrice's murder. They're closing the case."

CHAPTER EIGHTEEN

ONE MONTH LATER . . .

T HE AUDITORIUM DARKENED, dropping
the neon fuchsia, lime, and azure set into darkness. Two spotlights appeared, each one trained
on one of the finalists of *New Orleans Ultimate Baker*.

"So . . ." the host's voice boomed across the auditorium.
"Now we come down to the final moment, the moment
we've all been waiting for. Who will be crowned the
winner? Who is the *Ultimate Baker of New Orleans?*"

Roxy didn't envy the pair awaiting their fate. The
woman on stage looked pale and pinched, in stark contrast
to the towering, vibrant cake creation behind her that
competed with the neon set for attention, a picture of
bright, glittery deliciousness. Next to her, a brave smile
stretched across the male finalist's face, aware that he was
on camera, but Roxy could see his hands shaking as he
clasped them together, his cake a more restrained celebra-
tion of color, focusing as it did on form, the cake having
been created in the shape of a cheetah.

All power to them. Roxy was far from the shrinking
wallflower she'd been when she'd arrived on the coach from

Ohio with nothing but a suitcase and her cat Nefertiti in her carrier, but she wasn't sure her newfound confidence would stand up to a televised contest just yet.

"To the judges!" the host's voice boomed out of the blackness.

All of a sudden, a new spotlight illuminated the judges' table. Elijah came into sight.

Roxy looked across from her seat in the audience to the faces of her friends. They were monochrome in the glare of the spotlights. They'd gotten front row seats thanks to Elijah.

"I can't believe it!" Nat whispered in her ear, her British accent more pronounced than usual. It always got that way when she was excited, or angry, or upset—any kind of heightened emotion. "Our Eli looks like a real celebrity!"

"I know!" Roxy hissed, beaming from ear to ear. Life could be full of good surprises, as well as bad, Roxy was discovering. She'd never really believed that before, but living in New Orleans with her new friendship family, something akin to magic was always happening.

And Elijah really did look like a celebrity. He'd always had a penchant for exotic outfits when he wasn't in his baker's whites, but since his TV appointment he'd ramped up his wardrobe even further. Today he wore a hot-pink, sharply tailored suit, a black cravat with an orange cupcake pattern printed on it, and black suede shoes with orange laces! His black hair had been slicked and coiffed by the production team, and he'd been spray-tanned until he was almost the same color as his laces. His teeth were so white they could likely perform X-rays. He still looked like Elijah, just a Ken-doll version.

"Elijah . . ." the host was saying. "Kelly has voted for

Carson, and Julia for Marnie. YOU, sir, have the deciding vote."

Some sporadic whoops and yells came from the audience as Elijah placed his elbow down on the desk with a flourish, bringing his balled fist up under his goatee-covered chin. He stared intensely at the contestants, his eyes flicking between them and their creations.

"I love you, Elijah!" a random fan hollered from the audience. Banner-carrying women were sprinkled throughout the auditorium waving their support for him in love messages above their heads.

Evangeline stared straight ahead at the stage, enthralled. Roxy, Nat, Sage, and Sam looked at each other and grinned. It was surreal to see good old Elijah, their beignet-baking, jazz-singing, ivory-tinkling friend from across the cobbled street, as a celebrity.

Roxy caught Sam's eyes for a moment and felt a flutter in her chest. Those big baby blues were nothing short of dreamy. That lopsided smile . . . The way he could fix anything . . . But . . . She quickly looked away. No. Their relationship was a business one. And there was no way she could trust him. There was still something strange going on, too much mystery surrounding him.

"Marry me, Elijah!" another fan shouted, her high voice quivering with devotion.

Nat folded her tattoo-adorned arms over her chest and snorted. "Good luck with that one," she said under her breath.

"Right!" Elijah said loudly. He rose to his feet and puffed out his chest like an emperor about to make a proclamation. "I have made my decision!" He was so dramatic he might have been Julius Caesar in a Shakespeare play. He really knew how to work a crowd. A mischievous look

crossed his face as he ramped up the tension. "I . . . choose . .
. as New Orleans' Ultimate Baker . . ." He paused, a grin
slowly manifesting on his lips. His arm reached out, his
fingers curling into his palm like a magician's. "MARNIE
DELAHAY!"

He threw his hands in the air. Golden confetti burst
from the ceiling. Marnie sunk to her knees. The crowd
roared. Roxy wished she'd brought earplugs.

Next to her, Evangeline drummed the floor with her
feet. Nat leaped in the air and pumped her fist, while Sam
clapped and whistled. Roxy looked over at Sage, who was as
serene as ever, her flowing robes making her look like a
goddess who'd deigned to come down to Earth for a day.
She wore fuchsia to match the TV show's logo, and cerise
flowers were dotted among her soft Afro coils. She watched
the audience and everyone with delight. "I'm an empath,"
she'd once told Roxy. "I feel what others around me feel. I
can't help it." Roxy guessed she must have been in heaven
right then the way joy and high spirits pulsed through the
audience.

They were all still on a high when they stepped from
the auditorium. It was late afternoon, and they squinted in
the bright sunlight. "Help, it's hot," Roxy said, shrugging off
the denim jacket she wore over her blue sundress. "The AC
must have been blasting in there. It feels like a furnace out
here. I dread to think what late summer's going to be like."

Sam wiped his brow. "I could jump in the Mississippi
right now while simultaneously gulping a vat of iced tea."

"If all these blimmin' people would get out the way, it
wouldn't be so bad," Nat said. The crowd was spilling out of
the auditorium. One roughly bumped into her, and Nat
gave the woman a sharp elbow in return. The woman
turned around and said, "Hey!" but with one look at Nat's

tattoos, Doc Martens, and hard stare, she disappeared into the crowd.

"That's what I thought," Nat murmured under her breath.

"I'll hail a cab," Sam said.

"No, no, let's give Elijah a moment," Roxy said. "I think the Mississippi is too dirty to jump in, but we might be able to fix you up with that iced tea." She pointed down the street. "Why don't we go to Patisserie Paradis and wait until he comes out? A sort of homage to him and Patrice Marveau, who might have been where Elijah is now if he hadn't been killed."

CHAPTER NINETEEN

"GOD REST HIS soul." Evangeline crossed herself. "But I'm gonna take a rain check. I wanna check on Pinkie before I get back in the kitchen tonight. He'll be missin' me, and I've so much to tell him. I've had such a lovely day." Evangeline sighed happily. Sam got her a cab, and she was whisked away to her unsuspecting French pug.

The others walked to the café and, except for Sage, ordered iced teas. Sage got a strawberry crush. The group of friends sat by the window, watching the seemingly endless crowd pour out onto the street.

"Isn't it strange to see Elijah like . . . a star?" Roxy said, watching women pass by with their signs proclaiming their love for him.

Nat rolled her eyes. "It's just a bunch of crazy old women with nothing better to do with their lives." She sipped her iced tea through a straw, her dark eyes filled with disdain.

"Meow," Roxy said with a chuckle. "I'd say he deserves it. He looks the part, acts the part, even sounds the part . . .

You remember when he serenaded the woman guest judge? He's such a character."

"Yup," Sam said. "Always has been. Always larger than life. He knows everyone. The life of the party in every New Orleans hotspot. If they take the show national, he'd be the perfect ambassador for our city, trust me."

"I agree," Sage said. "He has the spirit of the city inside him. He's like a walking Mardi Gras."

"They won't take him national," Nat said. "He only appeals to crazies like us Southerners. Those California people would hate him. They'd think he was too weird. Anyways, they can't have him. He has to stay here and do the rebuilding."

With the money he was earning from his TV gig, Elijah had finally embarked on renovating his bakery with gusto—the realization of a dream he'd had for years. The interior of his humble bakery across the street from the Funky Cat Inn was to be torn down and rebuilt. Restoring the exterior, refitting the interior, expanding to the second floor, and building a garden out back would take place over the coming weeks.

Elijah had hired architects, landscapers, and restoration specialists to reimagine the space but also retain the historical features of the building. It was going to be a huge affair, modern with historical twists, a landscaped garden, and a sweeping balcony up above.

There would be a lot of disruption for a while. It would be a huge change for their small corner of New Orleans, which housed only the bakery, the Funky Cat Inn, and a quaint cemetery. But it was needed.

Ever since Elijah had begun his stint on the TV show, his bakery had been crammed with customers. It got so full that lines spilled into the graveyard in one direction and out onto the main street in the other. Their little secret spot in the city—ramshackle, yes, but full of quiet charm—had already changed.

Roxy was unsure about the change really. It was good for business—more people knew about the Funky Cat—but change was always unsettling, and part of her missed the hidden away aspect of the alleyway. She had liked the inn being incognito. It gave it an air of mystery and surprise.

The others had noticed too. Roxy knew that Nat didn't like it. Her attitude had gotten more acidic, and when that happened, it was usually because she was worried. Sage had noticed the change, and not just because she was spiritual and intuitive, but because they were like family and knew each other inside out. "Honey," Sage had said to Nat gently. "We've got to move with the times. Life is an ever-flowing river. Nothing stays the same for long."

"Well, what if I want everything to stay the same?" Nat said. "What with Evangeline retiring and now Elijah being a star and the world cramming itself down our alleyway . . . I don't know . . . It's just weird. I want it back how it was."

"But if nothing changed," Sage said, "you wouldn't be here with us, nor would Roxy. You'd be living your old lives. And maybe Evangeline would have sold up to the developer like she planned, and the Funky Cat wouldn't even exist. Yes, change feels uncomfortable. But if we lean into that discomfort, embrace it, we learn that we too can be as fluid as circumstances. And this fluidity helps us to morph and thrive."

"You should open a church with Dr. Jack the way you preach," Nat said evenly. "I know some people turn to the spirit to get by, but I'll turn to my music, thanks very much."

Roxy smiled. "And copious amounts of beignets."

"If Elijah's not too important to make them anymore," Nat said bitterly.

"You don't have to worry," Sam said. "I've known Elijah for over ten years now. Nothing can change him. He'll keep a clear head on his shoulders. Don't you doubt it."

Roxy gave him a small smile."It's weird sitting here talking about Elijah when it could so easily have been Patrice who got the job. And what's even weirder is the way his case was shut down. It was so sudden."

"Seemed fishy to me," said Nat.

"But who are we to argue with the police? We should leave them to it," Sam said. "Anyway, Elijah is doing a great job. He deserves his success."

"Talking of Elijah," Roxy said, looking now at the crowd outside the studio. It had thinned out. "I can't see him anywhere. Can you?" They all looked out of the window. It was getting difficult to see. A hot, hazy dusk fell over New Orleans.

"I'll call him," Sam said. Moments later he shook his head. "No answer. I'll try again."

"There he is!" Roxy cried. She pointed. Elijah was surrounded by a group of fans, signing autographs and taking selfies. As Sam called him, they saw him look at his phone, then put it back in his pocket without answering.

Roxy turned down the corners of her mouth. "We'd better go home without him. We need to prepare for his big dinner tonight. Even with the prep we did this morning, there's still a lot to do."

"Yeah, and we've got guests coming in," Nat said. "We can't have you stressed and shouting, now can we?"

Roxy laughed. "This, coming from you." Nat wore her heart on her sleeve, and that didn't always go down well with the guests—or Roxy for that matter.

"Hey!" Nat said hotly. "I'm much better than I was, thank you very much!"

"It's true," Sage said. "But you mustn't worry. You have an artistic temperament. We know that, and we all love you unconditionally."

Nat grinned. "Even if I . . . set Elijah's new bakery on fire to get his attention?"

"Oh my gosh!" Roxy said, getting up from her chair and swinging her jacket on. "You've got to stop!"

"I can't help my dark sense of humor!"

Sam had been standing by, bemused by this strange female jousting. Once again, he exercised his cab hailing abilities, thankful for something to do. By his side, Roxy remained cheery. She was excited about pulling off an extravagant dinner that night. But as she looked over at Elijah, she wondered if Nat might be right. That morning he'd arranged to ride back with them, but now he was preoccupied and hadn't called them with an update. He hadn't picked up the phone when they'd contacted him. This lack of care was unlike him.

Roxy called out Elijah's name. "Elijah! Elijah!" He didn't look up.

Sage put her soft hand on Roxy's arm and spoke to her gently. "Let him enjoy his moment. He'll remember us later. Let's share in his joy, even if it is from afar."

CHAPTER TWENTY

AS SOON AS the group arrived back at the Funky Cat Inn, the place turned into a hive of activity. To celebrate the end of Elijah's first series and the start of his reno, Roxy had offered to host a big dinner for him. Besides the friends, Elijah had invited his construction lead and restoration specialist. The next day, Elijah's old bakery would be demolished so he could start building the new one. In New Orleans, and especially at the Funky Cat Inn, they needed little excuse for a party, and the start of the project was easily reason enough for an evening full of wine, rich food, jazz, and laughter.

Elijah had invited the city site inspector Lacey Gregory to the dinner but had secretly been relieved when she'd declined the invitation. The city planning department and the construction industry were hardly natural playmates. It was like inviting the boss to your birthday party—necessary but inglorious.

Lacey had, as was her job, picked holes in every facet of Elijah's plans, requiring many revisions. "The phrase 'drunk on power' comes to mind, cher," Evangeline had said. No one was inclined to disagree, except for Sage, who was keen to find spiritual reasons for the woman's ornery attitude. Whenever Sage and Lacey happened to be in proximity to each other, Sage would hover a little away from the site inspector. Roxy knew Sage well enough to know she was sending Lacey "healing energy."

To get the project off to a good start, full of good vibes and goodwill, Elijah and Roxy had agreed upon a dinner in full-on, swinging Funky Cat style. They would have a huge New Orleans Cajun and Creole multicourse meal devised by Evangeline and prepared that night by her and Nat. Sam would play the sax, while Elijah and Nat would sing classics by Nat King Cole and other jazz legends. Sage would read her tarot cards, and Roxy's fluffy Persian cat Nefertiti would no doubt join them for a saucer of milk and the merry atmosphere.

When they got back to the hotel, Nat rushed to the kitchen to start fixing the food while Roxy attended to the dining room and the salon. She spread the white tablecloths, fresh from Sam's laundry, over the huge table where they'd eat together and got to organizing the rows of silverware they'd need for each course. There was a plaintive mewl behind her.

"Hi, Neffy, baby," Roxy said, briefly looking up as she arranged the steak knives. "Sorry I didn't come to see you right away. It's going to be a whirlwind tonight, so you won't get much attention." Nefertiti appeared to understand and mewled again, seemingly displeased.

Roxy couldn't resist. She laid down the last of the steak knives and scooped her white fluffball of a cat into a cuddle. She looked into her beautiful blue eyes and said, "I'm sure the guests will fawn all over you when dinner's done. And who could resist, huh? Who could resist?" She gave Nefertiti a tickle under her chin and squeezed her a little tighter. Nefertiti shut her eyes, smiled, and purred loudly before Roxy bent down to ease her onto the floor. "Sorry, baby. I've got to get back to work."

Once the table was laid, complete with candlesticks and wine and water glasses, Roxy headed into the salon. It was clean and tidy and looked beautiful. The gold and navy color scheme was accented by a gold chandelier and mahogany antiques that set off the light and dark walls magnificently. Nevertheless, Roxy spent a little time sprucing it up. She fluffed up the navy and antique gold velvet cushions, then gave each of them a fashionable karate chop to put a dent in them like she'd seen on Instagram. During the renovation of the hotel, Roxy had picked up a social media interior design habit and could still happily while away an hour each night marveling at the ideas she came across and imagining new projects for the hotel.

Next, she set the tarot table against one of the champagne-colored, satin armchairs. The table was technically an antique card table around which Roxy presumed people had played <u>bourré</u> and poker in days gone by but was now used by Sage to offer insight into someone's future as told to her by the tarot. She dusted the tabletop and the surfaces to bring the salon up to her standards. Now to check on the food.

A wall of steam hit Roxy in the face when she entered the kitchen. It smelled rich and buttery and wholesome. Nat was like a worker bee buzzing around a hive.

"Smells awesome!" Roxy proclaimed. "How's the soup coming along?"

"Excellent, of course!" Nat said, sounding offended. She could be crotchety at the best of times, and especially when there was a big dinner to prepare. "I'm working on the pie," she said as she whipped mixture in a bowl. "Pastry's all done, so now it's just the filling and the topping."

"Perfect," Roxy said. "I'm really looking forward to it." It was true; she was. The excitement of big dinners was often infused with anxiety. When they had important guests, or maybe a critic coming, everything had to be 100 percent perfect. But tonight, it was just them and their construction guests. It was to be a relaxed affair, and Roxy couldn't wait to drink up and chow down.

"What have we got on the menu?" Roxy asked. At that moment, the back door burst open and in came Evangeline, tying an apron around her waist.

"Crawfish and corn soup to start," she called out.

"Followed by crab cakes with Evangeline's secret dipping sauce," Nat shouted, now shaking vegetables in a sauté pan. Roxy raised her eyebrows. Evangeline wouldn't share the recipe for her secret dipping sauce with Nat. It had been the source—or sauce—of some arguments! How would they make it when the old woman was gone?

"And after that?" Roxy cried out happily. This call and response routine was one they had gotten into most evenings. It had the practical advantage of informing Roxy of what was on the menu, but it also raised the energy in the kitchen. It was a way to celebrate the food they were preparing.

"Steaks! Grilled outside in the yard. Marinated in a bourbon, lemon juice, soy sauce, and brown sugar marinade for a whole day. I'll spray them with more sauce while they're grilling for extra flavor."

"And dessert?"

"Pecan pie with a caramelized cream filling and a chocolate pecan topping. Both filling and topping infused with bourbon, like the steaks. Elijah's favorite," Evangeline shouted out.

"Cheeseboard with fruit to finish, although they'll likely be stuffed by that point," Nat concluded.

"Nah, they can take it in the salon and pick at it slowly while they enjoy the music and tarot," Roxy replied. "Anything you need me to do?"

"No, cher, all under control," Evangeline said briskly, taking some ramekins from a cupboard.

"How was Pinkie, Evangeline?"

"He was more interested in sleepin' than hearin' my story of the day at *Ultimate Baker*, so I decided to get on in here where I'm more wanted. Go get into your glad rags, cher. We'll be fine here."

"You're angels," Roxy said as she left the room. She couldn't help but chuckle to herself. If angels were anything like the oft-grumpy Nat and Evangeline, heaven would be full of raised voices and the sound of banging pots!

CHAPTER TWENTY-ONE

ROXY WENT TO her room to take a shower and change her clothes. She was a casual sort of girl. Her previous lack of confidence had meant the last thing she wanted was to stand out. Blending into the background had been her aim, and that was easiest to achieve in jeans and sweaters.

But her self-esteem and confidence had bloomed since she'd been in New Orleans. "Like a rare flower that only opens under the right conditions," Sage had said poetically one night at dinner. "A New Orleans flower."

Everyone had agreed, and Roxy tried not to blush. With newfound faith in herself, whenever they had a formal sit-down, she'd taken to wearing gowns bedecked with sequins and shimmer. The dresses lit up beautifully under the chandeliers and golden lamplight, so much so that she felt like an Old Hollywood movie star or a glamorous patron at a jazz club, back when women wore satin gloves and men tipped their hats.

Roxy got these dresses from a vintage-inspired dress-maker named Beulah. Beulah ran Beulah's Boutique on

Marie Laveau Street. For tonight's dinner, Roxy had opted for her boldest yet to celebrate Elijah. It had sequins from the neckline to waist and a bodice so tight it gave the impression that slight Roxy had curves. It was also emerald green.Where the bodice ended, the skirt bloomed into an ankle-length, slimline, cream net. She added long, cream, satin gloves that reached the crook of her arm.

Roxy teased and gelled her short, blonde hair into retro finger waves and wore large statement earrings—long drips of gold with an amber stone in the middle. On her feet, she wore gold satin pumps that Beulah had recommended, even if they didn't do anything for her height.

"Wow!" Sam said when she walked into the salon a little later wearing the dazzling gown.

Roxy was feeling so confident she didn't even blush. "Thank you, Sam," she said breezily. "You don't look too shabby yourself."

He laughed as he carried his saxophone case into the salon, ready for the music later. "Thanks," he said. "I don't think anyone looks too bad in a tux, though. We men just all look the same as each other."

Except for those with beautiful eyes, Roxy wanted to say but didn't. She felt her heart flutter all too often when she saw Sam and didn't want to encourage herself further.

Recently, Roxy had made the mistake of calling her mother, who had never been supportive or kind. It had been her first contact in many months and represented a misguided, overly optimistic attempt to build a semblance of a relationship. Dinah Reinhardt had been warm and apparently empathetic until Roxy felt comfortable enough to bring up Sam and her reservations about him.

"Ah," her mother had said. "He's either a lowlife or a genius. Or both. A low-life genius. A laundry is almost always a cover for money laundering, don't you know that?" she scoffed. "It figures you would get involved with someone like that. You never were a good judge of character or situations. I'm surprised that hotel of yours is still going. You sure you're not losing money hand over fist?" Roxy imagined her mother at the other end of the phone saying this amid a cloud of smoke from one of the high tar cigarettes she invariably smoked inside the trailer she lived in. "Get out more is my suggestion. I don't know why you're so shy, Roxy. You won't win any beauty pageants, but you're hardly Frankenstein." That was her mother's version of a compliment.

Before New Orleans, Roxy would have hurt for days over this conversation, but now she hung up and thought no more of it. She was a new Roxy now, a Roxy no one could tear down. This was her life, a life she had built and owned with strength and courage and passion.

Soon everyone arrived for the dinner. Sage and Dr. Jack were first. Dr. Jack's brown corduroy suit made him look even more like a cuddly teddy bear than normal. Sage matched him. She had changed into deep-chocolate robes.

The front doorbell rang, and Roxy raced over to welcome Elijah's construction manager, a woman named Annie Boolan. She was accompanied by a very tall man who was the consultant for the protection and restoration of the bakery's French architecture. He introduced himself as Xavier Jean-Pierre and bowed as he shook Roxy's hand. Roxy recognized them from the *Ultimate Baker* filming that had taken place at Elijah's bakery before he got the job. Elijah had told her he'd known Annie since his schooldays. She had, as a special favor to him, returned to the city from Boston, where she now lived, to take charge of his project.

Sam and Roxy quietly chatted to their guests as Nat

and Evangeline banged around in the kitchen. There was a notable absence though as they nursed their predinner bourbons in the salon. "Where's Elijah?" Annie asked. The construction manager was a surprisingly feminine and glamorous woman of around fifty. She had long, swishy red hair and Christian Louboutins on her feet. The color of the soles of her shoes was the same as her hair. Red. Xavier couldn't keep his eyes off her, although he was much younger than she.

"I'm not sure," Sam said, looking concerned. "His phone is off. It's going straight to voicemail."

"Leave him be," Evangeline said, coming in with a large silver platter bearing shrimp toast. She handed it around. "He's probably lappin' up all the attention, cher. The Lord knows he deserves it. His talent has gone underappreciated for years." She looked around at them as if to give them a warning. Roxy noticed Evangeline's eyes lingered over the restoration expert for a long moment. Admittedly, he was very good-looking, but she was sure that wasn't the reason for Evangeline's scrutiny. Evangeline was very protective of New Orleans' architecture and would no doubt be keeping her eye on the restoration part of the bakery project.

The elderly woman cleared her throat and continued. "Unfortunately, fame is a fickle business. It may chew him up and spit him out. My advice is that we're all here for him when the spotlights fade and he's back bakin' in the early hours every day without an audience. It will surely happen in time. He just needs to keep his feet on the ground."

Sam leaned nonchalantly against a pillar. "Aw, that's a little pessimistic, don't you think, Evangeline?" Roxy never failed to be charmed and impressed by Sam's Southern manners. "I'm sure he'll have a long and successful career in showbiz if that's what he wants. Anyway, he's not neglecting his roots. He's renovating the bakery. I propose a toast in his absence. May the work go swimmingly and the restored building come to a beautiful fruition." He held up his glass. "Cheers, everyone!"

"Cheers!"

Right then, there was a knock at the door. "Oh, great. That'll be Elijah!" Roxy said. She set her bourbon down and hurried into the hallway. She opened the door with a smile, saying, "Thank goodness you're here! We almost . . ." But she trailed off. It wasn't Elijah on the doorstep; it was Lacey Gregory, the city's building inspector. She too had been present with Annie and Xavier at the earlier filming.

Lacey looked as she had back then. Black combat boots, a black tee, and black pants made her look like some kind of ninja. Her black hair was pulled into a tight bun on the back of her head. Roxy somehow managed a smile for the woman who was glaring right at her. "Oh! Please come in. Join us for dinner. We're having a little celebr—" she said, recovering quickly.

"I'm not here on a pleasure visit," Lacey said witheringly. "I'm here to give Mr. Elijah Walder some very bad news."

CHAPTER TWENTY-TWO

"**B**AD NEWS?" ROXY said. In the salon, she'd felt wrapped up in a warm, cozy, golden glow of friendship. In the hallway, she felt the lonely chill of a draft. "What's wrong?"

"There are errors in the paperwork, and Mr. Walder won't be able to proceed with the groundbreaking tomorrow," Lacey Gregory said. "If ever."

"Ever?" Roxy repeated, stunned. "Elijah will be devastated."

"The building codes do not take 'devastation' of the emotional kind nor hurt feelings into account, Ms. . . .?" Lacey squinted.

"Reinhardt," Roxy said finally with a touch of condescension.

"The paperwork will have to be resubmitted from scratch."

"Ms. Gregory." Roxy turned to see the construction manager Annie Broolan strut toward them, her cheeks flushing as red as her hair and the soles of her shoes. She smiled warmly. "Lacey." Annie held out her arms. "I was sure I heard your dulcet tones. Is there a problem?"

Roxy looked between the two women. She sensed an argument was about to ensue and fast.

"There's going to be a delay on the start of works. A paperwork issue."

"A paperwork issue?" Annie said, frowning. "Really? A freaking paperwork issue? You know me, Lacey. You know I know the consequences of not dotting every i and crossing every t. You think I would make a mistake like that? Me?"

Lacey's eyelids drooped as she gave Annie a long, withering look. "You know I make it my responsibility to be the most conscientious site manager in the state—no, the nation —when it comes to health and safety. I will not compromise on that."

"Oh, right," Annie said sarcastically. "You're holding up this project the night before it's meant to start because of some triviality. Am I supposed to be grateful or something?"

"With your history, I did think you would appreciate or at least acknowledge where I was coming from, I'll admit," Lacey said. "Obviously I was wrong. I'll come by tomorrow to start the paperwork over."

"Over my dead body are we starting again."

"That's precisely what I'm trying to avoid, Ms. Broolan. Dead bodies. I would have thought you'd have wanted that too."

"Trying a new way to make my life as difficult as possible, more like. How are we supposed to get this project done with you breathing down our necks all the time? Mr. Walder loses business every day his project is delayed! What's he going to think?"

Lacey looked genuinely hurt by this. Her lips pinched together, the lines around her mouth showing. "That's not my concern. My job is to make sure all the paperwork is present and correct. Currently, it is not." Lacey Gregory blinked long and slow. "Ms. Reinhardt, I'll bid you goodbye. Ms. Broolan, I'll see you tomorrow. Have a good evening."

By the time Roxy closed the front door, Annie Broolan had stalked on her high heels back into the dining room. Nat sidled up to Roxy. "What's going on?"

"I'm not sure. Lacey Gregory has just shown up to say they can't start tomorrow. Paperwork issues, she said."

Nat groaned. "Elijah's not going to be happy about that!" she said, taking a swig of her bourbon.

"No." Roxy tapped her fingers against her thigh. "But let's not dwell on that now. It's not any of our business, and there's nothing we can do. Let's calm everyone down and enjoy the night. Demolition or no demolition."

"Right-o. You get everyone to the table, I'll get the food," Nat said over her shoulder. She disappeared into the kitchen. A few moments later, she reappeared in the dining room carrying five bowls of soup. After some training from Evangeline, Nat had learned how to carry numerous plates at once like a pro.

Sam looked concerned. "What's up?" Roxy asked him.

"I'm getting worried about Elijah. He's still not picking up. I think I'll quickly drive down to the studio and see where he's got to."

"All right," Roxy said. "I'm sure he's fine, but I guess it'll put our minds at ease."

Nat overheard them as she brought out three more bowls. "He's fine, trust me." She deposited the bowls and returned to the kitchen. Roxy followed. As soon they had passed through the swing doors, Nat turned to her. "He's probably taken a TV bigwig to a bar. Or been carried there by some crazy fan who can't believe their luck. He's probably forgotten all about us."

"Nuh-uh," Roxy said. "He knows we're putting this party on for him. He'd never miss that. Especially without calling. It's just not like Elijah at all."

Nat twisted her mouth and frowned. "Wanna bet? Fame is a heady drug, Rox."

Nat's skepticism about Elijah got on Roxy's nerves. Sam headed out to his Rolls Royce, and Roxy returned to the dining table.

"Please, come sit between me and Xavier," Annie Broolin said, her eyes wide. She nodded at the seat next to her, clearly keen to be separated from the restoration expert. "I do love your outfit, Roxy," Annie said. "It's beautiful. Very vibrant, just like this wild and wonderful city."

"I was about to say the same to you!" Roxy said. Annie wore a long, white dress with a blue floral pattern, topped with a bolero jacket of green palm fronds on a pink background. It shouldn't have worked, but it did. Around her neck was draped a long, delicate gold chain holding her half-moon spectacles. Her Louboutins were white. Somehow, she looked very put together and chic.

"Mmm, my compliments to the chef," Annie said as she sipped the soup from her spoon. She nodded at Evangeline, who disappeared with a half smile into the kitchen. Evangeline had been told her cooking was excellent for over fifty years. Praise didn't excite her much anymore; nothing much did, except Pinkie, her French pug, and *Ultimate Baker*. Nevertheless, she still wriggled self-consciously whenever she was complimented.

The steaks took a little while, so they ate warm baguettes with melted garlic butter while they waited. Roxy chatted to Xavier. She found him fascinating. He knew all about the history of their little alleyway.

"The workers who built these buildings were vodouisants. At the time, voodoo ceremonies were illegal. Vodouisants formed companies so they could make a living, but also so they could meet under its guise and practice their religion."

"Oh!" Roxy said. "And they built the buildings on this street?"

"Uh-huh, in the mid-eighteen hundreds."

"Wow!" Roxy said. "I never knew that! Don't tell Nat. She'll say it's cursed!"

Xavier flashed a smile. "Maybe it is," he said. "Though as far as I can work out—vodouisants don't write anything down, it's an oral tradition learned through initiation and apprenticeship—groups were more into blessings than curses."

"That's a relief," Roxy said with a laugh.She was glad of the distraction from her thoughts. She'd been nervously picking at bread, but she didn't feel like eating any of it. Finally, the steaks were brought to the table. "Excuse me," she said quietly to Annie and Xavier. She headed into the lobby and got out her phone. She called Sam. "Any news on Elijah?"

Sam sounded panicked and out of breath. "Not yet, Rox. I can't find him anywhere. No one at the auditorium knows where he is. He didn't sign out. Not a trace of him at any local restaurants. I'm just walking around now to see if I can find him."

"Okay," Roxy said. She felt nervous. Sam was usually such a laid-back character that hearing his anxiety put her on edge too. "I'm sure he's fine," she said. She didn't sound very convincing.

"Of course, he is," Sam said, equally aware that their words lacked meaning. Platitudes only.Elijah would never skip a party at the Funky Cat, especially not one in his honor. He was eccentric and flamboyant, but not arrogant.

Back at the hotel, Roxy didn't want to worry the others, so she took a deep breath and dredged up a smile before she returned to the dining room. But she found herself pushing her steak and sautéed Cajun spiced potatoes around her plate. *Please let Elijah be okay*, she said in her head over and over. *Please.*

CHAPTER TWENTY-THREE

THANKS TO ANNIE'S good nature and Xavier's fascinating historical knowledge of the area, the dinner went well, and Roxy had regained her appetite by dessert. Annie proved to be a good laugh, drinking too much wine and eventually ribbing Xavier as he tried to flirt with her. It lifted the mood. Besides, whose mood wouldn't be lifted by a caramelized cream pie with chocolate pecan topping?

"Food of the gods," Roxy declared as she took her first bite. Then came the kick of bourbon. "Oof. Nat, you've been very liberal with the liquor! Do you want us all collapsed in a heap by the time we get to hear you sing?"

"Singing sounds better with bourbon," Nat said with a wink. "You know what Elijah always says? The more greased the wheels, the smoother the ride. Where is he, anyway? Sam catch up with him yet?"

Everyone seemed to be listening in on their conversation. "I'm sure he's fine," Roxy repeated like a mantra. Perhaps the more she said it, the more likely it was to be true. "You know, maybe his new management insisted he do interviews or something." It was meant to be a convincing diversion, but Roxy realized it could be true. It put her mind at ease, and by the time they got to the salon for Sage's tarot reading, she felt much better.

"Who's got a question?" Sage asked as she shuffled her tarot deck.

"I do!" Nat said. "Will I totally flop at singing tonight as I'm going a cappella without Sam's sax and Elijah's piano?"

"You don't need cards to know that, cher," Evangeline said. "Now stop attention seekin' and settle down." Evangeline, perhaps surprisingly, took the cards very seriously.

"Man, this is why I miss NOLA," Annie said. "You don't get tarot readings after dinner in Boston, I'll tell you that much. I have a question, Sage, a serious one."

Sage looked at the construction manager, her expression open and serene. She nodded.

"What's happened to Elijah?" Annie asked. "I've known that man since he was a kid. It isn't like him to not turn up to a party."

Sage paused for a moment and looked down at the cards. Roxy looked around. She expected Nat to draw up her lip skeptically, maybe let out a little derisive snort. She expected Evangeline to repeat her speech about letting Elijah enjoy himself. But they didn't say anything, nor did they make a sound. No one did. They appeared as worried as she was.

"Okay," Sage said, laying the cards out in a spread, facedown. "Please come and pick one card, Annie, and give it to me. Take a moment before you choose it. Breathe deeply, and focus on your question, then pick up the card you're first drawn to. Try not to overthink it. It should feel almost automatic when you reach for it."

Annie slipped off her expensive heels and padded over

the thick, mink-colored rug in stockinged feet. She pulled a card and handed it to Sage. Sage turned it over and laid it faceup on the mahogany surface of the tarot table.

Everyone who was close enough to see the card gasped, Roxy included. It was a black card with a white skeleton. "DEATH" was written at the bottom in red.

"Wait!" Sage commanded, raising her hands. It was the loudest Roxy had ever heard her speak. "This does not mean literal death. The death card means something is coming to an end. Something is dying. It could be the end of something good or the end of something bad. It's not easy to tell. All we know is there is major change in progress."

"Major change," Nat repeated with a heavy sigh. She went over to the gold retro drinks tray she'd picked up on Etsy and poured herself a bourbon. "Major bleedin' change." She plonked herself back down on the couch and sipped moodily. "I reckon I'll be singing the blues tonight."

"Who else wants a reading?" Sage asked. Roxy watched her carefully. She saw Sage giving herself her own lightning-fast reading under the tarot table and saw two other horrible cards come up. First was THE DEVIL and second was THE TOWER. The latter depicted a tower on fire, people running away from it. Roxy had seen Sage do enough readings to know that the tower card nearly always meant bad news. She was sure Sage's surreptitious reading was about Elijah, and even though she wasn't sure if she believed in the cards herself, her heart sank. Could something really have happened to her flamboyant friend?

They tried to enjoy the rest of the evening, but Elijah's absence hung like a cloud over everything. Annie laughed too loudly. Xavier got an underwhelming reading from Dr. Jack. Nat sang a song with a sad melody about there being no love in the world, obviously written by someone in the depths of heartbreak. The song was so depressing, Nefertiti joined her, caterwauling her little heart out. Roxy had to remove her from the room.

They were about to call it a night when they heard the front door open. Everyone froze. Was their evening going to have a happy ending? Or were lives about to be set on fire like the tower in Sage's tarot card?

Elijah's voice boomed through the Funky Cat, but it was slurred and too loud. Sam helped him stagger in, Elijah's arm around his shoulder as Sam carried the slighter man's weight. In his free hand, Elijah grasped an open bottle of champagne. "Elijah, I really think—"

"No!" Elijah said thickly. He raised his hand like he had at the contest, but this was a drunken flourish. "It's time to par . . . tayy! Shorry everyone. I'm in demand everywhere! The life of a celebrity, huh?" He straightened up, looking almost sober for a moment. "Sho, where's my birthday cake, huh?"

Roxy surprised herself. She was furious. All that anxiety over Elijah's safety and he turned up embarrassingly drunk. "It's not your birthday, Elijah. Sam, please take him home. Maybe stay with him and make sure he doesn't do anything stupid."

"Hey!" Elijah said, pointing in her face indignantly. "Every day is my birthday, Roxy, and you'd do well to remember it!"

Roxy glared at him, her hands on her hips.

"Sorry, everyone. I should have taken him straight home," Sam said. "See you tomorrow. Come along, buddy."

Elijah hovered next to Roxy, grinning, daring her to react. There was a splattering sound, and Roxy's feet suddenly felt wet. Elijah had spilled champagne all over her shoes—the special satin pumps she'd bought to celebrate his success. Fury bubbled up in her again as Sam dragged Elijah away. Roxy stepped out of her wet pumps and marched to the kitchen with them. Evangeline hurried after her. "I'll sort the floor, cher. You get to bed."

"What an idiot. What an absolute idiot he is." Roxy leaned against the counter, anger rendering her almost speechless.

"I know," Evangeline said. "He is. Don't worry about the mess though, cher. Me 'n' Nat will mop up."

"I'll make sure the guests are okay," Sage said, joining them in the kitchen. "Good thing Elijah is their client and not the other way around. You go on right to bed."

The door opened, and in walked Nat. "It's just champagne, Roxy. I'm sure your shoes will be alright."

"If not, there's always Sam and his magic laundry potions." Sage smiled.

Roxy let out a deep breath. She felt so let down. "Are you sure you don't want me to help clean up?"

"Of course," Nat said. "I'm heading out too. Not staying here for the mood."

Evangeline said nothing but gave Roxy a stern look. Sage caught her gently by the shoulders and turned her in the direction of the door. Roxy grabbed a plastic bag, popped her shoes in it, and headed back into the salon. She managed to wave goodnight to Xavier and Annie. Once in her room with the door locked, she chucked the shoes into the shower and aggressively turned on the water. She didn't know if a shower would stop her shoes smelling like a winery, but it made her feel better.

She was furious with Elijah. For making them all worry. For ignoring Sam's calls. For not turning up when the dinner was in his honor. She was furious with Nat for being right about Elijah's uppityness, and with herself for being so naïve.She felt such a fool.

She'd thought her perfect New Orleans family would always be there for one another, would always treat each other well. Now they were divided; a crack was showing. A big one, a chasm perhaps. Would it make everything crumble? Roxy felt her foundations shaking under her feet. What had happened to Elijah, the lovely, cheery man who took them around town, who had long discussions with her about building a business, who got up at the crack of dawn to make them the best beignets in New Orleans?

"He had no right, Nefertiti," she said once she was in bed. Fueled with rage, she'd wanted to rip off her green sequined dress. She'd managed to calm herself enough to remove it carefully, yet not enough to hang it on the hanger. She'd tossed it over the back of the chair carelessly, just like she felt Elijah had tossed them all aside, her especially. "He had no right." Thankfully, despite her temper, the food, alcohol, and late hour had done enough to counteract it. She soon fell asleep, sleeping fitfully but long and dreaming of burning buildings and fleeing people.

CHAPTER TWENTY-FOUR

B Y THE NEXT morning, Roxy's anger had left her and been replaced with sadness. When she looked over at her green sequin dress laying forlornly on the chair, she felt empty. The day before everything had seemed so simple, and all on the right track: Elijah's success, the start of his plan to rejuvenate his bakery, the future of their businesses entwined in partnership side by side. Now the renovation couldn't go ahead, and she didn't feel so jubilant and supportive of Elijah's success. The businesses no longer felt *simpatico*.

Roxy had awoken as the sun was rising, and after watching it for a while, she took a long, hot shower and smiled at herself in the mirror. Despite how she felt, she didn't want to give a bad impression to the others by moping around.She headed to the kitchen to make coffee and was startled to find Evangeline buzzing about making beignets.

"Morning," Roxy said brightly. "What are you doing here?"

"You're up early, cher," Evangeline said, ignoring her

question. "Did you sleep well? Coffee's in the pot. I'm just makin' beignets, and then I have to get back to Pinkie."

"Beignets?" Roxy said as she poured her coffee.

"Well, it's not like Elijah's goin' to be up and at 'em this mornin', is it now? Anyway, the less said about him the better. He'll be nursin' a ragin' hangover today."

"And then he'll get the bad news about the construction not going ahead. I wonder what they're going to do? I mean, the construction teams were all set to start."

"Well," Evangeline said briskly. "N'awlins ain't all jazz and java, cher. They'll work it out."

The doorbell rang, and Roxy went to answer it. On hauling open the heavy, wooden front door, she found a huge bunch of white roses on the doorstep. Roxy took the card attached to the flowers and read what was written there.

"To the fabulous, far too kind, and hopefully forgiving, wonderful Roxy. I'm very sorry for being a drunken brute. I hope these beautiful flowers that remind me of you begin to make it up to you. E. XX"

Roxy sighed. She didn't know what to think. The flowers *were* beautiful. She felt the residue of her hard, hurt, angry feelings melt away with the softness of the note. Roxy sometimes wondered if she forgave the people who wounded her too easily. Was she doing so right now? She looked up. Standing in the courtyard was Elijah, his hair tousled, his eyes red-rimmed. He smiled sheepishly.

As she sat down at a table in the dining room, Elijah placed a plate full of hot beignets and a coffee in front of her.

"Evangeline's?" Roxy said.

"No," Elijah said, sitting next to her. "Mine. I didn't know she'd made any. I made these for you just now. To say sorry, of course. Please forgive me, Rox. I couldn't stand to have you mad at me. Honestly, I can't remember what happened, but Sam filled me in on all the gory details, and I'm mortified, honey. Truly."

"So, you haven't seen anyone? None of your construction crew?"

"Not a soul," he said. He looked embarrassed. "They haven't started the construction, probably because, like a fool, I overslept and didn't meet with them. After last night they probably thought the whole thing was off. Looks like I'll be buying roses for everyone."

"It has been called off." Elijah frowned, puzzled. "The work's not going ahead today, Eli," Roxy said quietly.

"What? Why not? Because of last night? Oh, no. What have I done?" Elijah's hands flew to his face.

"No, it's not because of that. It's a paperwork issue. Something wasn't quite right. Lacey Gregory from the city planning department came over last night and said she'd be over today to discuss. She stopped the work going ahead. Annie spoke to her. She was ticked off." The sound of raised voices in the courtyard carried through into the dining room. Roxy looked out of the window. "Uh-oh. No need. Lacey's already here and arguing with Xavier and Annie. Let's go!"

Roxy and Elijah rushed out front as ahead of them, Xavier, Annie, and Lacey stood outside the cordoned-off bakery with hard hats on.

"Remember, all the historic architectural pieces have already been preserved and put into storage," Xavier was saying. "They will not be damaged by the demo."

"And what exactly can you do if we go ahead with the building work?" Annie said with venom. "Make us knock it down and rebuild it?"

"Yes, basically," Lacey said. "I don't make the rules."

"Actually, it seems you do, or are attempting to," Annie replied. "Last I heard the paperwork was approved last week."

"My subordinate didn't go through it with enough of a fine-toothed comb," Lacey said. "In my view, the health and safety regulations are not met."

"Hey," Elijah said as he and Roxy strolled over. "What's going on? What do you mean the health and safety regulations aren't met?"

"Trust me, they are," Annie said. She chucked a nod at Lacey. "This one just enjoys ruining people's dreams."

"Standing in the way of progress," Xavier agreed. "I've been involved in hundreds of similar projects. There's nothing wrong with the proposed measures."

Elijah was smooth. "Lacey, we're on a tight schedule. I'm losing business every day, and we can't reopen as everything's been removed from the inside. How can we make this go through as quickly as possible? As in immediately." He smiled a bright, white, made-for-TV smile.

"Don't hold your breath," Lacey said. "When the city board sees the issues I've highlighted, the project won't go ahead without numerous appeals and modifications."

Elijah turned a shade of purple. "Are you freaking crazy?" he cried. "But that will take months!" He pulled out his phone. "We're doing this renovation whether you permit us to or not. In fact, I'm calling the whole crew now to get them down here."

"You can't do that, sir. You are not approved to do so."

"So, freaking sue me." Elijah was steaming now. "Do you know who I am?"

CHAPTER TWENTY-FIVE

"**E**LIJAH..." ANNIE SAID.

"You will leave me with no choice but to call the police," Lacey said.

"Do it," Elijah spat, ignoring Annie's warning. "Hopefully it's Johnson. He can stand right in the path of the backhoe."

Roxy hung back as Elijah phoned the construction team. Lacey stood at the end of the cobbled street where it met the main road, making her own calls.

Are you freaking crazy? Elijah's words circled around inside Roxy's head. They confused her. He'd been so humble with his apology to her one moment, then acting like a diva the next.

Around the corner of the Funky Cat swaggered Nefertiti. Shadowing her was the ginger cat. When the white, fluffy feline spotted Roxy, she abandoned her friend and wound her way around Roxy's ankles. Both watched the stripey orange cat stalk away.

"Ooh, Nefertiti, have you made a friend?" Roxy tickled her under the chin. "Or got yourself a man? Hmm? Now, I'll warn you. Johnson's coming over, so you might want to find a better place to relax." Johnson disliked cats and always glared at Nefertiti like he was facing off with a tiger. The disdain was mutual. Nefertiti had hissed at him, much like Roxy would like to do on occasion.

Annie went inside the hotel to change into appropriate construction wear. Xavier sat down on a chair outside the bakery and watched the commotion. A van from ALHA-09 arrived, and Roxy watched a couple of familiar faces jump out and get set up. Zach and Mickey, the cameraman and sound engineer from *Ultimate Baker*. Jocelyn was with them.

"What are they doing here?" Roxy asked Elijah.

"Wha—oh, they're here to document everything. For a bit for the show, or just posterity, we'll see."

Roxy went inside to make coffee for everyone. She found Nat in the kitchen. It was nearly midday, but the hotel worker was grabbing her first coffee. She hadn't been around at breakfast.

"Oh, Rox, I'm sorry I'm so late. I knew Evangeline was on breakfast duty, but I slept right through my alarm." She looked genuinely apologetic.

"Meh, nobody died. Besides, there's drama outside. Even though Lacey's told him to halt the construction work, Elijah wants to go ahead regardless. Lacey's calling the police."

Nat looked up at the ceiling and sighed. "I'll have to find an errand or two to run." When possible, Nat slunk into the background whenever Johnson was around. Normally that would have been difficult for someone with red, patent leather Doc Martens and an armful of skulls and roses tattoos, but thankfully for Nat, Johnson seemed to prefer investing his time in his ongoing feud with Roxy.

"Actually, I think I'll stay inside and clean the bathrooms, if that's okay," Nat said. "After I make some food for the construction workers. I'll do po'boy sandwiches, right?"

"Great, yep. A mix, maybe some salami, ham, some cheese, BLT. Pile them high with fillings and salad. I have a feeling today is going to be long and busy."

Roxy was right. On Elijah's call, a huge number of construction professionals swarmed into the courtyard. Sam arrived at some point, as did Sage, who was to perform a spiritual blessing on the site. There were so many workers that Roxy lost track of them, but at one point she spotted Sam huddled in a corner with one of them. He held a po'boy in his hand but seemed to have forgotten about it, his intense conversation with the man taking all his attention.

"Look, Neffi," Roxy whispered to her cat, who had stuck around despite the commotion. She mewled to be picked up for a cuddle. "Sam's crazy about po'boys. I've never seen him hold one for so long without wolfing it down. Must be an important conversation, huh?" She felt her stomach tie itself into knots. There hadn't been any questionable incidents with Sam for a good while, and she'd let her suspicions recede.

Now, seeing him in deep conversation with a strange man brought all her doubts flooding back. She'd spotted him before making conversation with men she'd cross the street to avoid. They were always suspicious-looking guys. What was Sam doing with them? She imagined him running a narcotics ring; the men he met pushing drugs onto the streets as Sam "washed" the money at the laundry like her mother had insinuated.

Roxy tapped her cheek. Was she being ridiculous? Probably.

"Yo!" Roxy turned and saw Johnson's sidekick, Officer Trudeau, walking down the alleyway toward her.

"What are you doing here?" Roxy said, smiling. Trudeau was younger than Johnson and quite pleasant when he was on his own. When Johnson was around though, Trudeau barked orders and made cutting remarks as he tried to impress his boss—although he lacked the conviction he needed to be truly frightening.

"The boss got called to a homicide case, so he sent me instead."

Roxy fetched him a coffee, and they sat on the bench together watching the comings and goings. Nefertiti snaked around Trudeau's ankles, proving her prejudices didn't stretch to all in law enforcement. "Johnson said the issues aren't critical; the build can go ahead. He just sent me to tell everyone that, Lacey Gregory included."

"Wow," Roxy said. It was unusual for Johnson to be even remotely amenable.

Trudeau leaned into Roxy and said in a lowered voice, "Between you and me, he'll grab any chance to undermine the city planning department. Long time ago, they wouldn't let him build an addition to his home without putting him through two years of appeals. He never forgets things like that. He has a long memory, and you know how he bears a grudge."

"Ah, well that explains it," Roxy said. "It does sound like the city is being overzealous."

Trudeau shrugged, then looked up and down the alley. "A lot of change happening around here, huh?"

"Tell me about it," Roxy said.

"So who's in charge? From the planning department I mean."

"A woman named Lacey Gregory, but I haven't seen her

in a while. Maybe she gave up and went home. Everyone was giving her a pretty hard time."

Trudeau shrugged. "Ah, well." He popped a beignet in his mouth and chased it with a long swig of coffee. He seemed far more interested in enjoying the sunshine than in locating the city's planning department representative.

Roxy looked over at the bakery. "I think they're about to start work. I must close all the windows to keep out the dust. I reckon I'll have to get the facade pressure-washed when they're done."

Trudeau looked up at the Funky Cat Inn, which was a gorgeous shade of hot pink. "Yeah. It's gotta be a pain for you, all this construction. I expect it'll be good for business, though. In the end."

Roxy saw respect shining in his eyes. Both she and the officer were tiny town, poor, rural kids who were bettering their lives. It made her warm to him even if she didn't appreciate his actions sometimes. She smiled. "Yup."

"Anyway, I'd better get going." He popped the last beignet in his mouth. "I'm working a big drug case. There's an underground ring in the city, and we're trying to bring it down."

"Oh?" Roxy said, her heart thumping.

"Yup," Trudeau said again. "Really mind-blowing stuff. Anyway, thanks, Roxy, for the fuel." He looked over at the bakery. "Let the games begin!"

CHAPTER TWENTY-SIX

THAT NIGHT, ROXY awoke with a start. Her cell phone was ringing. She snatched it off the nightstand and swiped. It was Johnson. Her stomach sank. She bit her lip with her top teeth. A call at this hour could never be good news.

"Miss Reinhardt," Johnson barked on the phone.

She sat up, immediately wide awake. "Detective Johnson."

"Lacey Gregory of the city planning department. Do you know her?"

"Barely, but I know who she is."

"When was the last time you saw her?"

"Umm, at some point yesterday. Why?" Small talk was never Johnson's strong point, and clearly, he dispensed with it entirely at two a.m.

"Her husband has filed a missing persons report. The last time she was seen was outside your little establishment. Care to explain that one?"

Roxy gulped. Her mind raced. "I don't know anything

about her being missing. I saw her in the alleyway. But that was hours ago."

The sound of a big gust of air reached her as Johnson sighed. "Why are you always in the middle of trouble?"

"Honestly, I don't know. It's not my intention. Are you sure she's not just at the office doing paperwork?"

"At this hour?" he said witheringly.

"Well, she did seem very enthusiastic about her paperwork," Roxy said. "I don't know, I guess there are a lot of possibilities. She could be out at a bar, or. . . attending a voodoo ceremony! She's only been gone a few hours. Isn't it protocol not to start worrying or making anything official for forty-eight hours or something?"

"Stop telling me how to do my job. Do I tell you how to fold napkins?"

Roxy sighed. "Look, I don't know where she is. She's not here, I know that."

Johnson harrumphed. "Well, make sure you tell me if you see her." There was a pause. "I'm keeping my eye on you, Miss Reinhardt."

"That's fine with me as I've done nothing wrong."

"As usual." Johnson hung up.

Roxy sat in the dark, trying to remember when she'd seen Lacey Gregory last. The planning department official hadn't been there when Trudeau had shown up, and before that her memory was a bit hazy. She cast her mind back.

The first day's work on the bakery had gone smoothly, and now the interior was nothing but four walls and rubble. Construction workers had come and gone, but Roxy didn't have a clear memory of Lacey since she'd called the police after Elijah insisted that the work go ahead.

Roxy sighed as she looked at her phone, the numbers 2:15 glaring back at her. She drew back her blackout curtain to peer out of her window. Later that day, the rubble would be loaded on trucks and removed from the site. Even though only the interior had changed, the alleyway already looked so different: a building site with cordons and tape and dumpsters. Disconcerting.

Roxy comforted herself with the vision of what was to come. On the outside, the stucco would be replaced and painted mint green; the large six-over-six windows would stay but shutters would be attached with strap hinges. On the ground floor, a large French door would welcome bakery customers, while ornate verandahs would wind around both the first and second floors. The project's second stage would encompass the building of a patio and a garden.

Elijah had discussed it all with Roxy over coffee, and she liked to think with a suggestion here and there, she'd made some contribution to the project even if she was a little worried about all the changes. Between them, Elijah and Roxy were turning their alleyway into a little oasis of peace, rest, and calm in the center of the city.

Roxy pulled back her blackout curtain further, trying to imagine it. But the scene looked far too eerie in the orange light of the streetlamps. Right now, it looked like a natural disaster had struck, the kind of change nobody wants.

She heard a click, and her attention was drawn to a movement in the far corner of the alleyway. Nefertiti chose that moment to jump up onto the bed, surprising her. "Princess!" Roxy hissed. Nefertiti took no notice and pawed at Roxy's comforter, trying to get settled.

Roxy peered out again, straining to see. She looked around but spied nothing, until another click got her attention and she saw a man on a bike cycle among the shadows of the alleyway buildings and into the street at the end.

"It's him again, Nef. That man. What's he doing coming around here on his bike. Who is he?" Satisfied that he'd gone, Roxy got back into bed. "Come here, hon," Roxy said, snuggling down and placing Nefertiti on top of the soft comforter, against her leg where she was less likely to get pummeled. Nefertiti was quite happy with this arrangement and settled down, tucking her paws underneath her, purring loudly. Soon Roxy fell asleep again, neither the man on the bike nor Detective Johnson able to come between her and her slumber.

CHAPTER TWENTY-SEVEN

W HEN SHE AWOKE in the morning, Roxy left Nefertiti sleeping on her bed and made her way to the dining room, where she found a table laden with mountains of pastries and Sam alone, munching on one, a cappuccino and the morning paper in front of him. Roxy couldn't help but smile.

"Morning," he said, smiling back. He nodded at the pastries. "I think Elijah's gone slightly crazy."

"Huh." She stared at the pile of soft, puffy pastries, many of them lightly dusted with powdered sugar. "How is he making them with the bakery torn down?"

"He's rented a small premises on the other side of town so he can take care of some of his regular clients. Care to help me make a small dent?"

"I think I will," Roxy said. She sat opposite him and picked up a beignet. "So . . . I take it he's happy enough with how things went yesterday. Today'll be about cleaning up the rubble."

"Yes," Sam said. "But I'm sorry he treated you so badly the other night. I hope his apology was good enough."

"It was, but I'm thinking Nat might be right about him being affected by his new high profile. When he found out about the delay, he got very loud and aggressive with Lacey Gregory. He even said, 'Do you know who I am?'"

"Did he?" Sam said with a chuckle. "Well, let's hope he comes back down to Earth real soon and joins the rest of us mere mortals."

"Talking of Lacey Gregory, Johnson called me in the middle of the night and told me she was missing. As usual, he seemed to think I had something to do with it. Anyway, seemed a bit strange. I hope she's okay."

Sam froze, a beignet in his hand, midair. "That doesn't sound good. Maybe . . . maybe she was upset Trudeau said it could all go ahead?"

"Maybe," Roxy said. "But I actually don't recall seeing her while Trudeau was here, or after. Let's hope she turns up today. Maybe she stormed off in a rage, humiliated when she heard the construction could go ahead. Went to drown her sorrows in a bar and got too drunk to go home. I don't know."

"Hmm . . . well, let's hope she's alright." Sam didn't sound convinced.

Despite her upbeat posturing, Sam's concern mirrored Roxy's own, and a ripple of discomfort slid through her body. Rattled, she sat for a few moments in silence. Then, "You know, yesterday Trudeau said something shocking. He said there's a narcotics ring they're investigating in the city."

Sam's face was blank, expressionless. "Oh?" he said casually. He brushed some crumbs off his hands.

Roxy plunged on. "Yeah, they're money laundering through businesses and stuff. Apparently, Trudeau says they've got a bunch of dirt on loads of people and are about to do nighttime raids," she lied.

"Ah, that's good," Sam said. "I hate drugs and what they do to people. I don't know how traffickers and dealers sleep at night." He looked down at his newspaper. "Maybe we'll see a reduction in violence. Wherever drugs are, violence follows."

Roxy regarded him closely. He didn't sound guilty. He didn't look guilty. But maybe he was just a great actor. She continued to watch him for a long moment.He caught her eye and chuckled awkwardly. "Is everything okay?"

"Oh, yeah, fine, fine, sorry. I've not woken up yet."

He smiled again, a warm, friendly, affectionate smile. Roxy felt butterflies dance around her insides. "So . . . where's Elijah now?" she said, wishing Sam didn't have such a powerful effect on her.

"Outside, getting started," Sam said. "They all are. Annie wants the site cleaned up, and Xavier is documenting the historical site features. Then they can get on with the refurb. Elijah's convinced the TV show will go national, and he wants to make sure the bakery is all done and good before he hits the road."

"Sounds like the crew's going to need some serious sustenance. I'll go and see how Nat's do—"

Like a streak of lightning, an earsplitting scream reached them from outside. Sam and Roxy rushed to the window. In the alleyway, Annie, her head flung back, screamed through a stretched, twisted mouth. Construction workers downed tools and stared. Behind Annie, Xavier carried the limp, lifeless body of Lacey Gregory out of what was left of Elijah's bakery.

He set her down on the cobblestone, removing his hard hat and placing it on his chest. Lacey's feet flopped out to the side, her big, black, oversized boots like clown's shoes, her face covered in plaster dust. Xavier crossed himself, his head bowed, Annie's screams still echoing around the alley.

CHAPTER TWENTY-EIGHT

"OH MY GOSH," Roxy whispered. "Is she dead? She can't be dead, can she? Can she?"

Roxy knew her speculation was pointless. No body flopped like that except a lifeless one. Sam and Roxy raced outside from their position at the window. Roxy punched a number into her phone as she made her way through the lobby and into the cobblestone alley. "Detective Johnson, I think you'd better come down here," she said.

As soon as Roxy had stepped through the doorway of the Funky Cat, she could see Lacey Gregory was most definitely dead. There was a purple tinge to her white, dusty skin. Blood matted her hair. Dust from the rubble covered her clothes. And if that evidence hadn't been sufficient, the reaction of those around her would have been.

The construction crew inside the building now slowly seeped from the wrecked building into the alley to look at the even more devastating sight on the ground. Xavier stood by Lacey's body as still as a cloud on a windless day, his head bowed. Annie had stopped screaming but had moved to Xavier's side, breathless, her hand at her throat.

Roxy's mind whirred. Lacey hadn't been seen since early the day before. She hadn't been seen since her argument with Annie and her call to the police. Where had she gone? And why wasn't she around when Officer Trudeau had arrived to say they could continue their demolishing?

Roxy continued to consider the possibilities. They must have checked the interior of the building numerous times. Had Lacey's death been an accident? Was she in the building when parts of it were torn down? How was it that no one noticed she was in there?

Everyone stood in stunned silence, until Roxy spoke without realizing what she was saying. "You shouldn't have moved the body. You might have contaminated the evidence."

"Evidence?" Annie said, her voice shaking. "What do you mean? Do you think . . . do you think she was . . . murdered?"

Roxy's thoughts roared. "I don't know, but there will have to be an investigation either way. She had to be dead or at least unconscious before the demolition. Otherwise, she'd have heard it starting and gotten out of there. Where was she found?"

Xavier lifted his head. "I went in to check the state of the walls. There was a cabinet that had remained intact despite the machines tearing down the interior yesterday. It felt heavy, heavier than it should have been. I found Lacey inside it."

"So, she *was* murdered" Roxy said. "And bundled inside a cabinet. Perhaps whoever they were hoped that she wouldn't be found, like, ever. That she'd disappear with all the other rubble into the landfill."

As she said this, the sound of running footsteps reached

her. Elijah had been alerted. He arrived at Roxy's shoulder. When he saw Lacey's body, he laughed; just a chuckle at first, but soon he was cackling maniacally. "Murder? Lacey's been murdered?" he said before erupting into more hysterical laughter. "On my project?"

"It's the shock," Sam said, appearing at his shoulder. "You need a cold glass of water. Maybe several. Come." He carefully guided Elijah into the Funky Cat, quietly shutting the front door behind him. Roxy, despite her horror, was struck by Sam's care for his friend.

She glanced again at Lacey's body. Roxy had only seen her as a pedant, a stickler for rules which frustrated progress. Now, in death, she saw her as a cherished wife, a daughter, maybe a mother. A human being, doing her best. Now, all that life was gone, crushed under so much rubble.

Nat joined her. "Sam told me . . ." she began, but trailed off as she caught sight of Lacey in the middle of the alleyway. She clapped her hand over her mouth, her big, black eyes expanding with shock until her tough gal persona reasserted itself. "Oh, great. Another extended season of making coffees for Johnson and his pals."

Nat's crassness spurred Roxy into action. "I think everyone should go inside. I don't care that they are dusty building workers. Cold water, like Sam said, or sweet tea for the shock. Make sure they all eat, Nat. I don't want anyone passing out. I'll stay here and wait for Johnson. You take care of them all."

Nat nodded, glad for something to do which would keep her out of Johnson's way. "Come on, everyone. Let's go."

The workers traipsed inside, leaving Roxy alone with the body. Nefertiti joined her, padding out of the front door

and winding her way through a jungle of construction workers' legs. Roxy sat on the bench, then stood up again, rest-
less. "So much for Sage's blessing of the project. It's been a
disaster from the get-go."

CHAPTER TWENTY-NINE

W HEN DETECTIVE JOHNSON stalked
into the narrow, cobbled street, Roxy caught
sight of him immediately. He hadn't noticed
her when he stooped down to pet a mangy dog lingering on
the corner. Roxy almost gasped. If she was a gambler, she'd
have bet on Johnson booting the poor thing out of his path
without a second thought. As it was, she watched in fascina-
tion as Johnson spent a moment with the dog, bending
down, cupping the dog's chin in his hand, and looking into
its eyes with something akin to care.

But when Johnson straightened and looked up at her,
Roxy flinched. His expression was inscrutable, but even at
this distance, she could see that his eyes were steely and
uncompromising. It only took a second or two for the indif-
ference to fall away, to be replaced with disdain and
contempt. Johnson squared his shoulders and lifted his chin
from his thick neck. His eyes bored into hers like lasers.

He stomped over, then looked wordlessly between her
and the dead body of Lacey Gregory. It was a surprisingly
quiet approach; Roxy could hear a small bird tweet in the

solitary tree beside the Funky Cat. Normally Johnson charged around like a bull, his bald, meaty head sunken into his broad shoulders, his neck as short as his temper.

Finally, Roxy broke the silence. "It was murder, I'm sure of it. It can't have been an accident or suicide."

He stared at her. "Get me a café au lait."

Roxy sighed. "Are we really going to do this?"

"And get me three beignets. I need food. I wasn't even out of bed when you called me. And don't tell a single person inside I'm here, got it?"

Johnson turned away and spoke into his radio while Roxy went inside the Funky Cat. When she returned with his beignets and coffee, he scoffed them down at lightning speed. "Right," he mumbled through a mouthful. A crumb clung to his salt-and-pepper stubble. "Same routine as always. I'm hauling you all into the station for questioning. No more sitting around the dining room getting your stories straight." He smirked. Then he looked down nastily at Nefertiti and said, "You included, *princess.*"

"*What?! Nefertiti?*" Roxy exclaimed, wondering if he'd gone mad. "You can't—"

"It's called a joke, Miss Reinhardt," he said, amusement dancing across his face. "Do try not to be so earnest and naïve."

Roxy knew it was pointless to react to the personal comment. "I'll go inside and tell them all to get ready."

"You'll sit your behind right here and wait for a squad car."

"Yes, sir," Roxy said, staring him down. Her voice was perfectly polite, but the look in her eyes was dangerous.

"I see you're picking up some good old Southern manners now," Johnson said. He stared right back. "Well . . . *bless your heart.*"

Roxy might not have been from the South, but she knew exactly what *that* meant. She grinned at him as he got up, dusting off beignet crumbs. Her smile was so fake she bared her teeth like a wolf. If only she could be so intimidating! That was the annoying thing about being five feet zero, small-boned, and pixie looking. She got carded when she bought liquor, every single time. She certainly didn't look like a part-owner or manager of a successful, albeit quirky, boutique hotel.But she was.

When the squad cars arrived, Johnson herded the group of construction workers and hotel staff outside to the main street and ordered everyone into them in pairs. Annie with Xavier, Sam with Sage. Roxy ended up with Elijah. She noticed that Nat was missing. Nat must have hidden away when the cops came looking. Roxy wondered if Johnson would notice. Elijah gave Roxy a trying-to-make-the-best-of-things grin, but it didn't feel right at all. Nefertiti mewled up at her from the sidewalk before the car door closed.

"There's a bowl of cat food in the kitchen, baby," Roxy said. "I'll be back soon."

"You hope," Johnson said before slamming her door shut.

When they got to the station, Johnson insisted on interviewing them all separately. They were there for a long time. Trudeau was assigned the role of babysitter. "Make sure they don't talk to each other, use any devices, or anything else," Johnson barked at him before he went into the interview room. With no means of passing the time—it hadn't occurred to anyone to take a book—what had been a shocking, drama-filled day became an excruciatingly boring one rather quickly.

Roxy was the last person to be interviewed. It was nearly dinnertime by then. Lunchtime had long passed with only a few sad sandwiches provided by Trudeau. Roxy's stomach rumbled as she walked into the small room with a metal desk. Cold, uncomfortable chairs were bolted to the floor.

Johnson looked up and sneered. "Having a nice day?"

Roxy was too tired to think of a smart answer, so she simply slid into the hard, plastic chair in silence. What a world away it was from the soft luxury of the Funky Cat. They went through the rigmarole of stating her name and date of birth for the tape, then Johnson began questioning her on her movements the previous day.

"I was sitting with Trudeau when I noticed she was missing," Roxy said. "I'm not sure how long Lacey had been gone by that point. I thought she must have returned home or gone back to the office, and I told Trudeau as much."

"You had motive to kill her."

Roxy wasn't taken aback. This was standard Johnson questioning. "Yes, I know. She was threatening the development. But it's not a very strong motive. The work on Elijah's bakery will be a boon for the Funky Cat and the street in general. But while increased bakery business is good for exposure and a nice place for our guests to get pastries, the clientele doesn't exactly cross over. Bakery customers don't typically need a hotel; they're locals. And the hotel's doing just fine. We're turning bookings away, to be honest. I'm not trying to save a failing hotel. It will be nice—a fancy, updated bakery across the way—and that's about it. So while it's technically true I have a motive, it is a spectacularly weak one. I suggest you look at people who have more to lose with the project not going ahead."

CHAPTER THIRTY

JOHNSON'S EYES SHONE nastily. "You mean like your new celebrity friend Elijah Walder? Are you turning him in? Trying to give me hints and don't want to say something directly? Don't worry, snitches *don't* get stitches under my watch. You could go into my specially designed witness protection program."

Roxy thought she'd rather end up in one of Evangeline's "specially designed" Creole seafood boils. And snitches get stitches? What was he, twelve?

Johnson saw her hesitate. "I know you'd have to give up the Funky Cat, but I'm sure you'll survive without your little project." He said it like she was a girl collecting stickers, not a grown woman running a very successful hotel she'd renovated.

"I'm not turning Elijah in. I'm—"

"Then perhaps you are an accomplice."

"What?"

"Covering up the crime is punishable by law, Miss Reinhardt."

"I'm not covering up any crime," Roxy said tersely. "I'm

not saying Elijah did it *at all*. No way. I have no idea who did it. Loads of people had the opportunity to kill Lacey. There were many people there yesterday."

"I know," Johnson said evenly. "I interviewed that laundromat guy who always seems to be skulking around. He said the same thing."

"Sam doesn't skulk," Roxy said. She felt her face get hot. Sam had looked a bit shady if you'd a mind to see things that way as he huddled in the corner with a dodgy-looking man she'd never seen before.

"I'm sure he can help us with a *good few* inquiries," Johnson said, raising his eyebrows.

Roxy couldn't resist. "What do you mean *a good few*?"

"Don't worry your pretty little head about it," he said. His patronizing of her enraged Roxy. She felt a white-hot flame of anger start in her stomach and explode from the top of her head. "Anyway," Johnson continued. "Did you see anything out of the usual yesterday?"

Roxy wasn't going to tell him about Sam's intense conversation with the mystery man. Her heart still beat a little faster from the "good few inquiries" comment. Did he have anything to do with the narcotics ring Trudeau had mentioned? Maybe Sam *was* involved in something shady, and his empire was about to come crashing down.

With that thought, Roxy's heart just about stopped. If Sam was caught doing something illegal and his assets confiscated, what would happen to the Funky Cat? When Evangeline retired, he'd stepped in and bought the place, giving half the shares to Roxy. Would she lose it? Would she have to pay him half the money to buy him out? She didn't *have* any money apart from what was in the company bank account. It was a healthy amount, but not nearly enough to buy the hotel outright.His fortunes were inextricably entwined with hers. Oh, who could she trust?

"Oi!" Johnson barked. "You're thinking. Stop thinking. Start talking."

"Sorry, I'm just tired and hungry," Roxy said. "I was thinking about what we're going to make for dinner."

Johnson raised an eyebrow. "Uh-huh."

"Okay, to sum up, I didn't see anything strange. I saw Lacey first thing and then not after that. There were plenty of people around that day."

"This is what doesn't make sense," Johnson said. "So many people around, and no one saw anything? Something stinks. Maybe you're all in it together."

"You should hope so," Roxy said. "I'm sure one of us will crack sooner or later. Then you can get them a plea deal and they can take all of us down with their dramatic and shocking testimony. Easy work for you."

"You watch too much TV."

"With respect, I think you do. *All* of us in this together? Don't be silly. That's fiction. In the fantasy section."

Johnson sighed. "Do you have *anything* worthwhile to contribute?"

"No," Roxy said. "I saw nothing unusual. I know nothing about the crime. And all I can do is guess. I know how against amateur sleuthing you are, so I won't say one word more or put forward a single idea."

"See to it things stay that way," Johnson said. "I don't want you creeping around with a magnifying glass, making a nuisance of yourself. Now go. Go! And take all your miserable little friends with you. Where'd your tattooed friend disappear to, anyway?"

"I have no idea. Goodbye, Detective Johnson." Roxy collected all her dignity and stalked out of the interview room before Johnson could ask her anything more about Nat, or Elijah, or Sam.

The construction workers had already left, but Roxy's friends had hung around waiting for her. They were all hungry. They looked miserable. Johnson hadn't done them the courtesy of providing a ride back to the Funky Cat. He'd turned them out onto the street.

Roxy took charge. "Let's go have dinner at House of Hebert. *That's* got to chase our blues away."

"Roxy, what a good idea!" Elijah said. "None of us are in our finest, but who cares?" That was an understatement. Those involved in the construction had on workwear. Elijah wore a faded, tatty T-shirt and jeans, clothes he'd presumably thought suitable for a construction site. Even Sam looked a little disheveled.

Nevertheless, Sam turned to the out-of-towners, Xavier and Annie, and grinned. "Ready for a crazy night?"

Annie grabbed an elastic from her wrist and tied her red hair up in a topknot. "Don't forget I'm a New Orleans native, Sam. Boston is just a colder temporary side trip for me right now." She cricked her neck from side to side and cracked her knuckles. "Let's do this."

CHAPTER THIRTY-ONE

T HE HOUSE OF Hebert was a sight to behold from the street. It was an old building. The archi-tectural style was classic New Orleans, but the architecture was the only classical thing about it.

Vivid colors exploded on the exterior walls. Murals of jazz singers, saxophone players, voodoo queens, and parade dancers with feathered headdresses stretched overhead. In between were painted fluorescent and technicolor swirls. The frames around the windows and doors were bright orange, and the grand front door was striped black and white. Roxy had only been there once before, but it was a place she would never forget. It was a beautiful chaos.

Roxy had texted Nat, and the quirky English girl showed up at the same time as Jocelyn, whom Elijah had invited. Jocelyn and Elijah had become good friends and were virtually inseparable. The makeup artist arrived breathless but excited to be included in the evening.

The group of friends walked through the atrium, which was a little shabby and bland, but emerged into the grand main room. It had a double height ceiling with a huge skylight that let in the muted, soothing colors of the dusky early evening sky. Huge brass chandeliers glittered from the ornate plastered ceiling that featured a "dragged" plaster finish—plaster embedded with gold tints. The rest of the décor was gold, orange, lime green, and flamingo pink. From the patterns on the walls, to the replica Louis-style dining chairs, tables, and couches, to the pillars either side of the huge stage, the restaurant was a raging storm of color.

"I can almost imagine how it used to be in the golden age of jazz," Xavier said, ever the history buff. "Here in New Orleans, the Jazz Age will never end, I'll wager. All the greats played here. Billie, Ella, Louis Armstrong."

"Talking of which," Sam said, "I wonder who's scheduled to play tonight?"

"They might not have live music tonight," Roxy said. "If not, you and Nat and Elijah should get up and have a turn. I'll bet you're as good as anyone else they have play here." Sam looked pleased and smiled at her, but both Elijah and Nat looked annoyed.

"As good as?" Nat said. "Gee, what a roaring compliment, Rox."

Elijah said nothing and went over to a couple of waitresses in neon uniforms who had been chatting away to each other. He stood in front of them, saying nothing.

One of them gave him the side-eye. "Yes?" she said. Customer service didn't appear to be the strong point here, but Roxy liked to think their lack of polish added to the eccentric, no-airs charm of the establishment. She also hoped her own guests thought the same about Nat and, on occasion, Evangeline!

Obviously, Elijah didn't concur. He continued to say nothing, staring the servers down, waiting for them to act. Roxy saw a vein throb in his temple. She watched his hands and jaw clench. She predicted another "Don't you know who I am?" moment.

Sam quickly walked over and jumped in. "Good evening, ladies. Table for . . ." He looked back and scanned their little crowd. Himself, Elijah, Jocelyn, Nat, Roxy, Xavier, Annie. "Seven."

They were led to a huge round table. "Who's playing tonight?" Sam asked.

"Lily and the Dark Spirits," the waitress told him.

Sam raised his eyebrows. "Huh, I haven't heard of them."

"They're a Gothic jazz group. They just started playing here," she said.

Elijah's lip curled as he draped his napkin over his lap disdainfully. "This place has gone downhill. Customer service, awful music . . . I dread to think what the food will be like."

The waitress taking the drinks studiously ignored him until she had to take his order. "A mojito . . . and a *smile*," he said to her.

Annie, who had ordered a brandy milk punch with a triple shot, looked at him across the table. "What's got your panties in a bunch, cher? Where's that sunny Elijah we all know and love?"

Roxy watched Elijah. He *had* changed. In fact, with his scowl and construction-ready clothes, orange skin, and bright white teeth, he was practically unrecognizable. Like a New Orleans hoodoo worker had spirited Elijah away and left some kind of shape-shifter in his place. A new spirit, with Elijah's body as its vessel. Roxy surprised herself by thinking that. It wasn't a thought she'd have had before coming to New Orleans. She wasn't remotely surprised, though, when a fortune teller came over to their table, offering her services to each of them while they waited for their main meals.

"Go on, then!" Elijah said, taking a ten-dollar note from his pocket. "Keep the change." He winked at her. "Hopefully you'll make my future appear brighter." Annie threw a twenty-dollar bill into the middle of the table. Xavier did the same, followed by Jocelyn and Sam.

Sam, ever the gentleman, pulled up a chair for the fortune teller. She was a deathly pale woman with startlingly green eyes and blonde, almost white, hair. But otherwise, she looked like an ordinary middle-aged woman who carried a little extra weight around her middle. If you passed her in the street, you wouldn't pay her any mind unless you happened to catch a flash of those intense emerald eyes.

Once the woman had scooped up all the money pooled in the middle of the table, she placed her hands on the surface and closed her eyes. Nat caught Roxy's glance. Nat barely tolerated mysticism when Sage was involved, and that was only because they were friends. When anyone else whipped out tarot cards or offered to look at her palms, she couldn't hide her disinterest.

"Spirits, spirits . . ." the fortune teller whispered. "I'm being drawn to . . . *YOU*." Her eyelids flicked open, the whites of her eyes shining. She pointed at Annie and made a beckoning motion, as if she were calling her spirit toward her.

CHAPTER THIRTY-TWO

"YOU, MY DEAR, have a dark and terrible tragedy lurking in your aura. It happened many years ago, but never fades."

Annie didn't react, but Roxy noticed Elijah stare at her, his eyes popping out of his head. They were old friends, and there was obviously history between them—history they hadn't shared with anyone around the table. Roxy wondered what it could be but was soon distracted as the fortune teller moved on.

"Aha!" The woman giggled. "The spirits are rushing in thick and strong now. All the messages are pouring forth. This is going to be easy." She chuckled. "Slow down, guys!" she said, presumably to the spirits.

Roxy got a bad feeling deep in her belly. She looked at the woman from under her eyebrows. She was skeptical. Was her intuition talking to her? Sage had taught her that a twisting feeling inside could mean something wasn't right, that she should pay attention to the sensation and what it was telling her.

Before Roxy first arrived in New Orleans, she'd had that

feeling a lot, her whole life in fact, the feeling that something bad was right around the corner. "Your intuition was corrupted by anxiety," Sage had explained. "It's not your fault, honey. It happens to most of us at some point. Trauma in your past probably caused it." But as Roxy gained confidence, that pit-of-the-stomach dread faded. How strange that it should return as she watched the fortune teller.

"You," the woman said, moving on to Nat even though she hadn't thrown any money into the center of the table, "your heart is soon going to soften through spiritual means."Nat kept her expression even, but a smirk settled on one side of her mouth. It communicated Nat's skepticism, and the woman quickly moved on, no doubt sensing that Nat would have little truck with what she considered the woman's nonsense.

"Now you." The woman nodded at Elijah.The baker leaned back in his chair, draping his arm over the ornate carved back and crossing his legs. A haughty look settled on his face. He appeared to own the place. "Hmm?" he said.

"You, sir, dark spirits are hardening your heart. You are amid a collapse that you have little control over."

"Do you think she's seen him on TV?" Nat muttered to Roxy, chuckling.

Elijah's expression didn't change, and he clapped his hands sarcastically. "Well, you *are* perceptive!"

"Not me," the fortune teller said. "The spirits whisper in my ear. I'm merely a humble channel. An empty vessel." Roxy frowned and shifted in her seat. The woman's words were making her uncomfortable.

The fortune teller continued. "You," she said to Xavier, "are wearing a mask that is soon going to slip. The spirits advise you to reveal your authentic self to the world soon, on your own terms, before your mask is ripped off to cruelly expose you. A shedding of illusions is coming for the city soon, in a special spiritual wave, and you won't be immune from it."

Xavier nodded. He smiled politely. Roxy knew him well enough already to know what he was thinking. He respected spiritual practice but from a distance. He was a historian, an observer, an anthropologist by nature. He didn't seem at all rattled by the fortune teller's words.

"You, next," the woman with the startlingly green eyes said to Jocelyn, her eyes blue, bright, and eager. The makeup artist looked like she was about to hear some juicy gossip. "Well, well, well. You're not as sweet or demure as you look on the outside, are you? You have motives nobody would guess, and the spirits won't even divulge to me what they are."

Roxy watched Jocelyn carefully. Her face fell on hearing the fortune teller's words. She nodded gravely, knowingly, her pink, giggly persona constrained by what the woman had said. But when the fortune teller moved on to Sam, Roxy saw Jocelyn's eyes dart from left to right a little too quickly. Roxy could feel her discomfort, a low-level panic. She wondered what it was about.

"And you, handsome young man," the fortune teller said to Sam. "You have good intentions, but you're hiding something that is the total opposite of all you stand for. Work out a way to clean up your act so you can live without the weight of secrets."

Roxy almost gasped out loud. She had to hold herself back. Maybe she was wrong. Maybe this fortune teller was the real deal.

"And you," the fortune teller said, finally turning to Roxy. "You will learn something, but I'm afraid it's not good news. You will discover something important, earth-shattering, that you will derive strength from." She paused, then gave Roxy a sympathetic look. "I'm sorry. I can only pass on what the spirits tell me."

The fortune teller reached out and squeezed Roxy's hand with her own. Her fingers felt like ice across Roxy's skin. She stared at the younger woman with her green, tiger-like eyes. "Be prepared."

CHAPTER THIRTY-THREE

A
FTER THE FORTUNE teller's unsettling readings, the dinner party tried to get back to normal by ordering a delicious Cajun feast, but it was a little too oily and bland. Roxy had pushed her bacon-wrapped chicken breast around her plate, found the Gothic jazz strange and haunting, and by the time they'd paid the bill, she couldn't wait to get out of there. The bright colors overwhelmed her.

Later, Roxy tossed and turned in bed, getting tangled up in her sheets and sending Nefertiti scrambling from the bed to avoid her flailing limbs. She'd had horrible dreams, as chaotic as the decor at the House of Hebert, a technicolor nightmare. Her imagination conjured up visions of Sam conducting drug deals from his maroon Rolls Royce before appearing on the roof of the bakery with a sniper rifle. A split second later, Jocelyn, Xavier, and Annie transformed into clowns who huddled over a grave at the cemetery that lay at the end of the Funky Cat's little cobbled street, arguing about Lacey's murder, each one of them wanting to take credit for it. In the dream, they spotted Roxy peeking at them from behind a tree and gave chase, bloody meat cleavers appearing in their hands.

Roxy awoke panting and drenched with sweat. She checked her phone and discovered it wasn't even six a.m. No doubt Johnson would be over soon, striding around the street like he owned it as he collected more evidence. He'd bark orders at her and maybe even Evangeline, as though they were his personal servants. He'd drop comments to imply that Roxy had something to do with Lacey's death or make vague insinuations that somehow she was at fault for bringing tragedy to the city yet again.

A new thought struck her. She picked up Nefertiti and hugged the cat's fluffy body to hers. "I don't know about all this spiritual stuff, kitty. It doesn't seem to protect against evil people and their intentions. Bad people don't sit around and ask some invisible entity for what they want; they go out and take it. This is the second murder inside a month that's touched me and my friends. I wonder if they're related. I bet Johnson says not. But I'm not so sure. He gave up on the earlier one rather quick."

Roxy turned her face to the sun that had started to stream through her window, and after a moment's thought, she quickly got up, pulled on a shirt and a pair of jeans, and squeezed out a pouch of food for Nefertiti before grabbing her phone and rushing out. "I'll be back soon, sweetie," she said to her puffball kitty absentmindedly, knowing that it would more likely be hours before she would return.

Sage and Dr. Jack would start their early morning meditation in fifteen minutes. She couldn't remember a time she'd wanted the comforting, calm, soothing presence of Sage more than she did right then.

Roxy wasn't disappointed when she reached Dr. Jack's botanica. She walked up to it, smiling her first smile of the morning. The shack, currently painted purple—Dr. Jack painted it a new color every two years—stood out among the sleek, modern buildings that surrounded it. It had resisted the march of time and opportunities for development for decades, but Dr. Jack maintained it well. It didn't look too dilapidated. He replaced the shutters, doors, anything that showed its age too keenly.

The colors Jack painted the store were something to do with planetary movements, but Roxy couldn't remember what exactly. It seemed Sage and Dr. Jack talked in another language sometimes, a language only they and the spirits and people in the spiritual movement understood. But the benefit of being in Dr. Jack's and Sage's orbit wasn't to do with what they believed and understood. It was about how they made other people feel. For Roxy, they made her feel warm and safe. As she approached the store, its windows jammed full of crystals and skulls and candles and all manner of mysterious, magical things, she felt a wave of calm wash over her.

"Roxy," Sage said in her mellow, smooth-as-honey voice. The tall woman hadn't turned around when Roxy entered, but she had the ability to sense who was close yet out of sight, their aura communicating with her. She was busy organizing a huge wooden tray with numerous compartments filled with crystals.

"Hi," Roxy said brightly. "I feel like I haven't seen you in ages." She watched Sage's slender fingers pick up the beautiful crystals with care and concentration.

Sage looked at her with her honey-brown eyes. They twinkled with life. "It's only been two days in physical time, but I sense a lot of spiritual activity. You have stories to tell."

"I do," Roxy said.

"Have you had a hot drink this morning?" Sage asked.

"No, I rushed right here as soon as I woke up."

Sage's eyes widened, and she put a hand on Roxy's arm. "Wait a little, honey. I'll brew something relaxing in the back room. Dr. Jack's in there with Mandala."

"Mandala?" Roxy said to Sage's disappearing back. "Who's that?" But Sage had already gone through the door to the kitchen.

Roxy spent a few minutes wandering aimlessly as she always did when at Dr. Jack's. Of course, New Orleans was a haven for magical-leaning folk. Dr. Jack had a regular clientele of witches, wizards, wiccans, hoodooists, and vodouisants who followed traditions Roxy had only the haziest knowledge of. But it wasn't only the experts and the truly devoted who depleted Dr. Jack's stock every week. Many New Orleans residents had a vague, hopeful belief in magic, and when times got tough, they hedged their bets with prayers alongside special powders, oils, and talismans.

Every Sunday evening, once the store closed, Dr. Jack mixed and brewed and blessed, making concoctions with unlikely names such as Good Fortune Oil, Archangel Michael Powder, and Go Away Devil Lotion. They sold like hotcakes, and as Roxy browsed, she noticed the Confidence & Attraction Serum needed restocking. Roxy made no judgement on whether she thought the items worked or not—she'd long given up on drawing such conclusions.

"Oh, no, Mandala, not out the door!" Dr. Jack cried from behind her. Roxy whipped around to see Dr. Jack flying toward the outer door as a little, black ball of fluff raced toward it.

"Oh!" Roxy said. "Mandala's a rabbit!"

Dr. Jack nodded and smiled. He scooped Mandala up

and the small rabbit snuggled into the crook of his arm and relaxed on his chest. "She's barely more than a kit. Tiny little thing, isn't she? Just six weeks old. It's her first day away from her mother, poor thing. I think that's where she's running to, back to her mother. It's barbaric, really. They should all live together forever in a warren I say." He smiled wryly. "Most people think I'm a hopeless sentimental."

Roxy smiled. "Only people who don't understand you."

"You're too kind, Roxy, as always."

"Can I come and say hello to her? Is Mandala a special name?"

"A mandala," Dr. Jack said, "is a spiritual symbol. We sometimes use them during our meditations. Here, give her a cuddle." He handed the tiny rabbit over. The little thing snuggled into Roxy and closed her eyes.

Roxy gave Mandala's long ears a gentle stroke with one finger. "Aww, she's so soft."

"Isn't she?" Dr. Jack said, beaming from ear to ear like a proud parent. He took up a piece of chalk and began to draw on the blackboard behind the cash register, where he usually noted down special requests from customers, unusual occult or magical items they wanted him to source.

Roxy cuddled Mandala and watched as Dr. Jack drew a circle and then intricate patterns inside it. "There you go," he said with a chuckle. "A very poorly drawn mandala. For Hindus and Buddhists, it represents the universe. For Jung —I don't know if you know of him, a great spiritualist, great psychologist—it represents—"

"The search for unity within the self," Sage said serenely as she entered with a teacup perched on a saucer. She deftly took Mandala from Roxy with one hand and handed the teacup and saucer to her with the other. They were navy, gold gilding the edges and gold stars scattered among the deep blue. The teacup contained a dark red liquid, particles of dried herbs floating about in it. It didn't look very tempting, but Roxy wouldn't dream of saying so. "Beautiful cup and saucer, Sage."

As usual, nothing got past Sage, not even a thought. "Don't worry, honey. The tea tastes a lot better than it looks."

Roxy bravely took her first sip.

CHAPTER THIRTY-FOUR

"UNITY WITHIN THE self? What does that mean?" The taste wasn't sweet, but it wasn't too bitter either. It was like drinking a garden.

"We're all complex," Sage said. "A chaotic mix of all kinds of influences. Some of them push and pull against one another." Roxy didn't usually like people preaching, but it never felt like that with Sage and Dr. Jack. She found it all very interesting, their take on life. "This creates an inner stress," Sage continued. "Or we can swing from one thing to the other in a dramatic way, which can cause all kinds of problems in our lives. Self-unity means owning all of ourselves, even the parts we don't like. That's how we find our way to inner peace."

"I get it," Roxy said. She wasn't sure she did—it was a little abstract—but her worries were pressing on her mind again and she wanted to move on to talk about them.

Sage looked her over for a moment. Roxy suspected she was assessing just how much comfort Roxy needed. "Come on, honey. Why don't we take Mandala out back so Dr. Jack can get on with restocking the incense sticks. A wiccan from out of town took all the neroli and jasmine for a baby naming ceremony." She gave Dr. Jack a loving look, which might as well have been a kiss. They were clearly very fond of each other but always denied any sort of romance. Roxy thought that might just be the only time they ever lied.

"Oh!" Roxy said when they went through the small kitchen and out the back door. She had no idea there was a little herb garden back there. It was equipped with a brand-new hutch and a run that still smelled of fresh wood. "It's beautiful, Sage. Like a secret garden." Old-fashioned high brick walls, rough with age, tucked the little yard away from public view.

Sage smiled and put Mandala in the run. "Have some exercise, sweetie. And I'll just get some greens for you. Hmm, that'll be nice, huh?" Roxy and Sage sat on a couple of patio chairs and Roxy sipped her tea in the early morning sun. Sage said nothing but looked at her with an open, kind face.

"We went to the House of Hebert last night," Roxy said. "Several of us got readings. It wasn't a very pleasant experience. All about secrets and hidden motives. Dark. Only Nat got a positive one. And, well, maybe me, but barely."

"Oh?" Sage said. "Did the fortune teller explain how to remedy them?"

"Hmm. Kind of, but not really. She told me to 'prepare.' She told Xavier he should reveal his true self before his mask slips. Sam is hiding something, apparently, and he should reveal whatever it is. Elijah's gonna collapse, Annie's had a dark past, and Jocelyn's motives are questionable. For what it's worth, I will confront something earth-shattering but be better for it. Sounds loads of fun. Nat was told that her heart would soften. I don't know. It was a strange experience."

"Let me ask you a question, honey. How did you feel after the reading was done?"

"Ugh, like . . . I don't know . . . horrible. Like there were spiders crawling all over me. I couldn't wait to get out of there."

"Okay," Sage said, suddenly businesslike. "You know, Roxy, she might have been a fraudster, or even worse . . . a dark worker."

"My gosh, what's that?"

"Someone who actively looks to upset people and throw them off spiritual balance. I'm sure you've met people like that in your day-to-day life, people who don't have spiritual knowledge. You know, people who bully and say nasty things and try to make you feel small. Well, dark workers are like that, but even worse. They use the powers of bad spirits to help them keep other people down, and . . . well, to harm people."

"What? Really!"

"Unfortunately, yes," Sage said. "And there's a market for their services too. Jealous of your neighbor's new, fancy car? Pay a dark worker and they'll help them get in a car accident through spiritual means. Or . . . want to break up a happy relationship so *you* can be the new girlfriend? They can help there too. They have oils and spells for all those kinds of things."

Roxy shook her head. "That's horrible."

"It is," Sage said. "Selfish people are everywhere. Even, unfortunately, on a path that's meant to be sacred and healing."

"Wow . . ." Roxy stared into her tea. "So . . . Do you think that woman could have been a . . . What did you call it again? A dark worker?"

"Possibly," Sage said. "I'm getting goose bumps even as

you're talking about her, which isn't a good sign. But then again, it is a little cool this morning." She smiled.

"I *did* get a bad feeling from her."

"Aha, that's your intuition working for you!"

Roxy grinned. It felt good not to be racked with anxiety all the time. "Yes!"

"Roxy, honey, don't worry about a thing," Sage said. "Life has downs. That's true. And they hurt. But it always picks up again later. Especially if you have anything to do with it. You're resilient and resourceful and have a tremendous inner power that many overlook. You don't need to worry about what the future holds. You've got it in the palm of your hand."

Roxy smiled at Sage across the table, a truly genuine smile. Being around Sage was so uplifting and empowering, you couldn't possibly feel down in her company. "Sage, did you get a call from Detective Johnson yet?"

Sage's eyes twinkled. "Alas, I haven't had the pleasure."

Roxy chuckled. "He'll call soon, I'm sure, since you were at Elijah's bakery doing your blessing on the day of the demolition. You know about everything that happened, right? With Lacey Gregory?"

Sage nodded gravely. "Yes, Nat filled me in. She sent me a text."

"Lacey was found in a cabinet, so her death is being treated as murder," Roxy said. "But . . ." She sighed. "It's going to be someone in our circle, isn't it? Annie, or Xavier, or a construction worker." She thought about how Elijah had changed but couldn't bring herself to say her doubts about him out loud. "No one else could have done it . . . could they?"

"I don't know what to say, sugar. Although I did see

many faces at the building site that I didn't recognize. Lots of people must be suspected."

"Yeah, the electricians, plumbers, demo workers. There was a guy talking to Sam. I guess it could have been him." Roxy felt relieved there were other possibilities besides Elijah. "Really, it could have been anyone. Anyone, if they wanted to murder Lacey, could have disguised themselves as a construction worker and done the deed."

Sage shook her head. "Annie was keeping an eye on things. Not just anyone can get onto a construction site. She had lists. I saw her checking off people."

"Oh. Surely that would make them easier to track down, wouldn't you say?" Roxy's mind was whirring, thinking through possibilities.

"I'd love to help, lovely. You and I both know that you can't help but use your intelligence on this case. It's just in your nature. But you know, I've told you so many times, hon, using divination to catch killers or thieves or whatever is highly advanced magic. The spirit world is full of illusions as well as truth, and on something as crucial as this, you can't afford to mess up."

Roxy hadn't wanted to get involved in the investigation, but her mind flitted from person to person as she considered who might have a motive to kill the city planning department worker. That was normal, wasn't it? If you thought you might be in the company of a killer, it would be perfectly understandable if you found yourself working out who the murderer might be.Wouldn't it?

Sage noticed the dilemma on Roxy's face and laughed. "You're a truth seeker," she said. "Your mind won't let you rest until you know what happened."

Roxy felt a little uncomfortable but laughed. "Maybe. Or maybe I'm worried *Johnson* won't let me rest until *he* knows what happened. The crime scene is right outside our front door. He's going to be hanging around. And while he does, he'll be thinking that Nat and I only exist to cater to his every whim."

Roxy sipped the last of her tea. The herbs left a pattern at the bottom of the cup. Roxy held it out to Sage with a grin. "Maybe you'll give me a better reading."

Sage smiled and took the cup gently, almost reverently. "Tasseomancy isn't my strong suit, but I'll certainly try." She peered into the cup. "Hmm. Well, I'd say this looks like . . . a lion. See the mane around here?"

"Oh, yes!" Roxy said, nodding enthusiastically. "You're right." The bits of herbs looked like nothing but dregs of her tea, but she wasn't about to say that.

"Lions are symbols of strength, royalty, ferocity, and determination. It makes sense that would be at the bottom of your cup."

"Why?"

"Because that's your character! Determined, strong, and ferocious. In a good way."

"Really?" Roxy said, incredulous. Then she laughed. "I'd expect to find a little mouse pattern to represent me." She had another thought. "No, a butterfly busting out of its cocoon."

Sage shook her head and smiled. "Don't live in the past, baby. No more mouse, y'hear?"

CHAPTER THIRTY-FIVE

R OXY STRODE HOME in an infinitely better mood than when she had left. It was just before nine a.m. The middle of the rush hour was somehow invigorating. Cars zipped up and down and around the streets, while people walked about their business or cycled on the sidewalks. The world was operating as usual, and in some way that made Roxy feel better. The murderer would be found, Elijah's shiny new bakery would be built, life would move on, and things would get back to normal soon enough. She was sure of it.

When she got to their little cobbled alleyway, she only glanced for a moment at the rubble laying beneath the windows of the deserted and quiet bakery. She didn't want to think about what had happened there the day before. Inevitably it would only tie her thoughts in knots as she attempted to work out who murdered Lacey Gregory.

Inside the Funky Cat, she found Nat loading the dishwasher with breakfast dishes. "Finished up already? That's a little early."

"Where did you disappear to?" Nat asked. She turned

and flashed Roxy a dark grin. "I was worried they'd be pulling you out of the rubble this morning."

Roxy rolled her eyes and grabbed a waffle from a platter on the counter. "As much as that would satisfy Johnson, I hope that won't be happening any time soon. Anyways, where is everyone?"

"Annie grabbed a snack and left with Elijah when he arrived with the morning's pastries," Nat said. "There's something going on with those two."

"There *is,* isn't there?" Roxy said, feeling vindicated that Nat had noticed too. "When the fortune teller spoke last night about a dark tragedy still affecting Annie to this day, Elijah looked like his eyes would pop out of his head and onto that horrible neon table."

"Hey! I love those tables!" Nat protested.

"Come on, surely not?"

"They're fantastic. Creative and artistic in a postmodernist, swinging sixties, Beatlemania kind of way, don't you think?"

"No, I don't. Anyhow, we digress."

"Don't add in extraneous detail then," Nat said with a mock pout that morphed into a smile. "I don't know about what that fortune teller told me, though. As if *my* heart is going to be softened by someone spiritual. I've been around Sage for how long now? And I'm still, well, skeptical isn't a strong enough word. The idea that I'm going to change my mind about that woo-woo stuff after all this time strikes me as highly unlikely. If it was going to happen, it would have happened by now.

"Anyway," Nat said, obviously keen to change the subject. "I don't know where the others went, but everyone's out. And since they're gone, I was wondering if I could take the day off. I want to pick up a few clothes in town, and over at the Lavalee Grand they're showing some old, classic movies. They're having a Hitchcock week. I'd like to go to the matinee if that's okay. They're showing *Dial M for Murder*."

"Sounds fun. Sure," Roxy said. "I don't see why not." She teased Nat with a grin. "Have you heard from George lately, huh? How's he getting on?"

George was a former guest who had been the assistant to a renowned psychic, Meredith Romanoff. They'd come to New Orleans for an event she was holding. Tragically, Meredith had been killed, but during his subsequent stay at the Funky Cat, George had taken a shine to Nat. And she'd blushed in his presence, even flirted a little.

But they were an odd couple. There was Nat with her Doc Martens, tattoos, band tees, and sarcasm who refused to believe in mandalas or hexes or healing while George had dedicated his life to pursuing the spiritual path. He was slim, preppy, and soft-spoken. He had pale skin and sandy ginger hair with freckles sprinkled across his nose. He was currently in a traditional village in Nigeria, learning about something called Ifa, which seemed to be a religious, spiritual, and divination method all rolled into one (according to Roxy's Google search).

"He's fine," Nat said, sounding cagey. "He logs into the local internet café once a week to send me a message." She finished loading the dishwasher but made herself busy arranging cupboards, banging pots and pans like she was a percussionist in a particularly rudimentary orchestra.

"Oh, right," Roxy said. "Do you know when he's coming back then?"

"No!" Nat said, with some force. "I don't keep track of his every move, do I? We're not in some kind of relationship, *any* relationship. I'm not *married* to him or anything!"

Roxy put her hands up. "Sor-ry." But she knew Nat well. Nat's protests were not because she didn't like George, but because she liked him a lot. "So, you don't know where Annie and Elijah went? What about Xavier?"

"I don't know. He just took off."

"Sounds like everyone's okay though. Keeping busy in the circumstances."

"How long before they're able to start back up on the building work?"

"Not sure. Johnson didn't tell me. But I should think it'll be a few days at least. Looks like I can get caught up on the bookkeeping and social media ads. Maybe even read a book! I can't remember the last time I did such an indulgent thing." She laughed. "The life of a hotel manager, huh?"

"You think *you've* got it bad," Nat said. "Try the life of a hotel skivvy!"

"Hotel what? Skivvy?"

"Look it up."

Roxy did just that. She scrolled and tapped her phone before letting out a laugh. "It means a 'domestic servant who performs menial tasks'! Okay, Cinderella."

Nat grabbed a broom and pretended to cry. "I can't go to the baaaaalll . . ." she wailed.

"Get out of here, you psycho. Enjoy your movie."

"You don't need to tell me twice!" Nat rushed from the kitchen to the unit where she lived, and Roxy grabbed another waffle to take to the office. She met Nefertiti in the hallway. The white puffball looked up sleepily from her place on the rose-pink, crushed-velvet chaise longue, then gently lay her fluffy head back onto her white paws.

"Hello, sleepy girl," Roxy said.

Nefertiti lifted her head again and let out a relaxed mewl, like she didn't really want a scratch but would tolerate one from her favorite person. Roxy sat down next to her. She plunged her free hand into Nefertiti's soft, long, white fur, holding her waffle in the other.

Roxy's mind wandered as she sat in the empty hallway. She wondered where everyone had gone as the velvetiness of Nefertiti's soft, soft fur soothed her while she munched on her waffle. She imagined Nat going to get changed before rushing out—Nat was always rushing—and Sage and Dr. Jack tending to Mandala in the botanica garden. Sam would likely be tossing huge bags of sheets and table linens around. Perhaps Elijah and Annie had business in the city. And Xavier, what might he be doing? And were any of them the killer?

CHAPTER THIRTY-SIX

W ITH THE FUNKY Cat empty, Roxy tried to turn her attention to all the things that needed squeezing in whenever she found the time—updating the accounts, sorting petty cash, replying to comments on the Funky Cat Instagram page, and making sure the bills were all paid and filed away.

But it was difficult to settle down to complete anything. Thoughts in Roxy's mind tumbled like the laundry in Sam's big machines. Her body buzzed with energy. The image of Lacey Gregory's flopping boots was seared in her mind. It didn't help that Roxy's office looked onto the street, the sorry state of Elijah's bakery a visual reminder of the site inspector's demise. Roxy pulled the blind down over the window to block out the view and returned to her computer. After she had spent far too long staring at a spreadsheet, wondering where her brain had gone, she launched a pencil across the office.

"That's it, Nef," she said, spinning in her chair. "I'm making a coffee. Then I'll give these accounts one more go. And then . . ." But she didn't finish her sentence. She trailed off and sighed. The truth was, she didn't want to be stuck in the office. She wanted a change of scenery. She wanted to head over to the botanica and browse crystals and cards or catch up with Nat in whichever weird and wonderful clothing store she'd no doubt ended up in. She was sure it'd be full of band tees and iron-on patches and vintage military jackets. But she needed to stay behind for the guests. They could return at any moment. Frustrated, Roxy meandered out to the lobby in search of coffee. As she turned toward the kitchen, a flash of white in her peripheral vision brought her up short.

An envelope lay on the floor. That struck her as unusual. Most correspondence these days was sent by email. What was even more strange was that there was no postmark and no address. On the front, all it read was "Roxy," penned by hand in block capitals. Someone had left it there for her to find.

Nefertiti padded up behind her. "Do you think Elijah's going overboard with more apologies?" Roxy said. She tried a smile, but her heart was hammering. She bent down to pick up the envelope. "Oh no," she said, suddenly jerking her hand away before she touched it. "I better not do that. Don't step on it, Nef, okay?"

Roxy rushed to the kitchen for some rubber gloves and a knife. The gloves were large marigolds and not really fit for purpose, but she managed to pick the envelope up and cut along the top with the knife. "There might be saliva on the flap, Neffi. Maybe DNA could be gotten from it." Her cat stared at her. Roxy thought she saw Nefertiti shaking her whiskers just a little. Figures. Even she couldn't believe how CSI her thinking had become.

Roxy gently slid the letter out of the envelope and sat on the floor to read it. The cream writing paper was thick and expensive looking, like it belonged to someone who still wrote a lot of letters by hand and cared about the stationery on which they were written. But the message on the sturdy paper was far from formal. The handwriting was in block capitals again.

DRUGS.

EVADING JUSTICE.

ACCIDENT? OH NO.

SECRETS.

POLICE CORRUPTION.

Roxy's mind was ready to explode. She read the list over and over, trying to make sense of it.

"DRUGS. EVADING JUSTICE." What Trudeau had said about a drug ring came to her mind immediately. Sam's face also popped into her thoughts. Roxy's stomach sank.

"ACCIDENT? OH NO." Well, that one explained itself, didn't it? As did "SECRETS."

"POLICE CORRUPTION." Roxy didn't know what to make of that. Johnson was unpleasant, of course, but corrupt? She doubted it.

Roxy sighed. "I can't make head nor tail of this, princess." She reached out to pet Nefertiti, but the cat had left, spooked perhaps by the letter or Roxy's reaction to it.

Roxy sighed again. She felt more confused than ever, and suddenly alone. Her friends seemed disparate and disconnected. From her and from each other.

Elijah had changed. He seemed a world away from the fellow local small business owner on whom she could test new marketing ideas or rely on to give her a boost when she hesitated over some initiative or other. And Sam always had a huge question mark hovering over his head. Perhaps her mother had been right about him.

Her other friends were busy elsewhere. Sage and Dr.

Jack were in their romantic magical bubble together, and as much as Roxy knew they loved her with a kind of warm, golden-hearted acceptance she'd never previously experienced, she knew she would never really understand them. The chasm between her world and theirs was too great. And Nat, despite her tough gal image, had great integrity and loyalty, but her singing secret undermined the closeness of their relationship. And as for Evangeline, well, she was off enjoying her retirement with Pinkie. Roxy didn't want to disturb her.

Roxy glanced at the letter in her lap. What did it mean? Did it have anything to do with Lacey's murder? And why did she have it? Roxy knew she should call Johnson. She didn't feel in the mood for his pointed insults and accusations, but she knew the situation would become a thousand times worse if he found out she'd delayed making a report. She stared at the handwriting on the paper.

When had the message arrived? Maybe when Roxy had been in the office with the blind closed. But Nat might have noticed it on her way out. Maybe she ignored it in her haste to buy her next band tee or pair of patterned, patent leather Doc Martens.

Roxy picked up the letter and envelope by the corners and went into the kitchen to find plastic bags to drop them into. After placing them carefully inside the zippered bags she found in a drawer, she went to make her café au lait. Nefertiti and the ginger tom hovered around the empty cat bowls, looking at her reproachfully. She gave them a small smile and pulled some cooked haddock from the refrigerator. She flaked it and placed it in a bowl, filling another with water and a third with kibble. As the two cats tucked in nose to nose, she flicked on the kettle and called Johnson.

"Ms. Reinhardt?" he answered with an impatient sigh, as if this were the hundredth time she'd called that day.

Roxy couldn't help but sigh in return. "I'm calling to report some evidence."

"Evidence of what?"

"Evidence in relation to the murder," she said. She tried hard to leave the irritation she felt out of her voice but wasn't entirely successful.

"What murder?"

"What do you mean *what murder?*"

He chuckled. "Oh, you mean Lacey Gregory. That case is closed. It was an accident."

CHAPTER THIRTY-SEVEN

"**H**UH?"
"THE CASE is . . ." Johnson began very loudly and slowly, as if she were both hard of hearing and incredibly stupid.

"Closed, yes, I heard you. But . . .? And . . .?"

"Oh, I'm sorry," Johnson said sarcastically. "I wasn't aware you were the assisting detective."

Roxy continued, fighting to stay calm. "On what basis did you decide it was an accident? How could it have been?"

"Construction site accidents happen every day. Her head was crushed, probably by a falling ceiling or something."

"But she'd been tossed in a cabinet—"

"Probably climbed in when she realized the ceiling was about to come down on her. For protection. Didn't help."

"But—" Roxy was astounded.

"Anyhow, I won't be troubling you further. Good day." The line went dead.

Roxy fought the urge to launch her phone across the room. Her hands were shaking as she placed it carefully on the kitchen counter. She stood watching the water inside her clear glass electric kettle bubble and roil with an energy that mirrored her thoughts. She reached for a coffee cup but froze just as her hand clasped the handle.

"No," she said, presumably to the cats. "No. It makes no sense. Lacey would have gotten out of the building. Everyone knew the teardown was happening." The words "POLICE CORRUPTION" flashed into her head, and she remembered what Trudeau had said about Johnson having his own plans obstructed at every turn. Could it be that the letter writer believed Johnson wouldn't investigate Lacey's murder properly because of a grudge against the department over his house renovations? Or for some other more sinister reason? It couldn't be, surely?

Roxy continued making her coffee. "It was murder," she said out loud, talking to the cats again. "Murder, for sure. And it's only been a day since it happened. *How* could he close the case already?" She went back into the hallway and snapped a picture of the letter with her phone before putting it in a plastic bag. She popped it on her desk, and by the time she returned to the kitchen, the coffee was ready for cream. She was about to pour it in when she decided not to.

"I'm not going to sit around and watch this unfold as a bystander, Nef. Neither am I going to let Johnson act like he's an aggressive dog and I'm his chew toy. I'm going to get to the bottom of this."

Roxy walked back into the lobby. She looked out of the window at the alleyway—the wrought iron gate that led to the cemetery at one end, the main street at the other. In between stood the hot-pink Funky Cat and the shell of the bakery. The sky was bright, an unending stretch of blue. It was quiet, peaceful. A bird cawed above.

Roxy felt a determination she never knew she had shoot through her. Her doubts faded. She felt the most confident, assured, and powerful she ever had in her life. Adrenaline pumped through her veins. Every time she thought of Lacey Gregory's body, she felt a new surge of strength. "No, Nef, I'm sick and tired of people bringing their evil intentions to our door and it affecting, and *infecting,* my business and my life. I just won't have it. I won't."

Roxy grabbed her jacket from the antique coat stand Nat had upcycled. It was black with gold claw feet. She wrote a note in block capitals with her cell phone number on it, put it in a plastic wallet, then taped it to the front door. After checking her keys, cellphone, and wallet were in her pocket, she locked the door behind her and went on her way.

Dread clutched her stomach in a vicelike grip, a horrible, sickening feeling. She cast a glance at the remains of Elijah's bakery. Images of Lacey Gregory's lifeless body flashed through her mind again. She hurried on. There was no time to be shocked, no time to be scared, no time to dwell. She set off at a brisk pace in the direction of Sam's laundry.

When he wasn't at the Funky Cat fixing something or other, Sam was at the laundry. Roxy always found comfort in the warmth and buzz of the machines whenever she visited. And of course, she felt she could happily drown in Sam's big, bright, dreamy blue eyes. Almost.

The fortune teller's words to Sam came to her—"clean up your act so you can live without the weight of secrets." The memory of these words was like a weight itself. Like an anchor, it acted to drag down any attraction Roxy might have for Sam, pulling it so deep into doubt it might never resurface. He was likely not only a drug trafficker but also a crazy con man who for some weird reason pretended to like her. For all she knew, he might even be behind Lacey's murder for some reason known only to himself and the shady associate she'd seen him talking to.

Roxy didn't know whether to laugh or cry at her own dramatic fantasies, and by the time she reached the laundry, she felt quite light-headed. It didn't help that she bumped into Sam, looking perfectly innocent and ordinary, in the doorway. He was on his way out.

"Roxy!" he said, his eyes lighting up.

"Sam," she said evenly, ignoring the giddy feeling inside. "Who was that guy you were talking to just before the teardown took place yesterday?"

Sam's brow furrowed. "Well, hello to you too. Which guy?"

"I don't know, some shady-looking guy with a hard hat on."

Sam's eyes flashed with recognition, but then he said, "Honestly, Rox, I don't know. I spoke to a lot of people on the site. Some were annoyed about the city's threat to the teardown. Elijah asked me to calm them and reassure them it would happen and the rebuild would go ahead. Sometimes construction work is difficult to find, especially for a big contract like that. The construction workers were worried for their livelihoods. It's understandable. I didn't know any of them personally."

Roxy watched him for a long moment. Why give such a long answer? Did that handsome face hide terrible secrets? Were his deep blue eyes searching hers because he had feelings for her or because he was trying to gauge whether his lie had landed? Why did everything have to be so confusing?

Sam tipped his head on one side. "Why do you ask?"

"Where are you going?" she replied, frowning. They were still hovering in the laundry doorway.

He grabbed the back of his neck briefly. "Nowhere, really. Just . . . to the mall to get coffee beans for my machine. I ran out a few days ago and . . . well, yeah."

He was obviously lying. Roxy thought quickly. "Oh, perfect. I need to go to the mall myself. I was going to send Nat to buy some cleaning supplies, but she's out for the rest of the day. Maybe I could ride with you?"

Sam looked at his watch. "You *know* there is nothing I would love more. But . . . after I go to the mall, I'm going to see my father, and trust me, you won't want to come along for that." He grinned, but his grin didn't reach his eyes. "Unless you like insults and the overpowering smell of furniture polish. He has his housekeeper buff his antique furniture to a sheen in her every spare moment."

Roxy didn't know if he was lying anymore. This was oddly specific. Sam's father was a plastic surgeon. Their relationship was fraught. "Maybe because of his job he's obsessed with cleanliness," she said.

Sam screwed up his nose. "The less time I spend trying to psychoanalyze my father the better. Trust me, I've wasted years trying." He chuckled. "He would probably puzzle Freud." He looked at his watch again. "I'd better go, but . . . tell you what. Why don't you come over for dinner on Thursday? My place. I'll cook. I'm sure Nat will take care of the guests just fine."

Butterflies created chaos in Roxy's stomach. "Sure," she said.*Had Sam intentionally distracted her again?*

"What do you feel like?"

"Surprise me," Roxy said.

"I was thinking Italian maybe?"

"Italian, Thai, Chinese, Indian, just about anything will do."

"Noted," Sam said with a sheepish grin. "See you then." He kissed her on the cheek and got into his Rolls, waving out the window as he pulled away. Roxy waved back. She wasn't sure what to think. The proposed dinner was a date, she knew that, not two friends getting together. There would be wine and dimmed lights. Maybe kissing. The thought made her stomach flip.

But . . . was it all just a means to throw her off the scent? Sure, they'd had their flirtations long before Lacey Gregory's corpse showed up. But she'd never been to his house. They'd never been on an official date. Why was he ramping things up now? Was it a genuine progression of their relationship? Or a cover to distract her from something sinister?

"Worry about it later, Rox." She surprised herself by talking out loud. If Sam was innocent, then she wouldn't jeopardize their relationship by acting suspicious. If he was truly guilty, then he might let some information slip.

She watched his Rolls Royce swing around the corner at the end of the street. She sighed. Mixed feelings were never comfortable, and with Sam, so much hung in the balance. Con artist, drug dealer, murderer . . . or part-owner of the Funky Cat Inn and possible love of her life?

CHAPTER THIRTY-EIGHT

O NCE SAM HAD left, Roxy felt in need of a bit of stability, so she stepped into a café a few doors down and bought herself a frappuccino with caramel for a little extra comfort. She gave Nat a quick call. The weather was heating up and the café stop provided two remedies—cool and shade.

"Hey, Rox," Nat said, her voice brimming with excitement down the phone. Upbeat and peppy was unusual for her. "You'll never guess what I've just bought."

"Tell me."

"Video coming through!" Nat said.

Roxy accepted Nat's video call and was greeted with the sight of Nat's face alongside a very loud pair of Doc Martens, all orange and black and green stripes. "Aren't they bloody spectacular?" she said, giving the boots a jiggle.

"They're . . . something!" Roxy said.

Nat stuck her tongue out. "They're African print. I'm going to take a pic and send it to George. Nigerian vibes." She winked. "Later, Rox."

Roxy had planned to tell Nat about the note, but she

hung up too quickly. It was so rare to see Nat animated and joyful. She'd even used the word "vibes," which was nothing short of astounding.

Roxy sank down in her chair overlooking the street. She sipped her drink. She thought about the note again. Was it from the killer or from someone who knew something? Maybe it was a random prankster? Maybe it was something Elijah would do these days with his new, fame-charged persona. Roxy knew she was getting cynical but couldn't help herself. She took another sip. The caramel was suddenly too sweet. The ice gave her brain freeze.She put it down.

She'd go look for Xavier. If she were to find out what really happened to Lacey, he seemed as good a place to start as any. Something about him made her feel at ease. Maybe it was his propensity to be factual rather than emotional. He was steady and logical. Besides, his detail-driven mind may have picked up things she'd missed.

She didn't have Xavier's cell number. But he was easy enough to find on Google with his distinctive name and professional profile.

"Uh, hey, it's Roxy. From the Funky Cat Inn."

"Hey, Roxy. How are you doing?"

"Um, I'm wondering if we could meet for a chat."

"If you have an appetite for history, excellent cuisine, and don't get motion sickness, perhaps you'd like to join me on the Mississippi for lunch upon the *Creole Empress*. I was just about to go alone, but I'd love some company."

A little after noon, Roxy was aboard the large paddleboat, which was just beginning its slow crawl along the Mississippi River. Her hand clutched a mimosa, and a smile spread across her face. "I need to do this more often," she said to Xavier, who was packed into a navy-blue shirt over freshly pressed khaki slacks. A beige sweater was draped casually over his shoulders, the sleeves knotted across his chest. Aviator sunglasses shielded his eyes. As he leaned on one leg, his hand in his pocket, the other resting on the boat rail, and the river glistening behind him, he looked like a catalog model. Roxy wondered about the little flirtation between him and Annie. With her fiery red hair and liking for designer shoes, they'd certainly make a head-turning couple.She didn't seem interested though.

"History, boats, cuisine"—he tipped his head as he raised his glass of white wine with a wry smile—"and good wine, of course. Do you enjoy history?"

"The history of New Orleans?" Roxy said. "Voodoo and mystery and culture and the best food on Earth? Well, I think anyone would be crazy not to take an interest."

"I do agree," Xavier said, looking pleased. "I've lived here all my life, and this is a city that just keeps on giving in terms of fascinating historical facts."

"Mm, yes, you're right there," Roxy said. "The other night, at dinner, I remember you mentioned our street was built by some . . . you'll have to forgive me, Xavier, I don't want to get the terms wrong. You said they were important. I want to say voodoo priests."

"Voodoo practitioners," he said. "*Vodouisants*, they call themselves. The people that worked on the buildings in the alleyway were vodouisants. They worked and worshipped together."

"Okay," Roxy said, quite sure she wouldn't remember. "Just out of curiosity, did those vodouisants . . . did they do all the horrible things people talk about? Curse people, kill people with voodoo dolls, all that stuff?" A strange thought struck her. "I mean, could they have sent out a lot of bad energy, so to speak, and . . ." She trailed off with embarrassment.

Xavier looked serious. "And?"

"I was going to say . . ." Roxy laughed at herself. "Could they have somehow left their bad vibes in the street, in the buildings? I mean, I know it sounds dumb, but I've heard the term 'residual energy' from Dr. Jack. Meaning a building —"

"Holds some type of energy from previous occupants or happenings."

"Oh yes, you know of it! Well, I was wondering if our street could be cursed. I know it's stupid. But we've certainly had way more tragedies than the average, and I was just wondering, you know, if that was a thing." She heard how ridiculous her idea sounded and felt herself flushing red. She was glad Nat wasn't there to laugh at her and tell her to spend less time with Sage and Dr. Jack.

"It's not an area given to rigorous study," Xavier said. "But I have heard many anecdotal accounts of hauntings and curses and the like which, upon inspection, do seem to have some measurable effect. Perhaps science will explain all these paranormal mysteries within the next century or so."

"That would be totally cool," Roxy said. She imagined scientists flooding the botanica to discover the mysteries that Dr. Jack and Sage seemed to understand already.

"It would indeed," Xavier said. "The scientific and spiritual communities are currently at odds. Perhaps with more knowledge they could come to a consensus. In general, the more one knows, the less one is afraid. It would be good to have resolution on this matter, but right now, there is none."

Roxy thought for a moment, looking out over the water. Her head spun a little, like when she was talking to Sage. "Xavier, Detective Johnson has closed the case. He says Lacey Gregory's death was an accident." She tried to read his face, but as usual, it was calm and not in the least expressive. "I'm sure it wasn't. She wouldn't have climbed into that cabinet of her own accord, now would she? I'm wondering if you saw anything, if you know anything that could help."

CHAPTER THIRTY-NINE

"LOOK OVER THERE," Xavier said, pointing across the river to the shore. "It's the Chalmette Battlefield."

"Okay," Roxy said. She frowned, two lines briefly appearing between her eyes before she let them drop. She was as interested in New Orleans sites and history as the next person, but Xavier had rudely cut across her question. It was almost as though he were avoiding answering it. Rather like Sam on their night out when she asked him about what else he'd done in his life besides own a laundry.

"The site of the Battle of New Orleans, January 8, 1815," Xavier said. "Against the British. The treaty ending the war was signed in 1814, but the war wasn't over." He gave a wry smile. "Oh no."

The boat's tour guide had begun talking over the public address system, and between that, Xavier talking over her, and the passengers moving around them as they prepared to disembark for the Chalmette Battlefield tour, Roxy's irritation was growing.

"Shall we leave with the rest?" Xavier suggested. "I'd like

to learn more." His eyes lit up at the thought of a history lesson.

"I'd rather stay on board if that's alright," Roxy replied stiffly. "There was a murder yesterday a short way from my property and I want to talk about it."

"I don't know anything," Xavier said just as abruptly. "Why would you expect me to? Do you think I'm somehow involved?"

"I didn't say that," Roxy said. "I didn't even imply it. As a matter of fact . . ." She trailed off.

Xavier smirked. "You know, *as a matter of fact* is a phrase rarely preceded by a fact, so it is a misuse of—"

Xavier was getting on Roxy's last nerve. "You do have a motive though," she insisted a little too loudly. "Maybe you were so angry the project couldn't go ahead that you killed Lacey."

"What? Are you accusing me of her *murder*?" Xavier smiled, revealing perfectly straight, white teeth. He looked out over the battlefield. "No matter, I bear you no ill will. It must be very disconcerting to have such a thing take place on your doorstep." He took a deep breath and continued. "However, I can assure you that I am in no way short of projects. And as much as I love history, architecture, and restoration, they do not induce such passion that I'm driven to homicidal thoughts if they are threatened, much less actions." He smiled again, but Roxy noticed his jaw working. She glared at him.

Xavier sighed. "Look, if you insist on remaining on board, perhaps we should go downstairs, get a snack or two, some lunch, maybe another drink at the bar before the hordes return."

"Fine," Roxy said, taking a deep breath. Xavier hadn't

seemed to take offense to her accusation, and she realized she sounded rude, so she added more gently, "Sure."

They went below deck and picked up olives and chips at the bar and a couple more mimosas before heading to a table. The dining room was bright, all cream and glass and gold. The sunlight streamed in, bouncing off the reflective surfaces. It was so bright, Roxy was sure it would give her a headache.

They picked at their snacks for a long moment, both silent. Xavier checked his phone, replied to a text message with a smile on his face, then with a dramatic gesture placed it facedown on the table. Roxy perused the menu and decided she would have smoked shrimp with remoulade, with creole bread on the side. It was an appetizer; she wanted to save room for dessert. She had spied Creole cream cheesecake with caramelized apple topping on the menu. She wasn't missing that for the world.

"I'm sorry I can't be of more assistance," Xavier said eventually. "All I can say is I deduced some bad blood between Lacey Gregory and Annie. The amount of bad feeling between the two goes way back."

"And that's all you know? You haven't asked Annie about it? You two seem close."

Xavier couldn't hide his reaction. His neck and face flushed, giving his dark complexion a red undertone. A vein popped in his neck. "The operative word would be 'seem,'" he said. "We are merely professional colleagues."

"You didn't know her before?" Roxy asked, peering at him carefully.

Xavier averted his eyes briefly. "Before? Before this project you mean? No. Look, I'm sorry, would you excuse me? I'm going to the bathroom."

"Of course," Roxy said. Xavier was frustrating her more

by the minute. He was obviously feeling under pressure but evading her questions. Roxy's eyes rested on his phone. He'd left it behind. Impulsively, she picked it up. To her surprise, the screen wasn't password protected. Before she even had time to think or consider the moral dilemma of reviewing someone's phone without their knowledge, she scrolled through his call log. She didn't know what she was looking for. Something, anything.

Her intuition paid off. She struck gold. There was a call to Lacey Gregory at eleven thirty p.m. the night before she died. It must have been after the dinner to celebrate the start of the building works and Elijah's drunken entrance. The call was just ten seconds long. That had to mean something. She quickly looked around and surveyed her surroundings. There was only the bartender present and an elderly couple at the other end of the dining room. Roxy was breathing fast. Her gut clenched. All of a sudden, she didn't feel safe. She had visions of Xavier pushing her off the boat.

Roxy quickly took a picture of Xavier's call log, grabbed her bag, and rushed up the stairs to the upper deck, all thoughts of Creole cream cheesecake with caramelized apple topping now far from her mind. She disembarked into the Chalmette Battlefield, rushing past cruise passengers and the tour guide on the main lawn.

With the words " . . . a symbol of American democracy and meritocracy winning out over the English aristocracy and elite mindset . . ." ringing in her ears, Roxy followed signs to the exit. She passed antique cannons and a grand colonial mansion as the early afternoon sun blazed down on her. Eventually, she cleared the battle site and reached a two-lane road. She found a tree under which to take shade and ordered a cab.

While she waited for the taxi to arrive, she considered what she'd just learned. A ten second call with Lacey Gregory. At eleven thirty p.m. the night before she was killed. But why?

Maybe Xavier had bribed or threatened her to keep the job open, and when she showed up the next morning unpersuaded, he killed her. But then . . . he had said he had more than enough jobs to be going on with. The motive didn't seem strong enough. Maybe he was hiding something. Perhaps that mask the fortune teller had talked of was about to be ripped off.

"To the Funky Cat Inn," Roxy said to the cab driver when it pulled up.She hoped he wouldn't ask her what she was doing there. It wasn't exactly a common place to pick up a fare.

"Sure thing," the cab driver said. "I hear it's a great little place." Despite everything, his comment made Roxy beam with pride.

She thought back to the House of Hebert and the dark worker as the cab made its way through New Orleans. They drove past rows of wooden houses with flags hanging over the balconies. Mardi Gras was a ways away, but she couldn't wait for it to come around again, the streets packed, glitter and confetti flying everywhere, the air pulsing with life and joy and rhythm, costumes flashing with color as people spun and danced. That was the side of New Orleans she had first seen in the TV commercial that inspired her to start her new life.

There was another life that lurked beneath the surface though. The magic of the city didn't spare it from the evils of human nature—greed, selfishness, cruelty, jealousy. Magic had its flip side. For just as there were people like Sage and Dr. Jack who believed in people's fundamental goodness, their potential to grow and change, and that the spirits helped them do so, there were hucksters and frauds around every corner, ready for some silver to cross their palm.

For the first time since she had arrived in New Orleans, Roxy felt her heart harden. Maybe Sage and Dr. Jack believed the world was all pretty crystals and sweet-smelling incense and fluffy bunnies. Perhaps they believed in unicorns. Maybe they always wanted to feel good, and that was all it was. That mysticism and spiritualism was just a way to feel positive all the time. But what about the truth? What was the truth?

CHAPTER FORTY

W HEN ROXY GOT back to the Funky Cat and the now shell of a bakery, she saw Elijah wearing a dazzling cerise suit, over which he wore a hi-vis jacket and hard hat. He was waving construction workers everywhere as they made way for a digger loading rubble into the back of a huge truck.

"You'll want to stop here," Roxy said to the cab driver, looking ahead. "Or your cab will look like you've been driving through the desert in a sandstorm."

Roxy clambered out of the cab and rushed toward Elijah. "Why are you doing this? You need to stop!"

Elijah's face crumpled, a mixture of contempt and confusion. "What?"

"You're tampering with a crime scene!"

"Didn't you hear? There was no crime, therefore this is not a crime scene. Johnson's ruled Lacey's death an accident." Elijah turned his back to her as he continued to direct the construction crew. Roxy hated how harsh his voice sounded, the steeliness, the hard as diamonds tone. Where was the adorable, flamboyant Elijah who had once been a lovable rogue? Now he just seemed a rogue.

"I don't think your decision is the correct one."

Elijah didn't look her. He kept directing workers. "Whyever's that?"

"Johnson doesn't like the planning department because they wouldn't let him build an addition on his house," Roxy said. "Doesn't that tell you something?" Elijah ignored her. Rage shot up like bile into Roxy's throat. She rounded on him and looked up, hoping her ferocity could make up for what she lacked in height. "You could have a *murderer* working on your new bakery."

Elijah looked at her witheringly. "For all I care, a *mass* murderer could work here if it meant my bakery got built. I'm on a tight schedule. Excuse me. Mickey! I'm ready for my close-up!"

"You've changed," Roxy said in disgust.

Elijah had turned away but rounded on her with fire in his eyes. "Yes, I have. That's what it takes. Can I bring Lacey Gregory back from the dead? No. So I'm doing the next best thing and getting on with my life and making it the best it can be. And getting this show on the road is what it will take. Besides, does it help you to have a murder investigation *and* a building site outside your hotel for weeks, possibly months, interfering with business? Of course not. I'm doing you a favor." Elijah sighed. His expression softened. "You're too good, Roxy. Don't you know that no one in this world is going to look out for you but you? People are selfish. You're on your own."

"That's not true!" Roxy retorted.

"Everyone's looking out for number one. If it benefits *them* to help you, they will. The moment nothing is in it for them, you won't see them for dust."

Roxy was speechless. That's what life had led her to believe before she arrived in New Orleans, but she had refused to accept it. Abandoned by her father, treated horribly by her mother, humiliated by her boyfriend, and bullied by co-workers, she really hadn't known much kindness, care, or loyalty in her life at all. Except for Nefertiti, but she didn't count.

Nevertheless, when Roxy had arrived, her New Orleans family had shown her that life could be different. Evangeline, Sam, Nat, Sage, Elijah, and Dr. Jack had become her safe circle, a place where she felt surrounded with support.Now though, it felt like her safe circle was crumbling. And fast. To hear such words from Elijah of all people was shocking.

"If that were true," Roxy said eventually, "there would be no love, no friendship, no family."

"Bonds are flimsier than we'd all like to believe," Elijah said. "The only relationship you can depend on is mutual self-interest. And it's to our benefit that we keep our mouths shut, our noses clean, and this bakery is restored as quickly as possible."

"So, you don't mind having a murderer around the place?"

"Look, Johnson says it was an accident."

"Aren't you worried someone might be out for you? Two people connected to you are dead."

Elijah went quiet. "I don't think I'm the connection. They were brother and sister, you know."

"What? Who?"

"Patrice and Lacey."

"What?"

"We were all together at school. Me, Annie, Patrice, and

Lacey. Lacey was in the grade below, Patrice the grade above."

"But that's terrible! Don't you think it suspicious they're both dead in strange circumstances just weeks apart?

Elijah looked at her and pursed his lips. "No, why would I? Johnson said that Patrice was killed after arguing with a homeless man, which seems perfectly feasible given his personality. And Lacey's was an accident on a building site, which isn't uncommon. Ironic given that she was the inspector, but not unheard of. Lacey shouldn't have been in that building. It was her own fault. Look, let's keep our heads down and make the work happen, eh Roxy? Focus on what we can control."

"And what about justice? Isn't that important?"

"I'm a baker . . . and a TV personality. You're a hotel manager. Not law enforcement, nor part of the legal system. Let's leave all that well alone."

"You sound like Johnson," Roxy said.

"Well, maybe he's got a point."

"Fine." Confused thoughts swam around Roxy's head as she walked away. The rubble clearing continued. Maybe she *was* too good, too self-righteous. People had said that to her more than once. Johnson, in particular, enjoyed calling her naive, earnest, and other belittling names.

Roxy found herself again wondering about the swiftness with which Johnson closed Patrice's and Lacey's cases. Siblings dead just a few weeks apart? It couldn't simply be an unhappy coincidence. Roxy sighed. What did it all mean? And what was she going to do about it?

CHAPTER FORTY-ONE

I 'M NOT INVESTIGATING. Roxy walked down the alleyway to the street. She hailed a cab. *I'm just going to buy a pastry at Patisserie Paradis. And if I end up talking with somebody who works there, it's just a friendly chat.*

Fifteen minutes later, Roxy was outside the café and bakery, looking down the alleyway that had been cordoned off weeks before. The dumpster was still there. Roxy considered checking it out but decided against it. It would look weird. Besides—she wasn't *investigating*. No, no.

Apart from a few people seated at tables drinking coffee, the bakery wasn't busy. It was well after breakfast and well before lunch. She walked up to the counter.

"Hi."

"Hey there." The young, blond guy behind the counter smiled at her as he polished it. "What are you having?"

Roxy looked at the various pastries in the glass case. She had to admit they looked sensational. Whatever kind of person Patrice may have been, he had a great team of bakers working for him.

"I'll take . . . a selection of macarons, please," she said, pointing.

"Sure," the guy said, still smiling. "Take a seat and I'll bring them over. Anything to drink?"

"Just drip coffee, please. Black, no sugar."

"Coming right up."

Roxy took a seat by the window and watched the people —inside and out—while she waited. Shortly afterwards, the blond guy came to her table and carefully placed the pastries and coffee in front of her.

"There you go," he said.

"Thanks." Roxy smiled back.

The guy stood at the table for a few seconds, then eventually said, "I've not seen you around before."

"Oh, I live on the other side of town," Roxy said. "Actually, I'm from Ohio originally."

"Ohio, huh? I'm from Arkansas. I came here to play music a few years ago and ended up staying."

"Yeah," Roxy laughed. "New Orleans is like that. There's nowhere like it, is there? I don't think I could handle living in Ohio again now I've been here a while."

"Yeah, right!" the guy said. He offered his hand. "Jake."

"Roxy," she replied. "Nice to meet you."

"Likewise."

"I'm surprised this place is still open," Roxy said. "I heard about the murder a few weeks ago."

"Ugh, yeah," Jake said, his smile disappearing. "He was the boss here, you know. The guy who was murdered."

"Who's running the place now?" Roxy asked.

"Nobody really. The pâtissiers—there's two of them who worked under Patrice—decided to keep it open rather than shut it down. For the customers more than anything. I'm not complaining. I need the money."

"Makes sense," Roxy said. "I guess Patrice had a partner in the business?"

Jake shrugged. "I don't know. Probably. He never really talked much about anything other than baking."

"Really?"

"No," Jake said. Then after a moment's thought, "Only that he lived with some guy a couple of blocks away."

"Down there?" Roxy said, pointing at the street beyond the window.

"Yeah. Fancy apartment block. Old French-style. Looks like a vampire's castle if you ask me—except it's right next to a McDonald's!"

Jake laughed. Roxy laughed too. She took a sip of coffee. "What kind of boss was he?"

"Patrice?" Roxy nodded. "Oh . . . man . . . I mean . . . What's that thing they say? You shouldn't speak ill of the dead? But you know . . . No doubt about it—Patrice was *really* hard to work with, and for."

"How so?" Roxy took a delicate nibble of her raspberry macaron.

"I've had tough bosses before," said Jake. "Guys who work you really hard or expect too much and yell at you about your work. But Patrice . . . he was something else. He loved drama. He was always getting into arguments with us over the stupidest stuff. Just before he died, he did a random 'inspection' of the pastries. He flew into a rage because there was one he didn't like—even though he had created it and trained the pâtissiers how to make it to his exact specifications. He'd tested it out before and said it was perfect. He was out of control, shouting and waving his arms about, not caring if customers saw him. He was terrifying. Sometimes I think he just wanted to argue and make life miserable for everyone."

"Sounds stressful."

Jake nodded, distracted by the memory. "It was. He was. Most people left within a few weeks. Even though Paradis has one of the best reputations in the city, the craziness simply wasn't worth it. People learned what they could and moved on as soon as possible."

"Hmm." Roxy swallowed the remains of her macaron. It was delicious. She took a quick sip of coffee. "So I guess he had a lot of enemies."

Jake's eyes opened wide, and he waved his hands in front of him. "Whoa! Don't go thinking anything like that now! Nobody here would have killed him. We're just rookie bakers and simple servers. I mean . . . sure . . . sometimes . . . just as a gag . . . we'd joke about poisoning a beignet and giving it to him, but I mean. . . that's all it was, a gag."

Roxy laughed. "I understand." She smiled. "Black humor. Stress relief."

"Exactly." Jake relaxed, then looked out of the window as he thought some more. "But you know . . . I even told the detective this—I wasn't too surprised Patrice ended up in that dumpster. I mean, of course I was surprised that he was killed. And like *that*. Horrific. But Patrice was so difficult. Always arguing with everyone. Even the guy he lived with. I never knew how he got away with it . . . I guess in the end he didn't."

Roxy looked outside again, down the street Jake had told her Patrice had lived on. She reached for her handbag and pulled out her wallet.

"You're going?" Jake said.

"Yeah. Thank you very much. It was lovely. The macaron *and* the conversation."

"Let me go get your bill."

Roxy stood and waited for Jake to return. She checked it and paid with her card, leaving a nice tip. "See you," she said, stepping past him to leave. Already, her mind was elsewhere, her feet carrying her with their own sense of direction and purpose.

CHAPTER FORTY-TWO

STILL THINKING OF what Jake had told her about Patrice, Roxy walked down the street where the baker had lived. Just as Jake had said, there was a large French building, several stories high, with huge sash windows. Long wrought iron balconies wound their way around the outside of the building, and carved pillars propped up the first floor. There were turrets, and Roxy could see why Jake had thought the apartment block looked like a vampire's castle. She stopped to appreciate the building. This must be where Patrice had lived.

Roxy wasn't sure what she was doing there, but she was intensely curious. Either way, it didn't matter. She couldn't do anything. She had no idea which apartment Patrice had lived in.

Just as she was turning away to head back home, an old woman walked up to the vast, wooden double-door entrance to the building. She looked like a New Orleans native—tough, colorful, and lively. The old woman reminded Roxy a little of Evangeline. Elderly, ornery, and a little broken down. Around her neck was a thick, purple scarf, and she wore a bright blue cardigan despite the temperature. She was carrying two heavy shopping bags, a baguette poking out of one of them.

The old woman set down her bags to fish for her keys in her big cardigan. The bags threatened to tip over, spilling all their contents on the sidewalk. Roxy immediately dashed to the woman's side. "Would you like some help?"

The old woman looked up at Roxy with a big, white smile. "Cher, I would like nothing more."

Roxy laughed and took both heavy bags from her. *I'm not investigating. I'm just helping an elderly lady.*

"They chargin' so much for groceries these days," the old woman said as she unlocked the big door and pushed it open. "And I *still* can't help myself buyin' too damned many of 'em."

Following the woman, Roxy stepped through the doorway into the big entrance hall. The building was even more beautiful inside. A black-and-white tiled floor. An elegantly curving staircase. Even the apartment doors were carved in delicate flower patterns.

"It's nice to have a well-stocked kitchen though," Roxy said. "Comforting."

The old woman closed the door and walked slowly to the stairs. "My husban' ain't complainin'," she laughed. "Oh Lord, that man can eat!"

The old woman took the stairs slowly, and Roxy followed with her bags. They stopped on the first landing, and once again the woman fumbled for her keys until she found the right one. The apartment entryway was packed with antique furniture and photographs.

"Just drop those bags there. Thank you so much, cher."

"Are you sure? I can bring them into the kitchen if you like."

"No, no," the old woman said with a broad smile. "If I make you work any mo' I'll have to pay you!"

Roxy put down the bags. She was about to say goodbye and leave when a thought struck her. *I'm not investigating. I'm just making conversation.*

"I was wondering," Roxy asked slowly, "if you know a Patrice Marveau who lived here?"

"Patrice?" the old woman exclaimed so loudly it sounded almost like a yelp. "Ain't a soul in this buildin' who ain't heard of him. The way he yelled and holla'd. Arguin' with that strange man he lived with. Bless 'is 'eart."

"Did you know he died a while back?" Roxy said.

The old woman shot Roxy a sharp look, her eyes narrowing. "Course I did," she said. "I ain't speakin' ill of the dead, cher. Just bein' honest."

"Of course."

The old woman shook her head. "Though it bein' quiet these nights . . ."

"Do you know which apartment he lived in?"

"Sure," the old woman said. "Ground floor. Number three. Used to hear if he was home every time I go out, every time I go in. Not anymore. Seems strange. Definitely quieter . . ."

"Thank you very much," Roxy said, turning to leave.

"Thank *you*, cher!" the old woman said, cheering up again. "Take good care of yourself now, ya hear?"

Roxy left the old woman's apartment and went downstairs. She found apartment number three and stood in front of the door for a few seconds, wondering what to do, what she would say if someone answered. *I'm not investigating. I'm just offering condolences.*

Carefully, as if it might attack her, Roxy reached out and pressed the doorbell. After a few moments, the door cracked open. Through the crack, Roxy saw a handsome man with sharply cut, gelled black hair and a chiseled face. He was wearing a red and green bathrobe. He held the door open only a few inches, but Roxy recognized him immediately.

"Xavier!"

CHAPTER FORTY-THREE

"ROXY! WHAT DO you want?"

"Oh! Um . . . hello," Roxy said meekly, suddenly feeling nervous.

"What is it?" Xavier asked. He quickly looked around, checking to see if Roxy was accompanied. "Where did you get to earlier?" he said. Seeing that she was alone, he relaxed a little. "I came out of the bathroom, and you'd gone. Pity, you missed a good time and some great food. The Creole cream cheesecake with caramelized apple topping was amazing." He opened the door a little wider so he could stand freely. He folded his arms.

Over his shoulder, Roxy could see the apartment was very clean and meticulously arranged. Just the sort of place she would have expected Xavier to live in, except for one thing—for a historian and restoration specialist, the décor was exceptionally contemporary.

"I-I'm sorry. I was feeling queasy and just had to get off the boat. The heat perhaps or maybe the food. I'm glad you had a good time."

Xavier nodded. "You could have texted. Anyhow, how can I help you?"

"I heard Patrice Marveau lived here. I met him a few times, and . . . and thought I would offer my condolences to . . . his friend. But obviously I'm too late. You must have just moved in."

Xavier let out a half sigh, half chuckle. "No, no. I've lived here for five years."

Roxy worked to keep the surprise from her expression. "You mean . . .?"

"Yes, Roxy dear, I lived here with Patrice until he died. Would you like to come in?"

Roxy hesitated, but Xavier smiled and opened the door wide. She stepped across the threshold. Xavier turned and led her into the living area; it was white and grey and chrome.

"I'm surprised, Xavier, your work isn't reflected in your apartment. I expected antiques, lots of dark wood."

"Good lord, no. Far too depressing. And I don't like to bring my work home with me. A complete break is what I want. Anyhow, Patrice. Patrice was one of the most difficult people you could ever choose to live with. The only family member who had anything to do with him was his sister, Lacey."

If Xavier had intended to shock Roxy with the news that Lacey was Patrice's sister, she denied him the satisfaction. She merely smiled sympathetically. "People keep saying that about him. That he was so very difficult."

"Hence my surprise at your visit. Please sit." Xavier gestured to a gray leather sofa. "No one else has visited in all these weeks since his death."

"Do you have any idea who might have killed him?"

"Killed him?" Xavier snorted and shook his head.

"None at all. The homeless man story is entirely too convenient and unlikely. But the police won't ever find out who killed him. Their list of suspects must have been the size of a yearbook. Patrice spent his every waking moment causing trouble and rubbing people the wrong way."

"So why did you live with him?"

"His work hours conflicted with mine. He was gone when I was around, so we didn't see each other much—him being a baker. Plus, the trauma bonding was effective."

Roxy frowned. "Trauma bonding?"

"You know, when someone is so awful, you're about to leave, then they do something nice, the endorphins rush in, and you suddenly decide they aren't so bad after all."

"Ah, yes. I do know something about that." Roxy thought back to her ex-boyfriend.

"Is there anything else I can help you with?" Xavier asked. He smiled, and a ripple of fear ran through Roxy's body. Xavier's smile was as oily as his hair. *Intuition, Rox. Trust your intuition.*

"Um . . . Is that . . .? Are they . . .?"

Xavier turned to see what she was looking at. "Patrice's ashes? Yes. I don't know what to do with them. I phoned Lacey the night before she died to ask her to take them. Of course, she never replied, and now I'm stuck with them."

Roxy's mind was filled with questions, but none of them seemed important anymore. She stood quickly and said, "I-I won't take up any more of your time." Xavier made to stand too. "I'll see myself out," Roxy countered quickly. "Thank you for your time. S-Sorry a-about lunch."

Xavier nodded and relaxed into his chair, crossing his legs. Roxy quickly shut the door behind her and hurried out of the building.

Back at the Funky Cat, Nat was in the back kitchen room purging crawfish. "Where've you been?"

"Oh, just out and about."

"Can I invite a friend of mine to dinner one evening? I'd like you to meet him."

"Uh, sure. Anytime. Listen, did you know Patrice Marveau and Lacey Gregory were siblings?"

"No!" Nat's eyes widened.

"And I went to his apartment today," Roxy told her, still pink from her outing.

"Whose?"

"Patrice's."

"You did? What did you go there for?"

"I'm not sure, but listen Nat, there's more. Patrice lived with Xavier!"

Nat's eyebrows rocked up close to her hairline. "No!" she repeated.

"It's true. Patrice and Xavier lived in this ultra-modern, ultra-cool apartment together near Patisserie Paradis! Don't you think that's strange? Xavier worked alongside his room-mate's sister, both of whom were found dead within weeks of each other. And . . ."

"And?" Nat had stopped her purging to pay close attention.

"Xavier even made a phone call to Lacey the night of the demo dinner. The night before she was found dead. He said it was to ask her to take Patrice's ashes away."

"Oh, what a tangled web we weave . . ." Nat said. Roxy frowned furiously at her. "What?" Nat countered. "Everyone in England learns Shakespeare. It's on a par with walking."

Click-click-click.

Roxy knew that sound. The noise of a bicycle mechanism. She peered out from behind her bedroom curtains, taking care that the streetlight didn't catch her face.

There he was again. The man with the bike in the alleyway. He wore a beanie brought down almost over his eyes. *Who was he? And what was he doing there?*

CHAPTER FORTY-FOUR

THE NEXT MORNING, Roxy didn't tell anyone about the strange man in the alleyway in the middle of the night. Partly because she wouldn't even know how to explain how strange it was, and partly because the next morning was so hectic.

Sam walked into the hotel while Roxy was having a quick coffee and beignet with Evangeline. As always, Roxy felt a slight tinge of embarrassment. He was so handsome her knees buckled a little, even though she was sitting down. It was something she thought she might never get used to. Today he was wearing worn denim jeans and a classic-cut, white T-shirt that made him look mighty fine.

Sam smiled as he approached the table. He picked up a beignet, dipped it into some chocolate, and took a bite. "Have the guests left?"

"Yep," Roxy said, smiling up at him.

"I guess you've got some laundry for me to do then."

"I do," Roxy said. "But don't you want to have a coffee first?"

"Later," Sam said. "I want to get a head start."

"If you say so," Roxy said, putting her coffee down and standing up. "Come and help me collect it from the rooms then."

She led Sam up the stairs. She wasn't deliberately setting things up so, but it seemed like she and Sam always found themselves alone somehow. She knew he was waiting for her to give him a signal about what was happening between them, but she always felt too preoccupied by other things or inhibited by her concerns to make a move. Sam was a perfect gentleman, and she knew he wouldn't push the issue.

"You know the drill," she said as she entered the room and went to open the windows and air it out. "Towels, pillow covers, sheets . . ."

Sam began collecting everything while she checked the cupboards and drawers for anything lost or out of place. "Did Nat ever say anything about her nightly jaunts?"

"No," Roxy said. "And I don't think she wants to. It's been a while and she hasn't said a thing. Why all the secrecy?"

Sam paused as he was pulling a cover from a pillow to think about it. "Maybe she thinks it would ruin her 'tough tattoo girl' exterior?"

Roxy laughed gently. "We're her friends though. I don't know why she would keep it a secret from us. We know she's tough. We'd be happy for her."

"Has she been acting differently?" Sam asked.

"Not at all," Roxy said. "She's the same old Nat. She's still skeptical of Sage's beliefs. And she still wears nothing but black." She shook her head.

"Roxy, all I know," Sam said with an affectionate smile, "is that you care about her. It's normal to worry. And I also know that Nat trusts you. I'm sure if she needed your help, she'd ask for it."

"You're probably right," Roxy said, sighing and relaxing a little. "But then again, Elijah trusts me too, and he managed to keep his audition for *Ultimate Baker* a secret for months! Don't forget—Nat still hasn't sorted out her immigration status. I don't want her doing anything silly and exposing herself."

Sam followed Roxy as they visited each of the other rooms where she had prepared the bags of laundry for him.

"You know, a while back," she began, "some guy turned up. Really late. Like, the early hours."

"At the hotel?" Sam asked.

"Yeah. Not inside. He just sort of stood outside for a bit, looking up at the windows as if checking for something, or waiting for something. I don't know."

"And? I sense there's an 'and.'"

"Well, he's turned up again. Twice more, including last night."

"What? Why didn't you tell me this before?" Sam said.

"Honestly, so much has been happening I almost forgot about it," Roxy said. "I've been trying to figure out what he's doing, but I have no idea. He seems harmless."

"But that's not okay. I'll stay tonight to catch him," Sam said resolutely.

"*Sam,*" Roxy pleaded, almost laughing at how sincerely concerned he was. "It's nothing. It's probably just some guy who has the wrong address."

"I don't care! Whatever his deal is, I'm going to find out," Sam replied firmly. "I've got the van parked outside. I'll stay there tonight and wait for him."

"You're going to stay awake all night just in case he comes along?"

"And tomorrow night, and the next night, and the one after that—if that's what it takes.'"

"But he may not show up again."

Sam simply shrugged.

Roxy laughed again, but she could tell there was no way she could convince Sam to change his mind. He might be the most accommodating, friendly, and generous gentleman most of the time—but once he decided to do something, she knew there was no way to stop him.

CHAPTER FORTY-FIVE

T HE DINNER THAT night was so energetic and lively that it ended later than usual. Evangeline got a cab home before midnight, and the two Turkish tourists retired to their room around the same time. They needed an early call for their morning flight home. Sage left exhausted after offering everyone tarot readings—and a whole book's worth of information about the cards. Elijah was also tired from providing the closing entertainment, some wonderful renditions of "My Bloody Valentine" and "Mercy, Mercy, Mercy." New guests—a party of six who had been the source of most of the excitement—were too drunk to party on anymore. The evening ended when they went up to their rooms, leaning on each other for support. Once again, Roxy was left alone with Sam as they cleared the table.

"Okay," he said as he brought the final stack of dirty plates into the kitchen where Roxy was tossing the tablecloth and napkins into a laundry bag, "here's the plan."

"Plan?" Roxy said, then she remembered.

"I'm going to move the van to a better spot," he said.

"Somewhere I'll have a good view, and where there's no lighting so he won't spot me. If you notice anything from your window, text me. And I'll text you if I notice something. Make sure your phone is charged and close by."

"You can't stay out there awake all night Sam," Roxy said. "And for that matter, neither can I." She shoved the laundry bag toward him. "Why don't you worry about something more important, like getting those wine stains out of that tablecloth."

"Do you think I can just go home and sleep knowing some weirdo might show up here at any minute? I can't believe you didn't tell me before this."

"After the long day you've had, you'll be asleep the second you sit down in that van," Roxy joked. "Besides, I told you, the guy didn't seem intimidating."

"*Didn't seem intimidating?*" Sam repeated in a shocked voice. "It's not *normal* for a guy to just stand outside your window every night, Roxy. It's *creepy*. Did you forget that someone died just across the way a few days ago? What if Johnson is wrong and it wasn't an accident?"

"I think he is wrong. And it's not *every night* and of course, I didn't forget," Roxy replied. "But . . . you think the man and Lacey's death are connected?"

"Who knows? I don't want to hang around to find out, that's for sure."

Roxy suddenly felt concerned. She hadn't thought that the stranger and Lacey's death had anything to do with each other before. But what if they did?

"Okay," Sam said, turning to go. "I'm going to head off to the van now. Remember: text or call me if you notice anything strange. Anything at all."

Roxy nodded, and Sam began walking out of the kitchen. But before he reached the door, she called to him.

"Sam," she said. He turned around. "I still think you're overreacting but . . . thanks." Sam smiled, nodded, then left.

Roxy finished up in the kitchen and then went to her room. She felt tired, but it was a different sort of tired. Not just the usual fatigue of a hard day. She felt emotionally tired. The situations she found herself in—Patrice and Lacey's deaths, Nat's secretive cabaret act, and the man outside her window—were like some difficult math problem that she was desperate to figure out, and for which she had all the numbers but couldn't put them together in a way that added up.

Nefertiti glared at her grumpily from the foot of the bed when Roxy entered her room. Roxy rubbed her cat's head a little. "I know you're angry at me Nef-nef," she said as she undressed, "leaving you to sleep on your own in a cold bed, and if I could make things happen differently, I would."

Roxy had a quick shower, changed into her pajamas, then put her phone on the charger. Before she got into bed, she turned off all the lights but her bedside lamp and moved to the window. Her curtains were drawn, but she moved them slightly so she could look down onto the street.

Sam had moved the van as he said he would. In the dark, it was hard to see him. She peered into the darkness until she could make him out. He was sitting in the driver's seat with his arms folded. His head was back, and she realized that he was already asleep. She laughed softly to herself.

"At least he tried, huh, Nef-nef?" she said. "It's the thought that counts, right?"

She stood at the window for a few more moments, looking down at the van and smiling. Sam really was a nice guy. It was obvious that he genuinely cared for her. That felt sort of new to her. She'd never had someone who put her at the center of their world. She couldn't think of anyone in her past who would camp outside her window all night because they were worried about her. Maybe her suspicions about Sam were misplaced?

Because there he was. A handsome, sweet man who cared about her so much that he was willing to stay out all night in his van to protect her. She could forgive him falling asleep as soon as he sat down. She smiled down on the dark street once again and was about to let the curtain fall. Then she saw something.

The stones on the road glistened, as if a weak light had shone across them. Roxy froze and continued to watch, just to confirm what she had seen. Seconds later, she saw where the light was coming from.

The bicycle slowly moved in front of the hotel until she could see it from her window. Even in the dark Roxy immediately knew that this was the man who had come around on the previous night. She watched the man get off the bike.

Roxy looked over at Sam, but he didn't move at all. She was sure now—he had fallen asleep. She considered not doing anything. She could just let Sam sleep, let the stranger look around, and then disappear. He didn't seem like much of a threat. But then she remembered what Sam had said about this man potentially being connected Lacey's death.

She let the curtain down gently then dashed across the room to where she had put the phone on to charge. Carefully but quickly, she called Sam.

"Gruh . . . mmm . . ." he grumbled into the phone.

"That's him, Sam," she whispered. "He's right there in front of you!"

CHAPTER FORTY-SIX

S AM HUNG UP immediately. The sound of the van door slamming outside penetrated the air, followed by a shout as Sam cried "Hey!" across the alleyway. Roxy dashed to the window just in time to see him grab the stranger. Compared to Sam, he looked even more harmless. Smaller and far weaker. The stranger froze as Sam approached, and before he could even think of running away, Sam had twisted his arm behind his back and was marching him up to the hotel entrance. Roxy quickly put on her big, fluffy slippers and dashed out of the room to open the door. She stood aside as Sam forced the man into the lobby.

"What's going on?" the stranger pleaded. "Let go of me!" He didn't even struggle.

"Thought you could just spy on innocent women, did you?" Sam said gruffly as he pushed the man forward. "Sit on the floor."

"*What?* No! I'm not . . . Let me go!"

"*Sit.*" The man sat cross-legged on the lobby tiles. "There you go," Sam said to Roxy, full of anger and pride.

He puffed out his chest. "One creep served right up! You going to ask him what he thinks he's doing? Or should I?" He blew out his cheeks and took a deep breath. He was panting.

"Sam," Roxy said slowly as the stranger groaned on the floor. "That's not a creep . . . That's . . . *George!*"

Sam looked at Roxy, then at the man on the floor, and noticed for the first time his red hair. He glanced at Roxy again. He frowned, thinking hard. "George?"

"Remember?" Roxy said. "Meredith Romanoff's assistant. The medium? George was her apprentice. He's supposed to be in Nigeria."

She went to the young man and carefully helped him to his feet. He was small and soft, with red hair and freckles. He groaned and winced in pain. He rubbed his shoulder where it had twisted during Sam's manhandling of him.

"Oh! *George!*" Sam said with a smile, then immediately sobered when he realized his mistake. The adrenaline coursing through his body plummeted. "Hey . . . uh . . . wow . . . I'm really sorry, buddy."

In between his wincing, George looked at Sam and nodded. Together, Sam and Roxy picked George up from the floor.

"Come on over here and sit down," Roxy said, leading him to the soft couch by the window. "I'll get you some painkillers and a drink."

"Thank you," George said, grimacing.

Roxy disappeared into the kitchen and brought back pills, water, and some fresh lemonade. She shared a quick look with Sam—who struggled to meet her eye—while George gathered himself.

"Look, I'm really sorry," Sam said. "I didn't realize it

was you. I thought . . . But . . . but I don't get it, George. What were you doing out there?"

"Yes," Roxy added. "The last I heard you were heading out to Nigeria to study Ifa?"

"I was, but . . ." George looked up at her from the seat. He stopped talking and stared into his lemonade. Roxy remembered what a sensitive, quiet guy he was. It was probably why Sage and others had said he had a gift for intuiting the spirits. He opened his mouth to speak, but only a whimper came out.

"Oh, George, it's okay," Roxy said compassionately. She sat down beside him and put an arm around his shoulders. "You can tell us."

The red-haired young man swallowed and sniffed, then looked at each of them again. "Will you promise not to tell anyone else?"

"Sure," Sam said.

"Of course," Roxy agreed.

"Well, I was on my way there—to Nigeria—on the way to the airport even . . . And I had this powerful feeling."

"What feeling?"

"I can't really describe it. The spirits perhaps, or maybe something else. I felt like I was leaving behind more than I was gaining by going somewhere else, if that makes sense. I realized," George continued, "that I didn't want to leave Nat." There was a long pause after he said that. "I think she needs me." Roxy glanced up at Sam and noticed that he was smiling, almost chuckling. "And I need her."

"I can understand that," Roxy said, trying to comfort him. "You two seemed to get along well."

"We had a connection," George said, "or at least, it felt like that. I don't know. I can't tell if it was a real spiritual connection or whether I just wanted there to be one. All my abilities to read, to commune with spirits, to see the other side—they all would go kind of crazy when I thought of her. I've never been good with girls."

"So you came back for her?" Sam asked.

"I guess," George said. "I wasn't sure what to do after Meredith died. I was sort of lost. I could always go to Nigeria, I figured, but I wanted to understand what was going on with Nat. If she would . . . If I could . . . If we . . ." He struggled to find the words, and Roxy squeezed him a little to show she understood what he was trying to say.

"But why stand around outside the hotel in the middle of the night?" Sam asked. "Why not tell us you were back in town? I don't get it."

"I'm not like you," George said, making it sound like an apology. "I'm not that confident or tough. When I don't know what to do, or when I have a problem, I turn to the spirits. I ask them to guide me."

"And did they?" asked Sam.

"Yes," George said, nodding confidently and looking up at Sam for the first time. "In fact, the first night after I returned to New Orleans I went where I felt, with nothing but the spirits leading me, and I saw her."

"Nat?"

"Yes. She was on Bourbon Street, and she was . . . she was with someone else. A man." Roxy and Sam swapped a look. George continued. "The next night I went back to the same place, and I saw her again— but this time she was with a woman. I didn't know what to think . . ."

"You've been *stalking* her?" Sam was incredulous.

"Well, not stalking her exactly."

"Sounds like it to me." Sam folded his arms.

"Look, I'm no threat, okay? I was just working out what to do. Waiting for a sign. I've seen her multiple times in that same area— sometimes with the man, sometimes with the woman. But recently, I haven't seen her at all. She disappeared."

"So, you came to the Funky Cat to see if she was here?" Roxy asked.

George sighed heavily. He sounded exhausted and weak. "Honestly, I don't know what I was doing. I can't tell anymore where the messages from my spirit guides end and my emotions begin. I just keep going all over the city looking for her, and then sometimes I come here and almost *will* her to appear. Oh . . . I know how stupid that sounds . . ."

"It doesn't sound stupid," Roxy said softly.

"And this man . . . who is he anyway, a boyfriend? Please don't tell anyone," George pleaded. "I feel such an idiot."

"Of course not," Sam said. "But I'll tell *you* something. When you want to be with someone, it's always best just to tell them."

George's eyes flashed then. "Pot. Kettle." Sam blinked several times in a rush, and he glanced away.

"The thing is, George," Roxy said, "Sam's right. You should speak to Nat yourself."

"No, I can't," George said quickly, pulling away from Roxy. "I'm too . . . I can't handle it. I've been going out of my mind and . . . I'm worried I've even lost my abilities because of all this. Oh no . . . ." George whimpered. He seemed on the verge of tears.

"Where are you staying now?" Sam asked quickly.

"In a small room over near Violet," George replied. "I'm almost out of money though."

"I'll take care of that," Sam said, pulling out his wallet. He handed George a wad of money so confidently that

George reached out to take it automatically. "Look, quit 'Nat-hunting' for a while. Get yourself together. Leave her to us. We'll figure out what's going on with her and get back to you as soon as we do."

"But—" George began.

Sam interrupted him. "We won't tell her a thing about you coming here or looking for her or anything. Don't worry." George nodded and sighed and slumped over again.

"Come on," Sam said. "I'll drive you home."

George got up and they all walked to the front door of the inn. Roxy unlocked the door and George went on ahead to Sam's car. Roxy quickly took Sam's arm to hold him back.

"Sam," she whispered quietly enough so that George wouldn't hear, "what are we going to do? How do we fix this? What about these friends of Nat? What if she already has a boyfriend?"

"Meh, we'll get her to clarify the situation. George just needs to get himself together and ask her out on a date. From what I remember, they seemed a pretty good match."

"I agree. But George is quite timid—and Nat can be scary at the best of times."

"Opposites attract," Sam said.

CHAPTER FORTY-SEVEN

ROXY DRUMMED HER fingers on the table. Something was bothering her. The closed cases. The anonymous letter. Lacey and Patrice being siblings. Xavier being Patrice's roommate. Masks, and secrets, and lies. It was all enough to push last night's drama with George from her mind.

Roxy pulled out her phone and dialed Detective Johnson's number. No one answered. Frustrated, she decided to head to the police station. What she had to tell him was important, and she wanted to say it to Johnson face-to-face.

It wasn't too far of a walk, so Roxy decided against hailing a cab and hurried there on her own. Marching through the streets gave her time to organize her thoughts and rehearse what she wanted to say. The police station wasn't busy, so Roxy stepped right up to the front desk, drawing the attention of the officer sitting there.

"I have to talk to Detective Johnson immediately. It's very important," she said.

The officer—a young woman with blonde hair in a ponytail and a bored expression—looked at Roxy casually.

"He's not here. If you want me to take a message, I think he's on duty this evening."

"No. It's important. I need to speak with him as soon as possible."

"I'm sorry, ma'am," the officer said. "But if you'd like to give me a message for him, I'll make sure he gets it and . . ."

Exasperated, Roxy could tell the officer wasn't going to budge. She looked around as she considered calling Johnson from her phone again. As she looked past the reception desk, down the corridor that led deep inside the station, she caught sight of a familiar face and immediately propelled herself forward.

"*Ma'am!* You're not supposed to go back there," the reception desk officer called after her, but Roxy didn't heed her words.

"Officer Trudeau!"

Trudeau looked at her. He squinted. She could almost see his brain cells spinning as he momentarily tried to place her. "You!" He stared into Roxy's face, waiting for her to explain herself. "Something I can help you with?"

"Yes," Roxy said. Trudeau glanced over her shoulder and shook his head at the young blonde officer in reception. She was gesticulating wildly. "I need to speak to Detective Johnson."

"He's not on shift at the moment."

"I know, but it's important. It's to do with the Lacey Gregory murder investigation. And Patrice Marveau's."

Trudeau looked at her for a second. He considered how serious and determined Roxy was. He smiled a little. "But both those cases are closed."

"Yes! I mean no!" Roxy said. "Oh, never mind, I just need to talk to him. He's not answering his phone."

Officer Trudeau nodded. "Like I said, he's off duty."

"But I need to speak to him now! Can you help me find him? If you give me his address, I'll go visit him myself."

Trudeau hesitated. "Hey, hey, he wouldn't like that. And it's completely against regulations."

"I won't tell him you told me where to find him. I promise."

"Hmm . . ." Trudeau groaned, then shrugged and sighed. He scratched his face. "I don't know where he lives. I doubt anyone here does. He doesn't disclose that kind of private information. Or any private information. All I know is that he's somewhere in St. Roch, I th . . ." Roxy's eyes lit up. "Hey!" Trudeau shouted at Roxy's retreating back. "You have no business there!"

"Thank you so much, Officer Trudeau," Roxy shouted over her shoulder as she ran for the doors. She quickly left the station, bumping into a couple as, head down, she pulled up a map on her phone. St. Roch was unfamiliar to her. No matter, she would trawl the streets looking for the detective if she had to. She considered asking Sam for a ride, but she wanted to speak to Johnson alone, so she ordered a cab.

As the cab moved through the city towards St. Roch, Roxy found herself staring out at rundown houses—many of them abandoned, many more of them in terrible condition. Occasionally she saw people, downtrodden and poor, carrying plastic carrier bags. Others relaxed on battered porches in front of bare, dry yards, overseeing the play of young children. Abandoned cars littered the sidewalk. This was a part of town that had been forgotten and left to decay.

"Where are we going, miss?"

"Please just keep driving, I'll tell you when to stop." Roxy had no plan other than she was hoping to spot Johnson or something she could identify as his outside his home. For half an hour they drove around.

"Are you sure you're doing the right thing? I mean, the meter is running, and this isn't the best part of town, miss."

"There!" Roxy pointed. A brown sedan with gold trim sat slightly askew in a driveway. Johnson's car. It looked as though the driver had merely aimed for its parking spot. A lack of care was evident.

The cab stopped outside the small house. It was little more than a shack. "This is the address you're looking for, lady?" The cab driver looked at the rundown cottage dubiously. "Are you sure?"

"Yes," Roxy said, also examining the old single-story house, her lips pursed. She could see that the weather-beaten wooden slats, at one time painted white, were now faded and split. Two dirty windows were set either side of a heavy but beaten-up green door. The yard was empty but for patchy grass and weeds. The whole place looked in bad shape, but there were some subtle signs of life—a few dog toys in the yard and several tiles on the roof had recently been replaced. "Would you mind waiting here a second? I shouldn't be too long."

"As long as you like, miss," the driver said, turning off his engine. "The meter's still running, though. And . . ." He looked around dubiously. "I might have to charge danger money."

Slowly, Roxy got out of the cab and walked up the path. She took one step onto the porch when a sound made her freeze in terror. A dog barked behind her. It was loud, hard, and angry. She spun around and immediately took several steps backward, slamming herself against the front door of the house as the dog jumped from the yard onto the porch, teeth bared, its eyes wild but focused. Trying not to scream, Roxy shut her eyes tight and hoped it wouldn't hurt too much.

CHAPTER FORTY-EIGHT

"**L**EO! DOWN, BOY!**"

At the command, the dog went silent, midbark. Carefully, Roxy opened one eye. She saw Leo now completely uninterested in her as he nuzzled a bone. Roxy turned to where the shout had come from—the side of the house. Johnson appeared around the corner, wiping oil from his hands on a rag. Out of work clothes, he looked different. He wore a dirty vest and old jeans, his plump but tough body not hidden under his ill-fitting suit for once. His patchy, sweaty skin flushed in the heat, his hair stuck up, and his face was riddled with stubble. But Johnson's consistently suspicious and pugnacious expression was unmistakable.

He stood looking up at her on the porch where Roxy was still pressing herself against the front door. He looked at her with disbelief. "What the hell are *you* doing here?" he growled, sounding as surprised as he was annoyed.

"I want to talk to you," Roxy said.

Johnson sighed heavily and shook his head. "*Jesus*

Christ," he growled as he moved toward her. "I can't even get away from you when I'm off duty."

Roxy stepped aside so he could push his way into the house. She carefully followed him. It was slightly cooler inside, but only because it was so dark, the dirty windows barely letting in any of the sun. "How did you find out where I live?"

"I . . ." Roxy began, but she trailed off, partly because she couldn't think of an excuse that didn't betray Officer Trudeau and partly because she was taken aback by the interior of the house. She knew Detective Johnson as a rough-and-ready type, but even she didn't expect his home to look like this.

Everything was rundown and filthy. There were cracks and marks across the bare walls. Every appliance and piece of furniture looked older than the detective himself. Tools and newspapers and boxes were scattered carelessly all about the place. The air smelled of stale alcohol and take-away meals. Pizza boxes, old newspapers, and empty beer bottles made walking across the room hazardous. Roxy couldn't believe it. Surely being a detective paid well enough to live better than this?

Johnson went to the old fridge, opened it, and pulled out a beer. He slammed it against the counter, popping the cap. Without offering one to Roxy, he moved to a worn-out armchair in the living room. Roxy felt fur brush against her bare leg. She jumped. Leo had padded inside to sit carefully beside the armchair, and Johnson reached down with his free hand to pat the large dog as he took a swig from his beer bottle.

"It's about . . . I wanted to tell you about . . ." Roxy began to speak but was distracted by looking for somewhere to sit. Eventually she shoved aside newspapers on the threadbare, brown striped couch opposite the detective's chair and carefully sat on the edge, reluctant to commit herself more fully. Who knew what dangers lurked deeper in those cushions? "It's about Patrice's murder. And Lacey's."

"Damnit!" the detective growled. "I *told* you not to investigate! What's wrong with you?" He took another angry swig. "Anyway, the cases are closed."

"It's just that—"

Johnson slammed the bottle against the arm of his chair. "I *knew* you were trouble the second you showed up," he continued. "Not for a second did I buy that whole 'cute and innocent' act. One second you're an out-of-towner running away from something, the next you're running a hotel, and now you're running about playing detective."

"I *wasn't* trying to—."

"I *know* you were nosing about," Johnson said, pointing one finger at Roxy, the rest wrapped around the neck of his bottle. He was still patting his dog with his other hand. "You can't help yourself."

"They were brother and sister!"

Johnson leaned forward in his chair to emphasize his point. "The cases are closed."

"And I have something else. Xavier, the restoration consultant on the bakery project for which Lacey was the city planning lead, lived with Patrice!"

"So?"

"And I received a note! An anonymous note! Surely, you're interested in that."

"Not really."

"If I didn't know better, Detective Johnson, I might think you were avoiding something. Your face is very red."

"Yeah, and it'll get redder if you don't beat it." He took

another swig of his beer, his lips squeaking against the rim of the glass. Roxy raised her eyebrows and waited. Johnson finished off his beer and, wiping his mouth on the back of his hand, threw the bottle onto another chair, where it landed softly.

"Now look, lil' Ms. Ohio, this isn't a game. This is bigger than both of us. Sometimes that's what happens. A man and his sister died. We—you and me—don't need to know why. Or when. Or by whom. There are other forces at work here. They're worrying about that. Now go home and forget all about it. Get on with your baking and playing house."

"So they *were* murdered! People are investigating."

"Go home."

Roxy sat up as straight as she could. "Make me."

Johnson's jaw clenched, and he let out a long exhale through his nose. He clasped his hands on his head and looked up at the ceiling before leaning forward, his elbows on his thighs, his hands dangling between them as he glared at Roxy, who steeled herself to meet his stare.

"We're dealing with killers here. Psychopaths. Criminals who know exactly what they're doing and wouldn't think twice about doing the same to *you*. And you're scooting about town in your short skirts and hot pants asking questions you really don't want the answer to, trust me. Well, eventually you're going to ask the wrong question of the wrong person at the wrong time. Then what do you think will happen?"

"I just wanted to figure out if . . ."

"Last time I checked, you were a hotel manager. And *I'm* a detective. Why don't we both stick to our jobs, okay? How would you feel if I turned up and started cleaning your guestrooms?"

Roxy laughed. She looked around. The idea of Johnson

cleaning anything seemed highly unlikely. "But Detective, you must pursue these cases. They must be reopened. Their killers haven't been apprehended. I've just given you a new lead." She reached into her bag and pulled out the anonymous note. "And . . . and I have another one."

Johnson flicked up his chin. "What is it?"

"Evangeline says Frank Ancelotti, the TV exec, the one who championed Elijah for the judge job, is mafioso."

"Don't say another word!" Johnson said, standing up so suddenly even his dog started.

"I don't understand," Roxy said.

"Good. Keep it that way," he said. "Just know this: all you're doing is getting yourself tangled up in something extremely dangerous. Now, for your own sake, Roxy Reinhardt, don't say anything else to anyone. And go home."

"But. . ."

"No buts," the detective interrupted, still standing. He pointed at the door. "I've got a very difficult shift coming up in an hour and I'd like to clean up. Please, leave and forget all about this before I start to wonder whether the only way to keep you out of trouble is to throw you in a cell myself."

Stunned and lost for words at his stonewalling, Roxy stood. The detective continued to point at the door, and she realized that trying to say anything else to him would be pointless. Even his dog seemed afraid to raise his head from his paws. She sighed and turned to leave.

All the way down the path and into the cab that was still waiting for her, Roxy struggled to figure out what had just happened. She couldn't understand why the detective was being so difficult. Johnson had been stubborn and frustrating from the first day she had met him, but refusing her help like this was beyond ridiculous.

"All done, lady?" the cab driver asked her as she got in.

"Yeah," she said disconsolately.

"Where to?"

"Do you know the Funky Cat Inn?"

"Ha! Who doesn't?" he said, firing up the engine and pulling out. "Everyone's talkin' about that place. I had a very nice Italian lady in my cab just the other day who couldn't stop talkin' about it."

Deep in thought this time, the cab driver's compliments passed Roxy by. She stared out of the window as the taxi turned and began to whisk her back through the rundown neighborhood. Nothing seemed to make sense. It was almost as if Johnson didn't even *want* to solve the murders. Confused, she replayed their conversation in her mind, searching it for clues.

Getting yourself tangled up in something extremely dangerous . . . Don't say anything else to anyone. And go home.

Distracted, the ad plastered to the seat back in front of her caught her attention. It was for *Ultimate Baker*.

"Thursday nights! 8-9:30! Hosted by Trey Ocean. ALHA-09."

"Sir," she said, leaning forward, her body working slowly to catch up with her brain. "Forget the Funky Cat. I need you to take me somewhere else, and *fast*."

CHAPTER FORTY-NINE

E VEN THOUGH SHE wanted to get there as quick as she could, it took Roxy a while to find Frank Ancelotti's address. She searched her handbag for his business card, and when she couldn't find it, she searched on her phone for his details. In the end, she tried Sam. He seemed to know just about everyone.

"Sam, do you have Frank Ancelotti's address?" Roxy was breathless.

"Somewhere. Why? Why do you want it?"

"I haven't got time to explain. I just need to speak to him."

"Rox—"

"Just give it to me, Sam!"

"Alright, alright. He owns a restaurant called Piacere. It means 'pleasant' in Italian. Are we still on for din—" The line went dead.

The taxi driver drove Roxy smartly through the city— straight into a traffic jam. "Protest march happening in the center of town. Streets are backed up," he informed her.

When the cab eventually stopped outside its destination, Roxy quickly paid and dashed out into the heat and then into the cool of the restaurant. Everything about Piacere communicated old-fashioned Italian—unsurprisingly considering its owner. It seemed more like an evening dinner sort of place, and it was very quiet when Roxy arrived at lunchtime.

Roxy pushed her way around the revolving door, which smartly deposited her in a dimly lit, cavernous room. Numerous round, white-clad tables topped with red napkins and unlit candles were arranged feet apart throughout. An Italian aria played quietly over the sound system, and Roxy could faintly smell the slightly acidic aroma of rich tomato and cream sauces coming from the kitchen. To one side was a beautiful, small mahogany bar stocked with wines and spirits. On the walls were black-and-white photographs of long-dead singers and celebrities, many of them signed. The whole place had an intimate, calm, romantic ambiance. Roxy immediately thought that even if Frank wasn't Mafia, this restaurant sure reminded her of the places she had seen in a lot of the movies.

Apart from Roxy, the only people present were two dark Italian waiters standing stiffly in front of the kitchen door and a young couple sitting by the window. One of the servers quickly approached her.

"Good afternoon, madam," he said with a heavy Italian accent. "How many for the table?"

"None, thank you. I need to speak with Frank."

"I beg your pardon?"

"Frank Ancelotti. I need to speak with him. Quickly. Is he here?"

The waiter stared at Roxy for a few seconds, then came to a decision. He gestured for her to follow him. When he reached a small table in the corner at the back, he pulled out a chair for her.

"Please wait here, madam."

Roxy sat down, and only then realized how anxious and out of breath she was. She tried to calm herself, taking deep breaths and closing her eyes as she figured out how she was going to say what she wanted to say. Nothing she rehearsed in her head sounded anything other than crazy.

After a few seconds, Frank emerged from the kitchen's swing doors accompanied by the waiter and another man in a suit. Suit man looked as serious as the waiters, but Frank wore his typical smile, but not, this time, his toupee.

"Roxy! What a surprise!" he beamed, opening his arms wide. Roxy stood up, and he hugged her warmly. Then he turned to the other men. "What is this? A restaurant or a desert? Bring the lady something to drink!" He turned to Roxy. "Are you hungry? What would you like? The fish is fantastic today."

"No thanks, nothing. I just need to talk."

"Of course, of course. But first you must try this wine. Very special—a classic Italian. I opened it to breathe half an hour ago. Lorenzo!" He briskly clapped his hands twice.

"*Si*," the waiter said quickly before dipping behind the small bar to grab glasses and the bottle.

Frank sat down, his smile unwavering. "What can I help you with, my dear?" he asked.

"It's about—"

"One moment," Frank said, getting up. He stepped away from the table and moved across the restaurant. Roxy watched him speak to the young couple who were just leaving. Frank, being Frank, was smiling and laughing and offering his thanks to them for choosing his restaurant. The waiter placed glasses on Roxy's table and poured wine while she sat at the table fidgeting. The longer she delayed, the more anxious she felt.

Eventually, Frank said goodbye to the young couple and returned to the table. "I'm so sorry. But I like to let my customers know they are appreciated."

"Yes, of course. I do the same with my guests."

"Please, go on. But try the wine first!"

Roxy sipped the wine quickly and nodded. "Yes, it's very nice."

"It's good, no?" Frank smiled.

"Very good. But Frank, please, I need you to listen."

"Go ahead."

Roxy took a deep breath. "It's about Patrice's murder. And Lacey's."

"Oh?" Frank replied, his smile straightening a little.

"Why is Detective Johnson refusing to investigate their murders?"

Frank spread his arms wide. "How should I know? Why don't you ask him?"

"I did. And when your name came up, he completely shut down and warned me off. Again."

Frank had been about to drink from his wine glass but was so focused on what Roxy was saying he placed the glass back down on the tablecloth without sipping from it. He pursed his lips and raised his glass again. This time he remembered to take a sip.

"But what does this have to do with me?"

"I don't know. I was hoping you could tell me." Roxy gripped her hands together so tightly her knuckles turned white, and her shoulders stiffened. She winced and opened her mouth to speak some more when, without warning, the air filled with the sound of police sirens. As the seconds passed, the volume rose sharply, the police cars approaching at speed. Tires screeched and car doors slammed. Roxy turned to look. The street filled with squad cars.

Doors opened, and she saw the heads of police officers taking cover behind them. She couldn't see any faces, but what she *could* see were gun barrels, and plenty of them. They were pointed at the restaurant.

CHAPTER FIFTY

A VOICE—AMPLIFIED AND distorted by a megaphone—boomed from the road outside. "Don't try to run, Ancelotti," the voice thundered. "We've got the restaurant surrounded. Don't do anything stupid. Come out with your hands up."

Frank ignored the instructions. Instead, he barked orders at his waiters. Roxy was stunned when she saw them produce guns of their own. Soon there were five men in the restaurant—the two waiters, the man in the suit, and two cooks in chef's hats—all carrying weapons. Big ones.

As if they were a highly trained tactical firearms unit (which perhaps they were), they assumed positions facing the doors, ready and focused. Frank ordered them around like a general.

"Lorenzo, behind the bar! Cover those officers to the right. Luca, Marco, use those tables as cover. Filipe, guard the back door; make sure they don't surprise us!"

"Frank! What are you doing?" Roxy exclaimed. She could barely believe what she was seeing.

"Please stay in the corner, Roxy," said Frank. She saw

he was carrying a silver pistol of his own. "I will try to get you out of this without you getting hurt."

"But what's going on?" Roxy stuttered. "I thought you were innocent!"

"I am!" Frank said. Roxy stared incredulously at the men with guns.

"Well, you aren't acting like it!"

"Of course I didn't kill Patrice. Or Lacey. Why would I?" Frank said, somehow managing to laugh despite facing the prospect of a shootout. "But I haven't always been so innocent. Johnson and me go way back. Back to the times when he was the only straight cop on the force, and I was involved in a bit of smuggling and theft—nothing too harmful, and certainly nothing I would ever get caught on. I always evaded him, and it's been eating at Johnson for years. Now it seems that the good detective thinks he can finally call in the debt and that it justifies this circus. Lorenzo! The curtains!" Frank flicked a glance at Roxy, who was now cowering under the table.

The waiter moved carefully to the windows and pulled a cord. The heavy, red velvet curtains dropped, the restaurant falling into darkness only dimly relieved by a lit candle left on the recently departed couple's table. The scene outside could now only be seen through the glass doors.

"Don't be stupid, Ancelotti!" the voice from the megaphone shouted. It was Johnson. "Nobody has to get hurt! Just come out slowly with your hands up."

"Just do what he says, Frank!" hissed Roxy. "You're innocent! You didn't kill Patrice! Or Lacey! There's no point anyone else getting killed!"

Frank laughed as he stood at the back of the restaurant, checking his gun. "That's not how the world works, my dear. Not mine, anyway. If I give myself up to Johnson, cops being cops, he'll find a way to put me in jail for the rest of my life—guilty or not. It's what he's wanted to do for years now. Johnson's just been biding his time."

"But what else can you do?" Roxy asked. Tired of sheltering under the table and forgetting herself as she argued for her conviction in justice, she stood up. "Shoot your way out of here? And then what?"

"I thought this day might come. Of course, I have a plan," Frank said. He laughed. "To escape and start a new life far away from here. Or alternatively . . . an honorable death." Frank looked at Roxy with a glint in his eye. "I've had a good life. You know, I bet heaven is like Italy." Frank picked up his wine glass and held it up to the light for a moment before sipping from it. "Better that than life in a cell."

"But what for? What have you done that would call for that?"

"Nothing really. But I have lived on the edge of things, Roxy. I've dangled from the precipice numerous times. There have been things you'd rather not know about. And I will spare you the details. I did not partake, but I didn't intervene either. Eventually, I turned over a new leaf, went legit. Oh, I know Alan and Paige merely tolerate me; I'm only an investor with no real skill in the TV world, but money makes the world go around, and it comes with a price. Nevertheless, despite my efforts, the past can catch up. Maybe this"—Frank nodded outside—"is my due."

"Frank Ancelotti," Johnson barked. He sounded even closer now. "We know you and your men are armed. You are a legitimate threat, and we *will* use force if you don't come out slowly with your hands up. This is your final warning."

Roxy felt her breath quicken and her heart thump. How

had she ended up in the middle of a shootout? Stuck between a mad Italian prepared to shoot to the death and a police detective who'd got his man completely wrong—was this really how she was going to die?

She hadn't felt this hopeless and desperate since that night in Ohio when she'd lost her job and her boyfriend all at once. Rock bottom. And here she was again.

Back then, she'd rescued the situation by taking a huge gamble. A massive risk. What if she could do that again here? Now?

Courage. That was what she needed. She'd had the courage to leave her whole life behind. The courage to build a new business from scratch. The courage to grab the man she was attracted to by the collar and kiss him. That's what it all came down to. Courage. Her past was small beer though, compared to this. Now, Roxy needed to confront a police department's worth of guns.

She lowered her shoulders. Straightened her back. Focusing on the restaurant's heavy wooden door handle, Roxy walked between the tables, past Frank, and past the armed waiters, refusing to consider what might await her when she opened the restaurant's front door.

CHAPTER FIFTY-ONE

"**H**EY! WHADDYA DOIN'?" Frank cried out. Roxy ignored him and pulled the door open, took a deep breath, and stepped outside.

She held up her hands and attempted to ignore the sound of shotguns and pistols being cocked. Nothing in her life had prepared her for this moment. She stared down the barrels of multiple weapons aimed directly at her. Not even her poverty-stricken childhood, workplace bullying, or abandonment had prepared her for the vulnerability she felt knowing that one small movement could end her life.

Roxy hesitated as she scanned the police cars and noted officers calmly staring back at her from behind their gun sights. She slowly stepped forward. Johnson stood behind an open car door directly in front. His eyes bored directly into her soul. He dropped his megaphone to his side and, after a few more seconds, indicated to his officers that they should lower their weapons.

"Clear the air," he shouted, though he was puce with anger seeing Roxy standing in the middle of the sidewalk, her hands above her head. She squinted in the sunlight like a dormouse awakening after a winter of hibernation.

Roxy stopped walking halfway between the restaurant door and Johnson's car. Beyond the row of police vehicles, she could see a crowd had gathered to watch the drama.

With a confidence she didn't feel and volume, Roxy shouted, "Frank Ancelotti did *not* kill Patrice Marveau! Or Lacey Gregory! You are all risking your lives for a wrong conclusion!"

The slew of police officers exchanged glances. They were unsure of what to think. The way Roxy had shouted was so authoritative that, despite her slight stature, it was almost impossible to doubt her.

Roxy resumed walking toward Johnson until she was close to him. Like an animatronic doll, she moved forward against all instructions and logic, almost daring Johnson to stop her one way or another.

"What are you doing?" he shouted, still stunned and angry. "Are you trying to get yourself killed? Stop!"

"I'm trying to get through to you, Detective Johnson," Roxy said, working herself into a fury as she considered how the detective ignored and mistrusted her. "You've got the wrong man. And while you're planning to shoot up a restaurant, Patrice's and Lacey's real killers are roaming free about the city!"

"His 'real killers,' huh?" Johnson retorted.

"That's right," Roxy said. "Zach and Mickey."

Johnson looked at her, confused. "Who?" he asked.

Roxy sighed, disappointed that the detective was so far behind her. "The head cameraman and sound operator at the studio. They work on *Ultimate Baker*."

"Cameraman? Sound? What are you talking about?"

"Nobody hated Patrice more than the crew," Roxy said.

"He was vain and difficult and always blaming them for how he came across. Every single member of the crew dreaded the prospect of Patrice being chosen because that would mean having to work with him."

"Marveau annoyed everyone around him," Johnson said. "That's hardly a revelation."

"The day after Patrice's body was found, I was at the studio. Zach had bruises all over his knuckles, and one of his fingers seemed stiff. He'd injured his hand."

"The camera operator? He works with heavy equipment all day. Probably just hurt himself doing that."

Roxy sighed, exasperated by the brick wall the detective was putting up. "Patrice was beaten and thrown into a dumpster days before the decision was made about the third judge job on *Ultimate Baker*. Lacey was hit over the head and dumped in a cabinet just as the wrecking ball was about to come down on the bakery. I am not sure of the motive for her killing, maybe she was onto them, but Zach and Mickey were there filming that day. They are the common link. I'm sure they had something to do with her death."

Johnson looked at her incredulously, then nodded at the restaurant behind Roxy. "Frank's guys are pretty tough, and direct too. Mafioso also have reason to want Marveau and Gregory dead. Mafia have their fingers in lots of the building projects in this town. The city goes along with them, overlooking and overseeing. It's too dangerous not to. Except an upstart, a perfectionist like Lacey Gregory, wouldn't play ball. Patrice's death was a warning to her. She carried on regardless. When she wouldn't bow down to them, they killed her. Lacey Gregory is a hero."

Roxy paused for a moment. The idea that Lacey was the main target in a double murder was news to her. That Johnson considered her a hero, even stranger.

"Then why did you say Patrice was killed by a homeless man and Lacey's death was an accident?"

Johnson didn't answer.

Roxy and Johnson stood staring at each other in silence. The cops around them stood down, bored now.

But Roxy wouldn't give up. "It makes more sense that Zach and Mickey were pushed so far by Patrice after the screen tests that they decided to take matters into their own hands." Johnson sighed and looked around him, reluctant but unable to dismiss Roxy so easily now.

Roxy continued. "I was just in there with Frank. He's ready to die. I think he presumed he would. He could have told me anything and it wouldn't have mattered. And still, even when it didn't matter at all, he told me that he had nothing to do with Patrice's and Lacey's murders. I'm telling you, Detective, he's not your guy."

Johnson stared at her for a couple more seconds, then glanced behind her at the restaurant before turning back to the car. "Okay, boys," he yelled at his officers. "Roll out. Santos, Pearle, Banks, and Barnes— get in there and arrest the lot o' them *if*"—he glared at Roxy—"they're still in there. The rest of you follow my car. We're heading to the studios to talk to a few people."

"Let me come with you," Roxy said, following the detective as he got inside his unmarked car.

"No chance," Johnson said. "You're lucky you haven't got yourself killed already. Remind me to arrest you for obstructing justice the next time I see you."

The detective slammed his door shut and left Roxy standing in the street as his car screeched away. Roxy watched them go until her heart leapt. Big, strong arms wrapped themselves around her.

"Roxy! What happened?" Sam said, hugging her to him.

He let go and spun her around, holding her by the shoulders and staring, concerned and stupefied, into her face.

"Sam?"

"I was worried when you said you wanted Frank's address. Then a friend called me. He said you were in a standoff with the police. What's going on?"

"Do you have your van here?"

"Of course."

"Let's go," Roxy said quickly. "We need to get to the television studio. I'll tell you everything on the way."

CHAPTER FIFTY-TWO

I N THE VAN, Roxy and Sam quickly lost sight and sound of the police cars, which had used their sirens to ease a path through the compacted traffic. Sam took a more creative route through the city, using backstreets and side roads that he was familiar with, but it still took them a while to reach the studio.

By the time they arrived, the police cars had already parked just outside the entrance. On the drive over Roxy had explained everything to Sam—her theory that the real killers were Zach and Mickey, her problem explaining it to Detective Johnson, and the standoff at Frank's restaurant. When they finally got to the studio, Sam pulled the car over and looked at her.

"I don't get it, Roxy. Why are we here? What's the plan? The cops have blockaded the building. Let's leave them to it. You've already risked your life once today."

"Let's just wait here a second," Roxy said, focusing on the studio building.

For a whole minute they waited. Sam went from staring

at the building—not sure what he was looking for—and then staring at Roxy, wondering what she was thinking.

Suddenly Roxy bounced out of her seat. "There! Sneaking out the side entrance! Quick! Sam! Let's do something!"

As soon as she said it, Sam fired up the van's engine and spun out into the street. He drove across it quickly, almost causing two cars to collide. The van mounted the sidewalk, Sam maneuvering it into the small alley into which a woman had emerged.

"Don't try to run, Jocelyn!" Roxy shouted. "It's over!"

Behind Roxy there was a commotion. Both she and Sam turned to see Zach and Mickey running, two police officers in hot pursuit. Their guns drawn, the cops trained them at the two men, shouting at them to drop to the ground. With cop cars blocking their path, the men did as they were told and slowed up, raising their hands. Pushed to the ground, they lay spreadeagled as they were cuffed and read their rights.

Roxy turned back to Jocelyn. She had gone. Roxy glanced up the alleyway. Ahead, running as fast as her little legs would carry her, her pink jacket flapping behind her, was Jocelyn. Blood pounding in her ears, Roxy sprinted to catch her. It took a few good strides. Roxy wasn't tall, and Jocelyn, while no expert runner, had a good start on her.

"Jocelyn! Stop," Roxy urged. "The game is up!" With every stride, Roxy gained on the makeup artist. She was close enough she could see the tread marks in Jocelyn's tennis shoes below the cuffed ankles of her sweats. Two more long strides and Roxy launched herself, flying through the air just before crashing into Jocelyn, grabbing her waist as she knocked the makeup artist facedown to the ground.

Roxy grabbed Jocelyn's wrists and pulled them behind

her back. "You're the ringleader, aren't you? Zach and Mickey were just your heavies, carrying out your instructions. What was it? Revenge for all the ways Patrice mistreated you? And what about Lacey? What did she ever do to you? Was she on to you, huh? Huh? Is that why she met you in the women's room? She told you she suspected you of killing her brother, didn't she? Or ordering your henchmen to do it. Is that why I saw her leaving the bathroom ahead of you and then you coming out all teary that time?" Jocelyn was a lot bigger than Roxy, and she struggled. In danger of losing her grip, Roxy did what she'd seen somewhere—TV perhaps. She put her knee on Jocelyn's back as she held her wrists.

Breathless, Sam ran up to help her, and together they turned Jocelyn over. When she saw her captive's face, Roxy sat back in horror. "Jenny!" The studio talent wrangler averted her eyes.

"Roxy! Can I help you?" This time the real Jocelyn appeared at Sam's elbow. Roxy stood up, astounded, casting glances between the two women. Perversely, considering the situation, she was most struck by the fact that the complexion of the sweating, panting young woman who had just run up to her perfectly complemented her peach and cream sweatsuit.

Roxy was so distracted by her mistake she barely noticed Detective Johnson walk up to them. "I thought I told you not to come here."

"You wouldn't have caught them if it wasn't for her!" Sam said, immediately jumping to Roxy's defense.

A little dazed now that it was really over, Roxy turned to the detective slowly.

"I had a feeling they would run the second they saw you and your officers," Roxy explained.

Detective Johnson grunted. "You and your *feelings*."

Sam, still defensive, said, "Sounds like you could do with a few more feelings yourself, Detective."

Johnson glared at them both a little more, grunted one more time, and turned back to his officers, instructing them to bring the now-handcuffed Jenny to the station.

"Come on, Roxy," Sam said, putting an arm around her and turning her back to the van. "I think that's about as much thanks as you're going to get from the detective today. Are we still on for dinner?"

CHAPTER FIFTY-THREE

I T TOOK SAM and Roxy so long to navigate the New Orleans traffic that by the time they reached the Funky Cat, the news had beaten them. Evangeline, Sage, and Nat were all pacing about the hotel lobby as they listened to the couple who'd dined earlier at Frank's restaurant being interviewed about the slight blonde woman who had later faced down the police with guns on the sidewalk. As soon as Roxy stepped through the door, she was overwhelmed by bear hugs, everyone glad that she was okay. Minutes after they arrived, Elijah also burst through the door.

"Oh my *God!*" Elijah exclaimed. "You *have* to tell me what's happening!"

Evangeline hurried to bring some of that day's beignets and some fresh coffee to the table as they all sat around, eager to hear Roxy's tale. Carefully, she explained everything—from her finding out Xavier was Patrice's roommate, to her noticing Zach's hands were injured, the revelation that Patrice and Lacey were siblings, and Johnson's strange insistence that the circumstances around their deaths were resolved.

"That day I was at the studio, the day after Patrice's body had been found, I saw Jocelyn coming out of the bathroom all weepy. I'd seen Lacey come out before her. I didn't recognize her at the time, but I realized after Elijah wanted his close-up at the construction site that all three of them—Zach, Mickey, and Jocelyn—had been there the day of the demolition. I thought that Zach and Mickey had killed Patrice, urged on by Jocelyn, because they hated him. I also suspected that Lacey had confronted Jocelyn in the studio bathrooms, and so they killed her too because she was onto them. But I was mistaken. Before Jocelyn appeared, Jenny had left the bathroom that day. She'd been flustered. I now think that Lacey had told *Jenny* she was onto her, and Jocelyn had overheard the conversation as she hid in a stall. The conversation had frightened her, hence her tears. I also suspect that the anonymous note was to put me—us—off the scent and was written by Jenny.

"When I was at his house, I realized that Johnson thought Mafia were behind the murders and that probably Frank was involved by the way he seemed to shut me down. So I went to see Frank to warn him. As you know, it didn't turn out quite as I planned."

The others asked questions, and Roxy answered them as best she could. She was still shaken and shocked by everything that had happened. Once she was done, the others talked among themselves, and she finally realized how exhausted and light-headed she was. "I think I'll have to skip dinner tonight, if you don't mind," she said to Sam.

Sam looked at her exhausted expression and chuckled. "Of course. I think you've done enough for one day."

"I can't believe the detective didn't listen to you. People might have been killed," Nat said.

"Detective Johnson is a man of very dense, closed-off energy," Sage said. "I suppose his job has made him like that. This was an occasion that called for a different type of soul."

"I remember when Roxy first came here," Evangeline mused, "there was more bite 'n' bark in a timid church mouse. Now look at her! Standin' up in front of a firin' squad! Good on you, cher!"

"It's incredible," Sam agreed. "I don't think a lot of people would have had the courage to do that."

"You're so brave, Roxy," Nat agreed.

"I *had* to do something," Roxy said, blushing a little.

"The first thing I'd have to do if surrounded by crazy men with guns," said Elijah, "is visit the little boys' room. Just thinking about it makes me shake with fear."

"Are you okay, Roxy?" Sam said gently. "You look a little pale."

"Yes, I'm fine," Roxy answered. "I'm just tired. It's been a crazy day."

"Get yourself up to bed, cher," Evangeline said. "We'll take care of the hotel. You work too hard as it is, and now you've a second job as a heroine. The press'll come swarmin' around here any minute. We'll take care of them for you."

Roxy laughed and was about to object—she never liked leaving others to do the work—but Nat jumped in. "Yes. Go rest, Roxy. We can handle everything here. You deserve it."

Roxy shrugged and sighed. "Thanks. I should probably take some time to get my head straight."

As everyone got up from the table, Roxy moved to help clear the plates, but Nat smacked her hand away. Roxy smiled back at her and then turned to leave. Before she reached the doorway, Elijah caught up with her and touched her arm.

"Hey," he said in a quiet voice.

"Hey," Roxy replied, equally hushed.

"I'm so sorry, Roxy. I have been such a fool. I don't know what came over me. I have been an absolute beast. Not just once, or twice, but at least three times." Elijah clasped his hands together. "Will you please, please, *please* forgive me? I swear I'll do better."

Roxy eyed Elijah's earnest expression. "The thing is, Elijah, you've apologized to me before and then carried on just as you were. Words without actions are meaningless. You'll have to prove you mean it to me."

"Of course, anything. I'll do anything. Tell me what to do."

"I want you to go back to being the fun, kind, humble person you used to be before you took on that judge's role. We are not impressed by your fame. We want the old Elijah back, capiche?"

"Yes, oh yes, I promise."

"And it will take time before we trust you again, y'hear?"

Elijah looked somber. "Yes, I understand. I'll work hard to make it up to you, Roxy. I promise. No more throwing my weight around, being unreliable or unkind."

"Good, glad to hear it. Now, go and help Nat and Evangeline. And tomorrow night, we'll have a big dinner. Invite your fellow judges and those producers, Alan and Paige. Frank, if he's no longer arrested. Also, Annie and Xavier. We'll make an event of it and show there's no hard feelings, put the past behind us. I'll see you in the morning." Elijah scuttled off, taking a pile of plates from Evangeline and holding open the kitchen swing door for her.

Sam came up to Roxy. "I managed to speak with George this morning."

"Oh, great. How is he?"

"Better. At least he's not wandering the streets at night anymore."

"Why don't you invite him to dinner tomorrow night?"

"Are you sure?"

"Yup, I'm organizing a big dinner tomorrow night to celebrate everything. Can you make it? I've told Elijah to bring his friends."

Sam's handsome face split into a big grin. "Sure. Sounds great. I'll bring my sax. It'll be like the old times."

CHAPTER FIFTY-FOUR

R OXY WAS UP early. The night before she had
crashed out quickly in her room and slept peace-
fully. Once Roxy had showered, dressed, and
given Nefertiti a good morning scritch, she went downstairs
to check on things. Judging by the rock music blaring out of
the kitchen, she guessed Nat was in there and that she was
alone. (Evangeline never liked listening to that sort of thing.)
Roxy turned toward the kitchen.

"Hey, you." Roxy stopped, startled a little, and spun
around to find Detective Johnson sitting on the small bench
by the front window. He looked tired and unshaven, still in
the same clothes he had worn yesterday at the confrontation
in front of Frank's restaurant.

"Detective," Roxy said, still stunned.

Johnson stood up and approached her. "Just finished my
shift," he growled, pulling out a pack of gum. He
unwrapped a stick and slowly put it in his mouth. "Thought
I'd drop by and update you on a few things."

Roxy looked at him, wondering if she was in trouble. He

offered her some gum from the pack, but she shook her head.

"Tell me what?" she asked.

Johnson shoved the gum back into his jacket pocket. "We got 'em," he said. "Forensics matched Patrice Marveau's injuries to camera equipment in the camera-man's van. His fingerprints were all over it, and so was a trace of Patrice's DNA. The sound guy confessed to being an accessory, getting Marveau down the alleyway where he got pummeled. He talked quite a bit when we put a little pressure on him.

"They confessed to the sister's killing too. They followed her into the building on teardown day under the pretense they were filming a bit for the TV show. They hit her on the head and bundled her in a cabinet. They didn't expect her to be found, but I guess because they weren't construction guys, they didn't know how to set it up so that she wasn't.

"And they both turned on the wrangler chick who hated Marveau's guts. Apparently, the sister was onto the wran-gler woman and let her know, signing her own death warrant in the process. I've been up all night pulling the truth out of them, compiling the evidence, and filling in the reports, but it's over. The three of them committed both murders."

Roxy reached into her bag. "I meant to give you this the other day, but I didn't get the chance. Perhaps it will help the case against them." She handed over the letter that had arrived anonymously on her doormat.

"Thank you," Johnson said.

"I put it in a plastic bag and everything,"

"I can see that."

"Would you like some coffee?" Roxy offered, hearing

weariness in the detective's voice. "I was about to get some myself."

"No. I need to get home to Leo."

"Of course."

"I just wanted to tell you that . . ." The detective trailed off, as if reluctant to say the words. "You were right."

Roxy nodded, knowing that it hurt Johnson to say that and not wanting to rub it in. "I'm just glad they were caught in the end."

Johnson sighed heavily. "It could have gone a lot differently," he said. "People could have gotten killed as we tried to arrest Frank Ancelotti. Zach and Mickey and the girl could have gotten away with the whole thing. You are a difficult person to deal with, Miss Reinhardt. You don't listen and you stick your nose in where it doesn't belong. Part of me wants to shout at you for getting in the middle of a shootout; the other part of me wants to apologize for not listening to you."

Roxy laughed to show there were no hard feelings. "I'll just presume you did both," said Roxy. Johnson nodded, and his lips widened—maybe the closest he ever got to a genuine smile.

"In my defense," he said, "there was a reason I didn't listen to you when you came to my house. I was told to lay off the cases because well, I shouldn't tell you really, but there's a big drug operation happening, and it was thought that the killings were related to that. The cases got shut down by the higher-ups, and I was told to move along.

"So, I kept telling you to be quiet, but you wouldn't listen. I needed you to stop sniffing around. If you knew something that could be used as evidence, I'd have had to involve you in the case. You'd have become a witness for the prosecution; you'd have to testify. There'd have been a price on your head. You'd be in witness protection for the rest of your life. Or dead. I was trying to save you that."

Roxy nodded, suddenly understanding. "So you didn't want to hear what I had to say because it might put a target on my back. Well, thank you, I suppose, for not listening to me," Roxy said, smiling a little at the joke. "But what was the standoff about?"

"I followed you after you left my house, and when I realized that you were going to Frank's place, I felt I had to act, big Mafia case or no. I couldn't let you walk into the lion's den alone. You could have gotten killed. I should have let you hoist yourself on your own petard, I suppose, but I couldn't."

"So you thought I was in danger, decided to ignore your bosses and haul Frank in, and save me in the process."

"Something like that. Even faced with all my generosity, you wouldn't go quietly!"

Johnson gave a half smile, then nodded as if that was all he had to say. He turned to leave, but Roxy felt a sudden urge. "Detective," she said. He stopped and looked back at her. "Can I ask you a question? A personal one?"

He turned to face her; his brows knitted together. "What?"

"I was just wondering," Roxy began, suddenly questioning the wisdom of what she was about to say. She pressed on regardless. "Why do you . . . live the way you do?" Johnson frowned, puzzled. "In that part of town. In an old house. Rundown. I was surprised."

In her head, the question had seemed sympathetic and friendly, an attempt to break through the detective's gruff exterior and relate to him as a person. As the words came out, however, she realized how judgmental and patronizing they sounded.

Luckily, Johnson seemed to take her words positively. He nodded slowly, as if he knew exactly what she meant.

"Same old story," he said gruffly. "Divorced a few years ago. She got the house, the car, alimony. I was left with nothing but my job and my dog. Then again, those are the only things I ever paid any attention to. That was the problem in the first place."

"Oh, I see," Roxy said.

Johnson did that strange half smile thing again. "You're a young woman with the skills to acquire and run a hotel, the confidence to face down virtually an entire precinct of police officers with guns, and the smarts to figure out two murders with a hundred possible suspects. What makes a woman like that leave Ohio for a place like NOLA?"

Roxy laughed gently. "I told you before, Detective," she said. "My boyfriend left me. I got fired. And my cat got excited over an ad for Mardi Gras. It's crazy, but it's true."

Johnson nodded again. Roxy wondered if he was thinking about the similarities between them—that both had experienced relationship breakups and hard times. She wondered if he was also thinking that she had taken an opportunity to start a whole new life, while he had succumbed to a life of emptiness in a rundown house surrounded by empty beer bottles and takeaway food boxes.

"Are you sure you won't have that coffee?" Roxy suggested again.

Johnson raised a hand to decline, as if too tired to speak now, and turned to leave for real this time. Roxy watched him, his shoulders slumped, shuffle out of the hotel. She sighed. She felt sorry for him.

"Thank you, Detective." Johnson half turned. "For everything."

CHAPTER FIFTY-FIVE

THERE WAS A party atmosphere in the hotel. Everyone was still talking about the dramatic events of the day before—especially now that it was all over the news. Even the guests had found out their hotel was managed by the heroine of a standoff who had captured the mastermind behind a double murder plot.

Roxy began to feel like a celebrity. Everyone was so keen to speak to her that she barely got any work done. Before she knew it, it was late afternoon, and she gave up. With a lot of guests turning up to dinner, it was all hands on deck in the kitchen. Sage chipped in to help, and even Sam took off his dinner jacket and lent a hand washing pots and cleaning surfaces.

Planning the meal had been the biggest challenge. Evangeline was taking the night off, so it was down to Roxy and Nat to prepare the menu. Roxy kept thinking of Paige and Alan. "What kind of food would make people like that relax and enjoy themselves, Nat?"

Nat had merely shrugged. "Whatever tastes good and fills their bellies, I reckon."

By evening, the whole hotel was blanketed with the sweet and savory smells of roasted meat, grilled seafood, buttery sauces, and rich marinades. The air conditioner blasted cool air over everyone to prevent them from overheating.

"Are you eating with us tonight, Sage?" asked Roxy as she tossed a pan over flickering flames on the grill.

"Have you got room?" Sage replied as she prepared a salad.

"Of course!" Roxy said. "Plus, you have to come so you can do your tarot reading. Guests always love it."

"Maybe not *these* guests," Sam said as he brought in another sack of potatoes from the outside store. He leaned over to whisper in Roxy's ear. "He's coming. George. He says he'll come. Tonight. I'm going to go pick him up." Roxy nodded surreptitiously as Sam slipped out the back door.

"I should go home to shower and change if I'm eating with you," Sage said.

"Me too, actually," Roxy commented, moving the pan away from the grill and wiping her forehead. "Nat? I think we're mostly done if you want to go and get ready for tonight."

"Sure," Nat said. "I'll just lay the table first. So it's you, me, Sage, Sam, Elijah, Paige and Alan, Frank, Annie, Xavier. Ten. Oh, and my friend. Eleven."

Roxy froze. "Who's that?" she asked casually.

"My friend. Remember I asked you if I could bring him to dinner sometime? He's coming tonight."

"Ah, right," Roxy said, her heart pounding as she thought of George. Were things gonna get awkward? "Sam's bringing a friend too. So that's twelve. Okay, I'm going to get ready. Time's getting on, and they'll show up any minute now."

Roxy checked on Nefertiti before she went up to her room. Her white cat was lazing about in front of the hotel with her new boyfriend—the ginger tabby. He was a little jumpy and protective of her, prowling as she lay lazily on the floor, occasionally flicking her fluffy white tail.

Roxy smiled at them, then went upstairs to take a long shower. She tossed on a satin, turquoise dress that she had bought herself as a treat. It had a plunging neckline, a low back, and folds which caught the light, making it shimmer, drawing attention to her. It was the sort of dress Roxy had always thought looked magical and beautiful on celebrities.

Until recently, that she could wear something like it had never occurred to her. As if it were not just a dress she was putting on, but an entire personality. Perhaps it was, she thought as she turned and looked at herself in the mirror.

Maybe it was New Orleans that made her feel so good in this dress. Its sophistication would have been out of place in her boxy little apartment back in Ohio, but here it coordinated with the elegant architecture of the French hotel she lived in now. All the sweet, rich food had filled out her body a little, and her formerly petite, boyish figure now had a few curves. She stood a little better, her posture a bit straighter, her chin higher. She no longer walked with her head down, as if ashamed of something or avoiding other people's eyes. Roxy no longer felt intimidated by such a beautiful dress. She felt fabulous in it.

She fixed her hair. Her short, blonde pixie-cut never needed much work, a bit of finger combing was all. She put on some chandelier earrings. After trying out a bunch of other accessories, she settled on a green pendant hung on a thin gold chain that Sage had given her. She also wore a gold bracelet and blush-pink high heels.

She looked at her watch. It was time to go. The sounds

of multiple people talking wafted up to her. The guests were arriving. Roxy checked herself one last time in the mirror, adding the final touch to her appearance, and plastered an elegant, welcoming smile on her pretty face.

The hotel slowly filled up with noise and people enticed by the gathering aromas of Nat's cooking as they readied for that evening's dinner. Elijah arrived after his TV shoot, early and happy to help out. Annie showed up dressed to the nines in a silky, white jumpsuit. Xavier stayed away.

Roxy descended the hotel stairs as executives Paige and Alan, Frank, newly released from custody, and Elijah stood talking loudly in the lobby. Alan wore a pinstripe suit and tie. Paige looked impressive in a tight, brown leather skirt and loose white blouse. Her brunette hair was radiant, the red highlights lit up by the light of the sparkling chandeliers. One by one, the guests caught sight of Roxy in her satin gown and stopped talking to look at her, open-mouthed and wide-eyed.

Frank whistled, then said, "Wow! Should have kept the cameras rollin', boys! That's a scene right there!" Newly released under caution, Frank had brought a bottle of "the wine we didn't get to enjoy last time."

A little embarrassed by his effusiveness, Roxy widened her smile at the compliment. "Dinner is ready when you are," she said.

"Fantastic. I'm sure everyone is as hungry as I am," Paige replied.

Alan, Paige, Elijah, Frank, and Annie followed Roxy to the dining room to take their seats. Nat and Sage had laid the table and were adding the final touches to the food. The aromas from the kitchen were exciting, and Frank was full of laughs as he spoke with Elijah. Roxy took her seat and looked around, enjoying the atmosphere. Annie and Paige spoke animatedly, like they were girlfriends of old. Alan entertained Elijah with stories of the most charming celebrities.

Sage came through from the kitchen wearing a beautiful green robe with a silver belt that showed off her slim waist and elegant posture. She had let her hair down to fall about her shoulders. She was followed by Nat. Even Nat was wearing a neat little black vest over a black, ankle-length skirt.

Later there would be music. Roxy couldn't wait to hear Sam play his saxophone as he usually did after dinner. Elijah would take up the piano, and Nat would sing. It was the highlight of such evenings. But first there would be food.

CHAPTER FIFTY-SIX

"**Y**OU'RE KILLIN' ME here!" Frank announced suddenly. "If I don't get to eat what I'm smellin' soon . . ."

"It does smell great," Elijah agreed. "What is it?"

"For the starter," Nat said, "we have chargrilled oysters. A New Orleans classic. They're grilled over fire with lots of herbs and butter, as well as a little cheese. They're very good."

Frank was already tucking in his napkin. "I'm drooling like a dog already!" he said, summoning a vision Roxy rather he hadn't.

"I'll bring the starters out now," Nat said, going to the kitchen.

"Can't wait." Alan smiled.

"Smells wonderful," Paige agreed as they sat down.

Roxy was pleased to see the two of them relaxing a little at the table. She had been a little unsure about inviting the two TV executives. She found them intimidating. Perhaps things really would go well tonight.

Soon the wine was being poured, and people started to

fall into conversation. Platters of oysters were placed in front of them. Squeals and coos of delight rose from the table at the sight. Then the noise died down as everyone focused only on eating.

When they were almost done with the oysters, Paige looked up at Roxy and said, "The rooms of the hotel are really beautiful."

"Thank you," Roxy said. "Sam and I worked on them together. We put a lot of energy into renovating the place."

"It sure is nice here," Alan added. "We might need a location like this in the future. Do you rent it out for shoots and things like that?"

Roxy thought for a second. "Well, we've never had anyone film here before . . . It sounds fun though. Call me any time and we can talk about it."

"I might just do that," Alan said.

Elijah looked at Roxy, his eyebrows raised. His expression said "look at you go, girl!" Roxy smiled shyly and looked down at her food. Despite the shenanigans of the past few days, her newfound confidence was still a little shaky. What did they call it? Imposter syndrome. Yes, that was it.

Nat cleared the oysters and disappeared into the kitchen. A couple of minutes later, Frank called from the other end of the table, "Are we going to eat or are you just going to torture us with these smells? Do I have to call my guys here and shoot our way into the kitchen? Ha!"

Roxy laughed and called back to him, "Sure, Frank. Give us one second. I'll just pop into the kitchen and give Nat a hand." Roxy elegantly left her seat and pushed through the swing door to the kitchen. She glanced at her watch. Sam and George still hadn't arrived. Neither had Nat's friend.

"How're you doing?" Roxy asked Nat as she entered. "Everyone's waiting."

"Yeah, yeah," Nat replied, sounding a little anxious. "The food's ready."

"What's the matter?"

"Nothing," Nat said, sounding unconvincing. "I'm just . . ."

She was interrupted by her phone. She quickly checked it and immediately the anxiety in her face disappeared.

"*Finally,*" she said, dashing for the door. "My friend's here."

Roxy blew out her cheeks but joined the others around the dining table as Nat ran outside. A few seconds later, she came back in with a tanned, happy-looking man. He was wearing loose slacks and a blousy, swirl-patterned shirt. He swayed as he walked, like Elijah, his eyes wide and interested in everything around him.

"Everybody," Nat announced. She looked very happy. "I'd like to introduce you to my friend: Larry Cross."

The others all greeted Larry warmly, shaking his hand and introducing themselves.

"Hi there," Roxy said. "Nice to meet you."

"Likewise," Larry said. Larry sat down at the table setting that had been readied for the missing Xavier, and Nat placed a couple of leftover oysters on his plate.

"Hey, where's Xavier tonight?" Elijah asked Annie. "There was no reply when I called him to invite him tonight."

"I've no idea," Annie answered. "Although I'm not entirely unhappy about it. He gave me the creeps."

Paige leaned over. "I hear he's skipped town."

"What?" Roxy said. "Whyever would he do that?"

"He's about to be exposed," Alan said.

"Exposed?" Elijah said. "As what?"

"As a conman. He is not the esteemed restoration specialist and historian you all thought he was. Our investigative journalism unit has been following him for months. We're making a documentary about him. We contacted him yesterday to allow him to give his side of the story." Alan looked about him. "And here we are. No Xavier Jean-Pierre."

"That's not even his real name," Paige added.

"My, my," Elijah said, his eyes wide. "What is his real name?"

"John Brown."

"Nothing wrong with a name like John Brown," Nat said.

"No, but it doesn't have quite the same ring about it as Xavier Jean-Pierre, does it?" Elijah countered with a heavy French accent. "Well, well, well."

"Sounds like that fortune teller was right," Roxy said. "She warned him about a mask slipping."

"She was right about me too," Annie said. "She mentioned a terrible tragedy that happened to me. Years ago, my ex-husband was killed on a building site that I was overseeing. It was eventually considered an accident, but there was suspicion for a while that I had killed him. It was amazing that the fortune teller knew about that. She was really something."

"She even was right about Jocelyn," Elijah said. "She's given up being a MUA. Said she'd always dreamt of something more, and now I've got to find someone else to make me look incredible. I wouldn't mind, but she's gone off to pursue her dream to be a wrestler!" Elijah looked pained at the thought.

"Are we all done with the starters then?" Roxy said

cheerfully. While she was pleased for Jocelyn, she wanted to move along from death and darkness. She was determined not to let a cloud settle over the sumptuous feast. There were murmurs of agreement and satisfaction around the table. "Good. Nat, would you bring out the main course?"

Nat nodded and got up out of her seat to go to the kitchen.

"What's it to be?" Frank asked eagerly. "I don't know how you're going to top a starter like *that!*"

Roxy laughed. "Étouffée. Crawfish and vegetables in a thick, nutty, savory sauce. Lots of herbs and Cajun seasoning. It's a stew, sort of like gumbo but thicker. Something of a specialty here at the hotel. We serve it with a selection of sides. 'Dirty' rice—that's rice with ground pork, celery, and a lot of herbs and spices. Okra fried in buttermilk. Cajun-spiced sweet potato fries. And lots of freshly baked po'boy bread to accompany it."

Frank whistled the same way he had after seeing Roxy in her dress. She smiled as the table started talking among themselves in impressed voices.

Nat arrived and started putting plates in front of everyone. Sage followed her, carrying the bowl of étouffée. The smell of the food was sweet, savory, meaty, and nutty all at once, and almost all the guests were distracted by it. They quickly started passing around side dishes and trying the food out while Sage ladled the étouffée onto their dinner plates.

"Mm-mm," Elijah said. "You won't find food like this anywhere else in America, or even the world. And I'll tell you why. Because this isn't just food here—this is *history*. You start with French cuisine—since this was once a French colony—and their particular taste for dense, savory flavors.

You add the Spanish and their liking of one-pot foods, the Creole, Acadians, influences from the Caribbean, from African slaves, and you start to get sweeter flavors, the complex spice blends. And because a lot of those people were poor, you start to get clever workarounds to bring about the flavors. Add in some of the freshest, best shellfish in the world, and you get something special. Something that could only happen right here in NOLA. There's nowhere else like New Orleans," Elijah finished, smiling. Roxy smiled right back at him approvingly. Elijah caught her eye and winked.

As they ate their way through the crawfish, Sage explained the different crystals she was wearing to Paige. Alan and Elijah talked business, while Roxy chatted with Larry. Eventually, Frank, who talked to no one, leaned back in his chair, patted his belly, and groaned. "Oh boy," he announced. "I'm about seventy percent crawfish right now."

The table laughed and Roxy said, "Well, let's fill the other thirty percent with dessert then. Everyone done with their main?"

Everyone nodded. They all looked sleepy and very satisfied. Roxy turned to Nat. She nodded at the empty plates. "Shall we . . .?

CHAPTER FIFTY-SEVEN

"THERE YOU GO, Frank," Roxy said as she placed his dessert in front of him. "This is a New Orleans-style apple pie—spiced with cinnamon and cloves. But the real specialty are the pralines, pecans in a caramel made from buttermilk. You'll love them." Frank nodded, already happily chewing on one.

The table was lively and chatty now. Sage had already pulled out her tarot cards, and Paige and Frank seemed intrigued. It was amusing to see the female executive relax. Gone was the brisk formality of earlier. Now she seemed more like a fascinated teenager. She was hanging on Sage's every word.

"What's that about singing?" Frank said, his eyes wide as he stole a praline from Paige's plate while she was entranced by Sage's reading of the tarot. "Is it time for music?" Frank opened his arms wide and quickly swallowed what he was chewing. "I'm right here!"

"You can sing?" Nat asked.

"I come from a long line of great male tenors," Frank said. He was serious.

Elijah and Roxy looked at each other. "Let's give it a shot," Nat said.

Soon they were all arranged: Elijah on piano, Nat as backup, Frank front and center at the mic stand.

It turned out that Frank was a terrible singer. But he knew all the words to New Orleans classics like "I'll Fly Away" and "On Mardi Gras Day." Also, he sang with such energy and enthusiasm it was funny and infectious—if a little out of tune. The guests around the table enjoyed it greatly, laughing and singing along. Even Paige and Alan seemed less frosty toward Frank as he made them laugh with another rollicking chorus. And soon he gave way to Nat. Like the club audience, they were absolutely silent.

After five songs, Nat took a short break. Midway through Nat's set, Sam had sidled into the room and joined her on his sax. Now they both sat down next to Roxy and Larry. "You look a little familiar. . ." Sam said, turning to Larry and squinting at him.

Nat rolled her eyes. "You can lay off the act now," she said, looking at Sam, then at Roxy. "Both of you."

"What do you mean?" Roxy asked.

"I saw you in the audience that night," Nat remarked.

Sam and Roxy swapped a quick, guilty look. Then Sam looked back at Larry and gasped.

"Hold on, you're . . ."

"Laverne de la Croix!" Larry said, using the camp, feminine voice he used for his character. He threw up some jazz hands, and Sam laughed.

"Wow," he said.

"We weren't following you or anything," Roxy said.

"Well, not exactly. You kept disappearing, and we just heard that you were seen hanging around town. We were out and about and wondered if we'd bump into you. I was worried you were in trouble since you didn't say anything about what you were doing."

"It's okay," Nat said. "I understand. I was going to tell you eventually."

"You *were* incredible," Sam said.

"Yeah. Really amazing, Nat," added Roxy.

"Isn't she?" Larry said proudly, putting an arm around Nat's shoulders. "She's become quite a hit on the club scene. People are coming from all over the state just to hear her."

"Most of them are coming for you, Larry," Nat said. She turned to Roxy and Sam. "Larry's been a regular on the club circuit for years now. We met when I was auditioning for a club night a few months ago, and since then, we've been doing our acts together. He taught me everything I needed to know about singing on the circuit. I wouldn't be doing it without him."

"Nonsense," Larry said. "Nat's a star. You can't keep someone as talented as her down. I'm lucky to have her perform with me."

"She's a star, for sure," Roxy agreed.

"By next year," Larry said, "we'll be filling out the Superdome."

Sam and Roxy laughed, but Nat twisted her mouth nervously. "I'm not sure about that," she said. "It's already becoming a bit too much for me."

"What do you mean?" Sam asked.

Nat sighed. "I have to wear a disguise. I'm terrified all the time I'm going to be found out. It's bad enough I work here at the hotel. Now I'm also singing? The whole reason I kept it a secret from you guys, used a fake name, and performed as a support act for Larry was to avoid any trouble. But now that our act is getting popular, I'm also a lot more worried. All it takes is for the wrong person to recognize me and start asking questions . . ."

"Oh, honey," Larry said, "you're going to be a star. And then none of this will matter."

"But why didn't you tell us? We would have kept your secret," Roxy said.

"I didn't want to involve you. I love singing and wanted to do more. But I didn't want to drag you into it. And I wanted something just for me. At first, it was exciting to have this secret. And I didn't want anyone to tell me I couldn't or shouldn't do it."

"There's one thing we didn't tell you yet either."

"Oh?" Nat replied.

"Yeah," Roxy said, looking at Sam.

"George is back in New Orleans," Sam said.

"*Really?*" Nat replied, unable to stop the beaming smile that instantly lit up her face. "I thought he was going to Nigeria to study some of that mumbo-jumbo of his."

"He changed his mind," Roxy said.

"He asked about you," Sam said, deciding to play it cool on George's behalf.

"Did he now?" Nat said, still smiling, swinging her shoulders side to side a little.

Sam looked over Roxy's shoulder. George was peeking around the doorframe.

"In fact . . ." Sam said.

"I'm here right now!" George stepped out just as Nat turned round.

"George!"

"Nat!"

Nat jumped out of her chair and ran to him. "You absolute silly. Stop being such a pussycat. C'm'ere." George, whether he wanted one or not, got wrapped up in a huge Nat bear hug followed by a long kiss.

Roxy and Sam sat back, relieved. "Well, that went well," Sam said, grateful that Nat's secret friend had turned out to be a drag queen and not a rival for her heart. He wouldn't have relished telling George *that*.

As the evening wound down, and as she waited for Elijah to bring her coat, Paige touched Roxy on the arm. "Are you serious about offering this place as a location?"

Roxy beamed. "Of course. With some notice and organization, I'm sure we could sort something out. We're very proud of the work we did here. I love the idea."

"Did you renovate the hotel then?"

"Virtually from top to bottom. Sam and I took over and threw ourselves into the project. Hard, dusty work, but we got it done. I had a vision, and Sam worked to see it to fruition. He's very handy. I couldn't have done it without him."

"Wow, impressive. Well, Roxy, thank you for a marvelous evening. I'm sure we'll be in touch. I might have a project or two for you myself."

"Your coat, ma'am," Elijah purred from behind her. Paige paused as he slipped the coat over her shoulders.

Sam was the last to leave. As he zipped his sax into its case, Roxy stopped him by taking his arm.

"Sam," she said gently. "Thank you."

"For what?"

Roxy lifted her head slowly and kissed him gently on

the lips. It wasn't passionate like the last time she had sprung a surprise kiss on him, but it was as tender and affectionate as a kiss could be. It was a kiss that said much more than simple words could. It expressed how much she trusted him, how much he meant to her, and how grateful she was.

As Roxy pulled slowly away, she saw Sam's handsome face alight with pleasure. He winked at her and quietly walked out of the hotel. Roxy went to the kitchen floating on air.

The fortune teller had told Roxy that she'd discover something important, earth-shattering, something that she would derive strength from. She hadn't known what the woman meant at the time. But now, she guessed standing up to a police department full of guns made kissing Sam small fry by comparison.

And what had the fortune teller said about Sam? Oh yes, that he should clean up his act so he could live without the weight of secrets. That still sounded ominous, but her heart was so happy, not even the fortune teller's words could dampen her spirit. Not now.

Alone in the kitchen, Roxy puttered about, stacking the dishwasher, wrapping leftovers, wiping counters. As she rinsed out her cloth, she noticed an envelope on the window ledge. On the front was Roxy's name written in Evangeline's hand. Roxy let out a quiet groan. What was it this time?

She slipped her finger under the seal and pulled out a folded piece of paper. In big letters, Evangeline had written: `"Take great care. Put this in the safe, cher. For when I'm no longer here. My secret dipping sauce recipe."`

Thank you for reading *Cajun Catastrophe!* I will have a new case for Roxy and her gang soon! To find out about new books, sign up for my newsletter: https://www.alisongold en.com

If you love the Roxy Reinhardt mysteries, you'll also love the sweet, funny *USA Today* bestselling Reverend Annabelle Dixon series featuring a madcap, lovable lady vicar whose passion for cake is matched only by her desire for justice. The first in the series, *Death at the Cafe* is available for purchase from Amazon. You can sample the series by turning the page and reading the first chapter. Like all my books, *Death at the Cafe* is FREE in Kindle Unlimited.

If you're looking for a detective series with twisty plots and characters that feel like friends, binge read the *USA Today* bestselling Inspector Graham series featuring a new and unusual detective with a phenomenal memory and a tragic past. The first in series, *The Case of the Screaming Beauty*, is available for purchase from Amazon and FREE in Kindle Unlimited.

If you're looking for something edgy and dangerous, root for Diana Hunter as she seeks justice after a devastating crime destroys her family. Start

following her journey in this
non-stop series of suspense and
action. The first book in the
series, Snatched is available to
buy on Amazon and is FREE in
Kindle Unlimited.

I hugely appreciate your
help in spreading the word
about *Louisiana Lies*, including
telling a friend. Reviews help
readers find books! Please leave a review on your favorite
book site.

Turn the page for an excerpt from the first book in the
Reverend Annabelle Dixon series, *Death at the Cafe* . . .

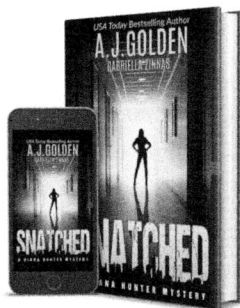

A Reverend
Annabelle Dixon
Mystery

death
at the
café

ALISON GOLDEN

JAMIE VOUGEOT

DEATH AT THE CAFE
CHAPTER ONE

NOTHING BROUGHT REVEREND Annabelle closer to blasphemy than using the London public transport system during rush hour. Since being ordained and sent to St. Clement's church, an impressive, centuries-old building among the tower blocks and new builds of London's East End, Annabelle had been tested many times. She had come across virtually every sin known to man, counselled wayward youths, presided over family disputes, heard astonishingly sad tales from the homeless, and still retained her solid, optimistic dependability through it all. None of these challenges made her blood boil, and her round, soft face curl up into a mixture of disgust, frustration, and exasperation. Yet sitting on the number forty-three bus to Islington, as it moved along at a snail's pace, was almost enough to make her take her beloved Lord's name in vain.

On this occasion, she had nabbed her favourite seat: top deck, front left. It gave her a perfect view of the unique streets London offered and the even more varied types of people. Today, however, her viewpoint afforded her only a teeth-clenchingly irritating perspective of a traffic jam that extended as far as the eye could see down Upper Street.

"I know I shouldn't," she muttered on the relatively empty bus, "but if this doesn't deserve a cherry-topped cupcake, then I don't know what does."

The thought of rewarding her patience with what she loved almost as much as her vocation—cake—settled Annabelle's nerves for a full twenty minutes, during which the bus trundled in fits and starts along another half-mile stretch.

Assigning Annabelle, fresh from her days studying theology at Cambridge University, to the tough, inner-city borough of Hackney had presented her with what had been an almost literal baptism of fire. She had arrived in the summer, during a few weeks when the British sun combined with the squelching heat of a city constantly bustling and moving. It was a time of drinking and frivolity for some, heightened tension for others. A spell during which bored youths found their idle hands easily occupied with the devil's work. An interval when the good relax and the bad run riot.

Annabelle had grown up in East London, but for her first appointment as a vicar, her preference had been for a peaceful, rural village somewhere. A place in which she could indulge her love of nature, and conduct her Holy business in the gentle, caring manner she preferred. "Gentle" and "caring," however, were two words rarely used to describe London. Annabelle had mildly protested her city assignment. But after a long talk to the archbishop who explained the extreme shortage of candidates both capable and willing to take on the challenge of an inner-city church, she agreed to take up the position and set about her task with enthusiasm.

Father John Wilkins of neighbouring St. Leonard's church had been charged with easing Annabelle into the complex role. He had been a priest for over thirty years, and for the vast majority of that time had worked in London's poorest, toughest neighbourhoods. The Anglican Church was far less popular in London than it was in rural England, largely due to the city's disparate mix of peoples and creeds. Father John's congregation was mostly made up of especially devout immigrants from Africa and South America, many of whom were not even Anglican but simply lived nearby. The only time St. Leonard's had ever been full was on a particularly mild Christmas Eve.

But despite low attendance at services, London's churches played pivotal roles in their local communities. With plenty of people in need, they were hubs of charity and community support. Fundraising events, providing food and shelter for London's large homeless population, caring for the elderly, and engaging troubled youths were the churches' stock in trade, not to mention they provided both spiritual and emotional support for the many deaths and family tragedies that occurred.

The stress of it all had turned Father John's wiry beard a speckled grey, and though he knew his work was important and worthwhile, he had been pushed to breaking point on more than one occasion. Upon her arrival, he had taken one look at Annabelle's breezy manner and fresh-faced, open smile and assumed that her appointment was a case of negligence, desperation, or a sick prank.

"She's utterly delightful," Father John sighed on the phone to the archbishop, "and extremely nice. But 'delightful' and 'nice' are not what's required in a London church. This is a part of the world where faith is stretched to its very limits, where strong leadership goes further than gentle guidance. We struggle to capture people's attention, Archbishop, let alone their hearts. Our drug rehabilitation programs have more members than our congregations."

"Give her a chance, Father," the archbishop replied softly. "Don't underestimate her. She grew up in East London, you know."

"Well, I grew up in Westminster, but that doesn't mean I've had tea with the Queen!"

Merely a week into Annabelle's assignment, however, Father John's misgivings proved unfounded. Annabelle's bumbling, naïve manner was just that—a manner. Father John observed closely as Annabelle's strength, faith, and intelligence were consistently tested by the urban issues of her flock. He noted that she passed with flying colours.

Whether she was dealing with a hardened criminal fresh out of prison and already succumbing to old temptations, or a single mother of three struggling to find some composure and faith in the face of her daily troubles, Annabelle was always there to help. With good humour and optimism, she never turned down a request for assistance, no matter how large or small it was.

When Father John visited Annabelle a month after the start of her placement to check on a highly successful gardening project she had started for troubled youth, he shook his head in amazement "Is that Denton? By the rose bushes? I've been trying to get him to visit me for a year now, and all he does is ignore me. You should hear what he says when his parole officer suggests it," he said.

"Oh, Denton is wonderful!" Annabelle cried. "Fantastic with his hands. He has a devilish sense of humour—when it's properly directed. Did you know that he plays drums?"

"No, I didn't know that. He never told me," Father John said, giving Annabelle an appreciative smile. "I must say,

Reverend, I seem to have misjudged you dreadfully. And I apologise."

"Oh, Father," Annabelle chuckled, "it's perfectly understandable. You have only the best interests of the community at heart. Let's leave judgement for Him and Him alone. The only thing we're meant to judge is cake contests, in my opinion. Mind those thorns, Denton! Roses tend to fight back if you treat them roughly!"

To get your copy of *Death at the Cafe* visit the link below:
https://www.alisongolden.com/death-at-the-cafe

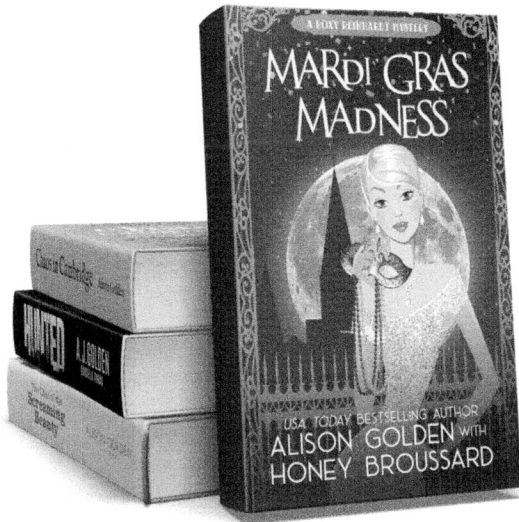

"Your emails seem to come on days when I need to read them because they are so upbeat."
- Linda W -

For a limited time, you can get the first books in each of my series - *Chaos in Cambridge, Hunted* (exclusively for subscribers - not available anywhere else), *The Case of the Screaming Beauty, and Mardi Gras Madness* - plus updates about new releases, promotions, and other Insider exclusives, by signing up for my mailing list at:

https://www.alisongolden.com/roxy

TAKE MY QUIZ

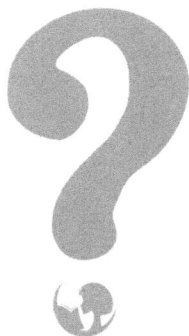

What kind of mystery reader are you? Take my thirty second quiz to find out!

https://www.alisongolden.com/quiz

BOOKS IN THE ROXY REINHARDT MYSTERIES

Mardi Gras Madness

New Orleans Nightmare

Louisiana Lies

Cajun Catastrophe

COLLECTIONS

Books 1-3

Mardi Gras Madness

New Orleans Nightmare

Louisiana Lies

ALSO BY ALISON GOLDEN

FEATURING INSPECTOR DAVID GRAHAM

The Case of the Screaming Beauty

The Case of the Hidden Flame

The Case of the Fallen Hero

The Case of the Broken Doll

The Case of the Missing Letter

The Case of the Pretty Lady

The Case of the Forsaken Child

The Case of Sampson's Leap

The Case of the Uncommon Witness

FEATURING REVEREND ANNABELLE DIXON

Chaos in Cambridge (Prequel)

Death at the Café

Murder at the Mansion

Body in the Woods

Grave in the Garage

Horror in the Highlands

Killer at the Cult

Fireworks in France

Witches at the Wedding

ABOUT THE AUTHOR

Alison Golden is the *USA Today* bestselling author of the Inspector David Graham mysteries, a traditional British detective series, and two cozy mystery series featuring main characters Reverend Annabelle Dixon and Roxy Reinhardt. As A. J. Golden, she writes the Diana Hunter thriller series.

Alison was raised in Bedfordshire, England. Her aim is to write stories that are designed to entertain, amuse, and calm. Her approach is to combine creative ideas with excellent writing and edit, edit, edit. Alison's mission is simple: To write excellent books that have readers clamouring for more.

Alison is based in the San Francisco Bay Area with her husband and twin sons. She splits her time between London and San Francisco.

For up-to-date promotions and release dates of upcoming books, sign up for the latest news here: https://www.alisongolden.com/roxy.

For more information:
www.alisongolden.com
alison@alisongolden.com

facebook.com/alisongolden.books

x.com/alisonjgolden

instagram.com/alisonjgolden

THANK YOU

Thank you for taking the time to read *Cajun Catastrophe*. If you enjoyed it, please consider telling your friends or posting a short review. Word of mouth is an author's best friend and very much appreciated.
Thank you,

Printed in Great Britain
by Amazon